CADEL

Freddie Exzell Bourn III

CADEL

A Novel

ISBN: 978-1-7351956-0-5 (Print)
ISBN: 978-1-7351956-1-2 (Ebook)

Cover Design by Berge Design

For my father.

I'm pretty sure we would have been good "adult" friends.

Contents

1.

Fuck these cruise ships.

Cadel sat on a bench near Pier 27 of the Port of San Francisco and, while admiring the massive ships, let his mind wander about the lives of the people who worked on them and how they made everything go so smoothly year after year after year -- and the shit they had to put up with on a daily basis. How did they deal with all the old, fat warblers, meandering up to the feed troughs to scoop mounds and mounds of food down their esophagi, without tasting anything, and then demanding to be entertained?

All those workers. And the ships kept coming and going and coming and going. Nonstop.

All those people who woke up every morning, drank their little cups of coffee, and headed off to try and please people who were incapable of being pleased.

How did they do it? How could they do the same thing day after day after day? He could not get his head around it.

And all those fat fucks.

Why did they even want to go on a cruise in the first place?

He imagined the sea and its majestic mysteries deep underneath the surface. The dark, quiet beauty of it all, undisturbed and unobserved, existing practically in another dimension. And these human garbage disposals merely wanted to float on top of all that majesty, consuming everything in sight, drinking fruity alcoholic drinks to numb themselves from anything remotely beautiful -- all the while hoping not to pass out before taking their heart medications.

The perverse nature of the whole thing revolted him to his core.

So what made him different? What set him apart from the masses? What made his worldview so much more important than theirs and why didn't more subscribe to it?

Was he actually smarter than them?

He allowed himself to consider the possibility and then forced the thought out of his head. He did not want karma to knock his head off.

But if he wasn't smarter than them, he, at least, knew he was not like them. He could never understand them, those lemmings, who probably also believed every damn thing they read on the internet.

And he knew it wasn't just the cruise ship Weeble Wobbles. It was humanity.

That was why he never felt part of anything. He never felt included. He was always on the outside.

And yet he let himself believe that he could change them, that he could educate them. He let himself believe he had the power to change things. The power of the pen -- or sticky keyboard -- could expose corruption and shine a light on the dark places of the world. He could inform the masses of the way things really were and maybe change things for the better.

So that was better than nothing, right?

Right?

He hoped so at least. Why then bother? Why go through what he went through to get a story?

He got up from the bench and felt the soreness of his mid-40s, white male body, which had experienced little-to-no exercise in the last 10 years or so. He gave a half-assed attempt at a stretch and went about his way. He could easily walk back to his job -- well, job within a job -- before his shift began. He would have plenty of time to get there, get situated, and might even have time for a smoke.

His job within a job. What did that even mean now? Which one was real, and which one was not?

He would be lying to himself if he did not admit there was a part of him that enjoyed being a cashier at a coffee shop. Money in and money out. Coffee made and coffee poured.

But he knew it was not his "real job" because being a cashier actually paid money.

Yes, the joys of being a "contract journalist."

The "good old days" of being a low-paid investigative journalist, which at least had some benefits, were long gone. He was paid by the story, and, sometimes, he might even be asked to write a story, but, even then, it was up to the editor whether he was paid or not.

He was luckier than most, though. He at least had contacts at a few papers. A few of his stories had been picked up nationally too, so he had some credibility and could get cash when he really needed it.

He also knew he was good. Not only at writing, but at breaking a story. His instincts were usually right on. And, right now, his instincts told him the story was right where was heading.

He had been working at The Coffee Shop for more than a year now, and that was where he knew the story was, even though he did not know all the details just yet. He just continued to trust his gut and work methodically. He was never one to go straight to the center of the story. He had to start at the outer edges and work his way in slowly, carefully, to the truth.

It was definitely not the way things were currently done in the newspaper business, which was why he knew he would never be able to hold down a real newspaper job. It took months of work to do the type of investigative journalism he loved. As a result, he could only do it on the outside and not as an employee of an actual paper.

At least, that was what Cadel told himself.

And now he was working at a coffee shop -- The Coffee Shop, that is -- all to break a story he thought was there, but could not quite put all the pieces together. He was close, though.

The Coffee Shop was anything but a true barista-style coffee establishment. The beans were the cheapest one could buy, and the equipment was bought at auction.

No one came to this place for the coffee, though.

Most of the non-addicts who came here to buy the swill, and maybe even drink it, did so purely out of guilt. The sign on the front door said it all: "Humanitarian Project Success" and then in smaller type: "Every employee here is working their way back to society."

So the place was chocked full of addicts and shitty coffee beans, and politicians could put a checkmark next to yet another feel-good project.

Cadel knew differently, though. He just had to prove it.

Drugs were involved, yes, but Cadel now suspected it was more than drugs. Prostitution, sure, and even …

"Excuse me."

Cadel snapped out of his haze.

"Yes?"

He looked around. He was standing in the parking lot outside The Coffee Shop. He lost himself like this more and more, and it was more than just daydreaming. His mind drifted to other dimensions, other times, other places, where he had complete control. It wasn't that he necessarily hated his own reality, it was that it just felt more natural at times to be anyplace but here. He had to force himself sometimes to look around and take notice of where he was.

He focused on the vision in front of him: a girl, who looked no more than 18, with dirty blonde hair, a nose ring, and the body of a 13-year-old boy. He knew her, yes, and, miracle of miracles, he liked her.

"Are you going in now or staying outside until your shift?"

Cadel looked at his watch. They had 10 minutes.

"Eh, let's go ahead and go in."

The Coffee Shop in its previous incarnation had been a shoe store, right in the middle of a strip mall. On one side had been a small spa, where women could get their nails done for cheap, and on the other had been a cell phone store. Now, there was just The Coffee Shop, surrounded by empty, abandoned spaces.

Yes, The Coffee Shop.

That was the name.

The. Coffee. Shop.

It was original, at least.

She walked in first, and Cadel noticed the gross, oogling eyes from the unkempt men, standing around. They were too far outside society to care much about societal norms. She took it in stride. If it bothered her, she exerted a lot of energy not to show it.

In contrast, there was only one set of eyes on Cadel, and they certainly were not lustful.

Mookie.

Mookie was not a nice person, even though there had been numerous humanitarian awards and feel-good, fluff newspaper articles to say otherwise.

Raised on the streets (check). Former drug addict (check). Turned his life around (check). Now, giving back to the community (check).

Except that it was all just the opposite.

Just an afternoon of internet searches, telephone calls, and background research at the local library painted a different portrait.

Middle-class upbringing (check). Stable home life as a child (check). College education at a large public university (check). Playing the local politicians and media for the fools they were (check).

Cadel knew Mookie was making a lot of money somehow. He felt it in his gut, but he just could not figure it out -- not yet at least.

Mookie was smarter than the average con man, but Cadel had just begun peeling the onion. All he had to do was be patient and wait.

"Hey, my two hardest workers, where ya been? Taking a smoke break from your day-long smoke break?"

He let everyone smoke in The Coffee Shop, including the workers. Mookie said it added to the "ambiance" of the place, harkening back to a time gone past. However, it was really because if addicts could not smoke, there would be trouble. Bad trouble.

Cigarettes and coffee. Not a better diet in the world.

His young friend lit up on cue, and Mookie looked at her with disgust. "Do you ever not smoke?" he said and put his head back in his newspaper. He was sitting at a small table, his table, in the back. Without looking up, Mookie said, "Get to work."

Yes, the life of a barista. Cadel took out the can opener and mutilated the industrial-sized can of beans.

"How's it going?" she asked.

Cadel looked at her.

"Oh," she said. "You're in a mood."

Cadel shrugged. He had only known her for a few months, and she was already nagging him.

Even though she was his only friend in this shithole, he knew it would probably mean trouble for him later. Even so, he had decided a while ago to acquiesce to her friendship overtures . . . but just a little.

"I would really like to go home and just sleep," he said after starting the pot of coffee. She handed him a tray of dirty coffee mugs, he placed them in the sink, and the two began their ritual of washing and drying.

She looked at him and understanding spread over her face.

"One of those nights, huh?" she asked.

"No, not that."

He looked down at his hands and placed them on the bottom of the sink. He let the soapy water slowly slink through his hands and down the drain.

"I'm just really tired," he said. He looked around the place. He was not the only one with dark bags under his eyes. The "customers" at The Coffee Shop were not your typical coffee shop customers. Sure, there were the occasional hipsters with the skinny jeans, dark horn-rimmed glasses, and man bags, but most were the type of folks you might see at a county fair.

Morbidly obese blacks (check); no-teeth whites (check); upper-class college kids, both black and white (check); and dirt-poor Hispanics (check).

The one thing they all had in common: the hollowed-out look of an addict too far gone.

Mookie ruled over them, and they did not care. And Cadel was beginning to understand why.

Not too long ago Cadel had heard about this place while snooping around a certain state legislator. He had heard the lawmaker liked little boys more than serving the good people of California, and, as he was digging into the good man's finances, he discovered several donations to The Coffee Shop. Never hearing of the establishment, Cadel showed up to have a good cup of java.

It was the most disgusting cup of coffee he ever drank, and, yet, the place was packed -- packed with homeless people and addicts and "doo gooders" and Mookie. The whole thing rang false, though. That day, he gave up his investigation into the legislator and dug his claws into this place. His gut had told him this was the story, even though he did not know quite why. This was what he had to expose, even though he did not know what it was he was going to expose.

"Hey, dummy!"

Cadel looked up to see Mookie's eyes glaring at him.

"Yessir?"

"How about helping them out?"

Cadel looked where Mookie was pointing.

Two men, one in his late 40s (although you could never quite tell with an addict), the other somewhat younger, were struggling to bring in some sort of rug. The younger one was holding his hand after dropping his end.

"Son of a bitch!" he said under his breath.

Cadel walked from behind the counter and picked up the end that had dropped. He and the older gentleman took the rug to the back of the establishment and dropped it.

Cadel pulled out a pack of cigs and offered one.

"No, thank you."

Cadel, taken aback by such a courtesy, looked at the man.

Long beard, motorcycle jacket, and ragged jeans. He was one of Mookie's long-time, right-hand men, Cadel knew, but he never had much interaction with him. Cadel admitted to himself that it was because he was intimidated by the man, and not just because of his size or demeanor. It was his eyes. They had life in them, unlike the deadness in a typical addict's eyes. This man's eyes were not only alive, but were bouncing all over the place.

Cadel looked back at the man, who did not look away. Cadel did not feel like getting into a battle of wills at the moment, so he made himself shrug, act as if he did not care, and meander back to his station.

He already knew not to fuck with this guy, but he made a note to himself also not to talk to him the way he talked to most of the people in The Coffee Shop, including even Mookie.

Cadel sighed. He could trace all the troubles in his life back to his smartass mouth. He could not control it, even if he wanted to. He decided long ago he would rather speak his mind than have people wonder what he believed. Sounds good in theory, but as a result, he had no meaningful personal relationships with anyone and his employment history was spotted at best.

The girl looked up from washing the coffee bin and smiled as if she knew exactly what he was thinking, but of course did not. Speaking of meaningful relationships destined to fail, who was this gal anyway? He had no idea, but she had latched onto him from the first time he met her. She seemed nice enough, although not really his type. Too skinny. Too pale. Too young. And he was not really into piercings.

She, no doubt, was first attracted to him because he was one of the few white faces at The Coffee Shop. She had a slightly rural, feral look to her, and, with her Southern accent, he assumed she had grown up with people who looked like her and thought like her. She wasn't racist, or, at least, Cadel had never heard her say anything racist, but he had never seen her have any meaningful discussions with people of color either.

Or maybe it was because she was just being careful, and Cadel had a friendly face.

Yeah, right.

Well, he could be charming when he wanted something, but he knew he was anything but friendly. Maybe that was what she was used to as well: unfriendly people, who were nice to her when they wanted something.

And Cadel definitely wanted something from her: an ally. So he was nicer to her than he was to most people, and he kept his sarcastic comments about her to himself. She seemed to appreciate that. In exchange, she did not unload anything about her past. She probably instinctively knew he was the wrong person to carry her yoke.

The only thing he knew about her was that she had a drug problem. He did not know what drug, specifically, but he guessed it was of the prescription persuasion. She still had her teeth, and there was no sign of rot. He also knew she was there on a court-ordered program. She carried a piece of paper that Mookie signed every day.

She was not the only person who carried around a sheet of paper Mookie had to sign. All the employees carried one. Cadel himself had to carry one, even if it was a garden-variety forgery. Mookie did not ask anything when Cadel showed up for the first day of work and asked him to sign it. He just grunted and, after signing, pointed to a mop.

Even with his newfound career kicking into high gear, Cadel knew Mookie had been suspicious of him and continued to be. It was the way Mookie looked at him out of the corner of his eye. Cadel saw it on occasion and thus knew he had to be careful, very careful, when it came to Mookie.

"Hey, Bukowski."

Cadel looked up to see the girl slinking over to him.

"Yes, Kowalski?"

"So, what are you doing this weekend? You told me you weren't working."

"I'm actually going to visit a friend."

"You have friends, Wojciechowski? Yeah, right."

Cadel looked at her until she looked back at him, which she eventually did.

"And what exactly do you have planned, Lewandowski?"

"I'm working. I picked up a shift. I have nothing else to do."

"Right."

Cadel knew she would probably do what most addicts did when they had nothing else to do: find something to place into their bloodstream rather than be bored. Or feel shame. Or face life. He seriously doubted she would end up working here over the weekend, but who knows?

He definitely would not be. And he was not completely lying about seeing a friend either. Jack Daniels was waiting for him back in his dingy apartment. He was going to be pretty busy, drinking himself into a stupor, thinking about his predicament, and possibly even writing a tiny bit.

Like most journalists he knew, the actual story would come last. For the time being, he made himself feel like he was actually working by typing in his notes, cutting and pasting his research, and writing out his theories. More than anything, though, he needed to get to the library and do some research. His apartment, predictably, did not have wireless, and he needed access to the relatively high-speed internet the library provided. He had several loose ends that needed closing before he began stringing all the story threads together. He would do that tomorrow.

In the meantime, he could not wait to feel the warm and fuzzies inside his belly. He would walk home, take out his notes, spread them across the table, pull out his old laptop, put in his headphones, turn on the tunes, and begin pouring. He loved losing himself in his own little world. There was no one to bother him, no one's feelings not to hurt, and no worries to gnaw at his soul. He considered it his weekly mini-vacation because it was by far the best 3-4 hours of his week. And, believe it or not, every once in a while, he came up with some pretty damn good ideas too.

He caught himself smiling and looked up to see the girl smiling back at him.

He put back on his somber mask and looked back down. Just a few more hours of this façade.

Later that afternoon, as he walked through the parking lot of The Coffee Shop, Cadel started getting that "ole time feeling" once again. He had a little spring to his step as heard the sirens singing their song, beckoning him back to his abode.

"See ya later, Kopowski."

He turned around to see his friend, standing in the doorway to The Coffee Shop. He smiled, waved, and let the current take him away from her.

As he walked on the sidewalk toward his apartment, he could feel the countdown begin. He could feel that urge in his gut, and he knew his brain would not be far behind with its justifications.

This was stressful. He needed a release.

If he wasn't hurting anyone but himself, what did it matter?

If it wasn't hurting the work, what did it matter?

No one would know.

No one would really care if they did know.

Cadel let it all wash over him. He knew he was at the point where it was futile to fight it, but he also knew he did not want to fight it. He liked it. He liked the release. He liked feeling good, even if for a small amount of time. He liked the flood of confidence he felt when the glass hit his lips and the warmth spread throughout his body.

As he got closer and closer, he became more and more locked in. There would be absolutely nothing that kept him from escaping to his own little world, where he was king and ruled all, tonight. A little twinge of shame hit his mind, as he thought that he would rather be here than anywhere else in the world. But he pushed that thought down as he saw the dingy, white stucco of the wall keeping the inhabitants of his apartment complex in check. And as his heart leapt with joy, the previous shame-filled thought left his body entirely.

When he awoke the next morning in his bed, soaking wet with sweat, he briefly basked in the glory of the morning before remembering who he was. Then, he let the pain, inside and out, wash over him.

As he pushed his legs over the side of the bed, he felt the first wave of nausea rumble up through his gut to his throat. He caught it in time, but knew the second and third waves would be much stronger. He waddled to the small bathroom and fell to his knees on the cheap linoleum in time to stick his head deep inside the porcelain ring.

The next few minutes were not pretty.

"Now, why, again, do I do this to myself," Cadel asked the toilet.

Time to get up, he told himself. He pulled himself up by the standalone sink and looked at himself in the mirror.

"Jesus Christ, what a loser," he said, admiring the way his greasy hair contrasted with the dark circles under his eyes. The fluorescent light also had a glorious way of bringing out every wrinkle on his face. "Maybe I do belong in The Coffee Shop … permanently."

He stumbled out of the bathroom and put on his jeans and t-shirt, both of which were on the floor next to his bed. He headed to the kitchen, and, once there, it did not take long for him to make coffee, get a cup, and head right back to the toilet. He sat on the cool toilet seat, drinking his hot coffee, and tried hard not to think about the night before.

Cadel looked at his watch. Mid-morning. Time to get to the library.

Cadel took a quick, cold shower, not because he was a manly man, but because the water heater was too little to make it through an entire shower with anything other than a lukewarm spray, bookended by scrotum-shrinking iciness. He considered it his penance and was still shivering as he got ready to leave.

As he walked outside, the sun blinded him, but, not for long, because, as he walked to the staircase and down the side of the building, the building's shadow enveloped him and he enjoyed the brief respite from the California sun. As he got to the bottom of the staircase, in his haze, he briefly noticed another shadow, out-of-place, within the staircase's shadow, but ignored it.

He ignored it, that is, until a brick hit him upside his head.

"Great, another concussion," he thought before he sank into warm darkness.

2.

Junie pulled a long, slow drag off the cigarette.

Yes, she had to look the part of a recovering drug addict -- nose ring, greasy hair, no makeup -- but the cigarettes, unfortunately, were not an act.

"But I love them so much," she mumbled to herself and flicked the butt on the pavement.

Her life as a 28-year-old detective was a fading shadow, but her current life as a washed-out teenager was just a present detached shell of reality. In actuality, she was floating between the two worlds and felt as lost as the addict she was supposed to be. The emptiness in her eyes, at times, did not feel like an act either.

"Thank goodness for a flat chest and bad skin," she mumbled to herself, knowing that most women would kill to have her youthful appearance, but not as a cover for an undercover operation.

She had to lose 10 pounds for this "role" to look more malnourished than normal. That was the hardest part: not eating and exercising more than normal. In contrast, it had been remarkably easy to establish herself as a barista at this so-called "Coffee Shop" under the watchful eye of Mookie.

He did not trust her, though, and he did not like her either. She knew that, but she did not care. She merely wanted to observe him and gather as much information about him as possible.

Later, she would take action, and she could not wait to take him down.

She walked through the front door of The Coffee Shop and took her place behind the counter.

"Where's your buddy?"

Junie looked up to see Mookie walking out of the bathroom, wiping his hands on his pants and staring right at her.

"He's not working this weekend. Said he was meeting a friend."

Mookie looked at her with his usual non-expression and then sat down at his normal seat in the back corner.

Junie knew her fellow co-worker was not meeting a friend. He was more than likely partaking in some sort of debauchery. She sighed. She liked the dumbass from the first time she met him … as much as she could like an addict. She knew from the beginning that his charm and sense of humor were his weapons: He probably used these fine-tuned armaments exclusively to get the type of score he craved at the expense of any and all relationships he may have had in his life.

But he made her laugh, which was her Achilles' Heel. A guy could be butt-ass ugly with no money in his bank account and a history of mental illness, but if he could make her laugh, her panties would be down to her ankles in seconds flat.

She met him after she had been undercover for about three months. He busted up in The Coffee Shop late one afternoon and proclaimed himself Lord of the Mop to the bemusement of no one but himself. After mopping floors for a month, and insulting everyone in the Shop in the process, he had been promoted to counter duty with her own sweet self. He had the necessary job skills: He was only late 80 percent of the time and had not asked anyone in the Shop for money. At first, she wondered whether he was a cop too, but as much as she hated to admit it, he was too smart to be a cop. He said things outside of what the 24-hour news and sports TV channels told him to say.

However, knowing things and being funny did not make him a good, stable person, she had to tell herself over and over and over again. He was here for a reason.

She looked back at Mookie, who was still looking at her from his seat.

"Hello?" he said. "You in there? Let's get back to work."

She shrugged her shoulders, and looked down at her hands in her faux, shame-filled addict persona.

She was really good at her job, but not so much at her fake job. Her coffee always tasted burnt because she never could get the machine as clean as it was supposed to be. Even the homeless patrons complained about her java, which was about as bad as an insult as it gets.

She was never much of a coffee drinker, so, as in most things she did not care much about, she half-assed it. There were so many complaints she often wondered why Mookie kept her behind the counter. She thought it might be because he could keep an eye on her without worrying about her doing untoward things (to other patrons?) out of his eyesight.

"Hey."

Junie snapped out of her fog and looked at the bearded man in front of her.

"Excuse me?" she asked as she tried to look interested.

"I said, 'Hey.'"

She looked again at the bearded biker man in front of her. She recognized him, of course. He was one of Mookie's "people," so she normally stayed away from him. He normally returned the favor, but today he seemed quite the Chatty Cathy. She gave him the biggest faux smile she could muster. "Sorry, honey, yes, what can I do you for?"

"Go get me some fucking coffee, you ugly little scarecrow."

Well, that was unexpected.

Junie, in her role as a cop was quite used to people yelling obscenities at her and threatening physical violence, but her senses told her this situation was quite different. This person was different.

She felt a deep stab of fear and a brief moment of panic. She turned quickly around, regained her composure, and walked towards the coffee machine with her back to the man. She poured the coffee, turned around, and looked at the man.

Most of the people in this place had a certain darkness, deadness, in their eyes. They were tired, exhausted, and just weary. Life had taken them for a ride, and most were more than ready for it all to end.

This man, though, was different. His eyes were full of a crazy energy. There was no telling what he was thinking or what he might do. She was scared, yes, but also oddly curious.

"I cannot wait to fuck your corpse."

OK, then, no longer curious.

Junie turned away from him again and acted like she was cleaning the coffee machine. When she turned around again, he was gone. Thank God.

Mookie had been under surveillance for over two years by the SFPD. He had blipped on the department's radar after several high-profile drug busts, where several of the perps had either been frequent guests of The Coffee Shop or one of Mookie's "employees."

Of course, this could all be explained away easily, and was, by pointing out that Mookie was in the business of reforming prisoners and getting the homeless on the straight and narrow. These were the people he was trying to help. He could not help it if they did not want to accept his helping hand and had slipped back into their old patterns.

Junie knew all this backstory and did not care. She despised Mookie from the first time she met him. She had done her research beforehand, so she had known he was not a nice person. He was a piece of shit. The lowest of the low. The way he looked at her, not sexual, but domineering. The way he was always sweating, the way he smelled, the way he adjusted himself in front of everyone … she despised all of him.

Nonetheless, she just could not put him away quite yet. He was too good. He was too smart. To clarify: She had gathered enough evidence to nail him on drug trafficking, which had been easy. She knew, though, he was also involved in prostitution and, to what extent, well, it was likely something deeper and darker than being a mere pimp.

But he was definitely a pimp. She thought Mookie might even proposition her at some point, but he never did, which, she had to admit, hurt her feelings on some level.

Ahhhhhh, yes. It always came down to "Daddy Issues."

She was from the South, yes … in fact, she was from the Deep South … in fact, she was from the deep, Deep South. Her family was your typical redneck family: little-to-no emphasis on getting an education, no one ever read anything (except the Bible), church every Sunday morning and Wednesday night, and, of course, swept under the rug, was a long history of alcoholism and abuse.

Her father left when she was only 11 years old, and her whole world fell apart. She had no idea how much she relied on him until he left. His mere presence had been the glue that kept her family together, and, when he left, her mother unraveled before her eyes.

It was easy now to look back on her life and see that was the time when she began looking for a man to fill the void in her life, whether it was having sex with slightly older, grosser guys or attaching herself to male teachers and coaches in somewhat inappropriate ways. She had always been looking for her daddy.

Her real father did come back to visit every once in a while, but it always ended with him either fighting or fucking her mother. Either way there was always an empty bottle of Blue Nun in the sink the next morning.

She could not wait to leave that small town, and she did. She had a distant cousin, who lived in San Francisco. She went to live there after turning 18 and never looked back.

In her mind, joining the Police Academy shortly thereafter had been the most natural thing in the world. She went online, filled out an application, and was in an itchy, ill-fitting uniform by the end of the month.

It was not long before she was a real cop, and not long after that before she was an actual detective. She was asked to go undercover, and she did. Everything had seemed so natural as if she was floating down a river with her body naturally bending to avoid every rock, log, and crevice along the way.

More than anything, though, the Academy and then the Department had been her first real family. At least, it was the first real organization in which she knew she was protected. She also knew if she worked hard and kept her nose clean, she would eventually be promoted.

Sure, things were not technically fair. She was not promoted as fast as her male counterparts, and she certainly was not paid as much either.

However, she knew where she stood. There were no surprises.

Until this assignment.

"You want me to go undercover as a drugged-out teenager and hang out with homeless people?"

Say whaaaaaaaaat?

Her superiors, though, had complete confidence in her, and she knew she was ready, even as complete panic nipped at her heels. She had done smaller scale undercover work, mostly drug busts, and had done reasonably well. This was a big-time assignment, though, and she was excited that this could also be a big-time jump in her career. Little did she know that her days would be spent making coffee and getting felt up by the homeless.

Junie looked up from the counter and caught Mookie's gaze. He had been staring at her, and he did not look away when her eyes met his. She knew in her role as a shame-filled runaway, she should look away immediately and feign a look of unworthiness.

She couldn't help herself, though. She met his gaze with a fierceness and rage she had long been suppressing. It probably had something to do with her anger at his bearded lackey just a few moments before too. Mookie continued to return the stare and, then, suddenly a smirk spread across his face. He looked back at his newspaper.

Junie felt a rush of pride in winning this very small battle. She vaguely knew, though, that by breaking character even for mere seconds she had put herself and the whole operation at risk.

She just couldn't help herself.

3.

Alexander stroked the stubbly, so-called beard below his chin and looked at the unconscious man lying on the ground before him.

He hated the position in which he had found himself, but he had no choice. In order to maintain the type of life he had built for himself, unfortunately, he had to return favors every once in a while.

This was a pretty big favor, though … as were all the others.

He had given up his less-than-legal ways a long time ago in exchange for his current life way off the grid. In order to get here, though, he had to ask a lot of a lot of people. Most were willing to help out in exchange for something immediate: cancelling certain debts, making introductions, handing over books of business, etc.

Other folks helped in exchange for something vague, something in the future.

Most of the time these favors involved girls, young girls. He tried not to think about it. Every once in a while, he made a deal to keep one and let her work on the Farm. Sometimes they would stay. Sometimes they would leave. He was OK with their leaving. At least they would not end up like the multitude of girls who were filtered through this place. He had an idea where the unlucky would end up, but he tried to put that out of his mind too.

He knew this was not an ideal situation, to say the least, and he hated that he had left himself, and everything he had worked for, so vulnerable, so exposed. He hoped eventually that "business" would slow down and maybe even stop altogether.

But, for now, business was booming.

The man lying before Alexander had been beaten severely. He had been in and out of consciousness since he had arrived -- so much so that Alexander had not been sure he would survive. Now, it looked like he was going to pull through.

For what, though, Alexander had no idea.

Would he stay here? Be picked up in the middle of the night?

These were the sort of questions Alexander knew he had to leave unanswered.

The man was in his late 30s, early 40s, it appeared to Alexander. Even with the man's eyes swollen shut, Alexander could see the beginning of crows' feet at the edge of his eyes. He was wearing an old Van Halen t-shirt, so he couldn't be all that bad.

Alexander guessed that the man had a certain affinity, if not outright religion, for all things Star Wars, David Letterman, and Seinfeld. He probably came from a broken home and, after years of self-parenting, could obsessively quote nuggets of wisdom from music, TV, and movies, ranging from the Beastie Boys to The Karate Kid to The Shawshank Redemption to Family Ties to Saturday Night Live to Prince.

He probably had deep trust issues and a self-defense mechanism comprised of bitter sarcasm and shame-filled rage. He probably never had a relationship lasting more than a few years and consequently wore those broken relationships as a heavy yoke around his neck, weighing him down more with each passing year.

Just a guess, though.

The man stirred and, for the first time since arriving, opened his eyes as much as they could open.

"Where am I?" the man asked through a hoarse whisper.

"Hold on. I'll get you some water."

Alexander went to the corner of the Barn where he kept an orange water cooler. He pushed the white spigot and poured the liquid in a metal cup for his guest.

As he was pouring the water, he heard the man stirring behind him. Alexander peeked over his shoulder and saw the man trying to get up as if to run away, not noticing the chain around his ankle. He watched as the man threw himself sideways, jerking the chain, and falling backwards onto the ground.

"C'mon, man, you might as well relax. Even if you didn't have a chain around your ankle, there's no way you could run away in your condition. At least try and get some strength before you attempt your great escape."

The man tried one more time to get up and fell back down as fast as he had risen. He let out a sigh and visibly gave up the fight, letting his muscles go completely lax.

Alexander walked back to where the man was, knelt down, lifted the man's head, and gently poured water down the man's throat. He put the cup down and sat down a few feet from his guest.

"Where am I?" the man asked again.

"It doesn't matter."

"Why am I here?"

"It doesn't matter."

A flash of anger crossed the man's face, and he looked at Alexander, "Well, what does matter?"

Alexander pondered this question and decided to put aside his deep, philosophical leanings for the moment.

"That you are alive and, for the time being, safe. I'm not going to hurt you, but I have to keep you here. The people who did hurt you are not here and will not be back for days … maybe weeks."

"I don't understand. I don't know …."

The man's eyes shut, and it appeared to Alexander he was content to know he would not be beaten for the time being. He was not looking for any other answers. Not now at least.

Alexander looked around and saw some horse blankets in the corner of the Barn. He got them, put one under the man's head and covered him with the other. He wanted him to be comfortable, but did not want to bring him into the Big House yet.

"OK. Rest now. No one is going to hurt you."

The man was already asleep or, at least, appeared to be.

Alexander left the Barn and walked the short distance back to the Big House. He knew he could not keep the man chained up like an animal for a long period of time, but he could not let him leave either. He was given strict instructions to keep him alive and on the property until he heard otherwise. He did not know if that meant weeks or months, but he had no option other than to do what he was told. This was obviously a special job, not one of the overnight holdings to which he was accustomed. As a result, he was keeping him in the Barn and not where he kept his usual, well, "deliveries."

Once inside the Big House he sought out some solid food to give his guest.

"Sir, the others are ready."

Alexander looked at the sprite, young thing in front of him. She was plain, but had a cat-like beauty to her, and was always eager to please. She had no idea how lucky she was to have wound up here at his abode. Outside the Farm she would be easy prey.

"Right. OK, I will head there now."

Nourishment for his guest would have to wait.

Alexander left the Big House and walked toward one of the Farm's gathering areas. He had built the first phase of it years ago. Now, it was big enough to seat over 200. From the beginning, he had envisioned an outside church -- like the "revivals" that moved through California when he was a child. His parents had dragged him to a few, and he still vividly remembered them, even though it had been more than 50 years ago. Although he never fell victim to that old-time religion, even at an early age, he had been mightily impressed with the preachers and their ability to manipulate people so easily.

The whole psychology of it fascinated him. Why would relatively intelligent people give lots of money to someone they hardly knew? What was it about a person who could captivate normally functioning citizens to listen for hours in the heat on hard, wooden benches? The music was OK, but not objectively good enough to have people swaying back and forth, sometimes even wailing at the top of their lungs.

He knew he was not near as charismatic as those preachers were, but he still thought about them at the meetings before his own so-called flock.

He never yelled or jumped up and down. He rarely even raised his voice. He was able to maintain a relatively calm demeanor. However, he remembered how those preachers would use guilt and shame to get those folks to do just about whatever they wanted.

And he certainly knew how to use those weapons.

"Good morning," Alexander spoke to the crowd, sitting on wooden benches on the sloping hill before him.

"Good morning," the crowd answered.

"Announcements: As you may have gathered, we have a guest staying with us in the Barn. Please do not approach our guest and do not speak to him, unless you are given instructions to do so. He is not part of our mission, and while, as all of you know, he may eventually be, it is not for any of us to say. It is out of our hands. He will be in the Barn for the time being. If his stay is a prolonged one, he will move into the Big House and stay there until he leaves."

Now came the time of the "talk" that Alexander loved the most: He got to preach his own type of a sermon.

"Why are we here?" Alexander asked his flock.

"Self-reliance," the crowd recited back.

Yes, it was cheesy, but what kind of recantation wasn't? Also, Alexander believed it was necessary to throw down the gauntlet every day. He wanted everyone here to throw his and her hat over the proverbial wall every day. He wanted loyalty, yes, but most of all he wanted commitment.

"Yes, self-reliance," Alexander repeated back.

"It won't be long until the outside world has completely imploded: first with a bang and then with a whimper. The only ones who survive and thrive will be those who know how to take care of themselves, who know how to feed themselves, who know how to clothe themselves."

He paused for dramatic effect.

"And especially those who know how to protect themselves."

Alexander knew that his so-called adoring flock had heard this talk hundreds of times, but he also knew there was comfort in repetition. If they knew what he was about to say, they felt they were "in the know." They felt special. They felt smart. Most of them had never had such luxuries in their lives.

And he knew they would do just about anything to maintain that security.

"Fuck America!" a scraggly looking young man, sitting on the front row, yelled to a scattering of murmurs of approval.

"Yes, America has lost her way. That is true," Alexander said, "but remember the principles this once great nation was founded on: freedom, independence, and liberty. It really isn't America, but the world, humanity, that has gone astray."

Alexander felt he was beginning to hit on all cylinders. It was hard for him to stop himself once he got going.

"We will always abide by America's founding principles, especially in the future, when things go bad. We have to remember always what it was that made this country great -- what made humanity great."

He had to throw in a little jingoism. Nothing made people more loyal than false pride.

"A new America," someone yelled.

"A new world," Alexander corrected them.

He looked at the crowd. Most of them were former addicts, prostitutes, or homeless … or all of the above. They were all previously on the fringes of society, the outcasts: The ones who the real Jesus would have saved if he had been born in this time. They would now be considered model citizens by the outside world. They were bathed, properly groomed, and experiencing good, clean livin'. Each was learning his or her own skill that would come in handy when there was no technology, cars, electricity, or even modern weapons.

Yes, of course, he had some weapons stockpiled, but that would only be for the initial chaos. They would have to know how to protect themselves once the bullets ran out. And they would eventually, but in the meantime….

He knew he was doing a good thing here. As a result, he bristled when he heard Mookie or his "employees" call this place a cult. This was anything but a cult. This was no more a cult than a church or a college fraternity. He just happened to know how to convert former outcasts into good citizens of a future world: They had to believe in what they were doing.

He was not the centerpiece of this organization. He was not the leader in a David Koresh or Jim Jones way. He did not have multiple wives, or even one wife for that matter, and he did not plan on conducting a mass suicide.

He wanted his flock to live fulfilled lives, but he had to teach them how to first. Frankly, he had a lot left to learn himself. He may not be their leader, but he was their guide.

And, sometimes, unfortunately, a guide has to do unpleasant things to get his followers to where they are going.

When Mookie first mentioned his idea of a halfway house as a cover for Mookie's business operations, Alexander felt like a gift had plopped into his lap.

It was hard not to feel like he had been chosen. Chosen for what, though? That had not been clear at first, but as he slowly amassed loyal followers, who would do just about anything he wanted, he eventually began to believe that, yes, he could lead the chosen few to the next phase of life on Earth.

He had enough people not only to survive, but thrive, and even be the next step in evolution.

OK, maybe that was overstating it slightly. After all, how could a former addict lead a bunch of outcasts to be the chosen ones. So far, though, as he slowly took it one day at a time, it did appear that he just might be the right person for the job.

No one was more surprised than himself.

At the very least, he could be the leader on an Isle of Misfit Toys in an ocean of the dying and the decrepit. He hopefully could provide safety and security in return for loyalty, adoration, and maybe even love, which was probably why God created the world in the first place.

After he finished the announcements/talk/lecture, Alexander dismissed them to go to their jobs. He headed back to the Big House by himself, wondering again what he was going to do with his guest. He decided the first thing, of course, would be to feed him -- if the man could hold anything down -- and then make sure his injuries were not that severe and treat the ones he could.

Alexander found himself wondering about who the man was and exactly what he did to put himself in such a predicament. He was obviously not the typical junkie. He did not need the usual cleaning and grooming rituals, typically reserved for first-time attendees. Alexander assumed his guest might even be educated, which would be rare in this place ... other than the occasional philosophy major, of course. Maybe he could have an actual conversation with his guest about something other than the Farm and the inevitable end of the world.

Yes, Alexander's marching orders were nothing more than to keep the man alive, but he thought there was nothing wrong with having a compadre with whom he could share a nice dinner conversation.

Alexander smiled and walked up the worn, wooden steps to the Big House.

4.

Mookie continued to look at the dumb, white bitch in front of him. For a long time now he had considered putting her in the "stream of commerce," but for some reason, some nagging sensation in the back of his head, he had not.

That changed just now, though. He saw how she looked at him, with a sudden, unexpected anger: A hatred he recognized only in those who were ready for their life expectancy to be drastically shortened.

Good, this is perfect timing, he told himself.

She was not exactly pretty, and she did not look young enough or "exotic" enough for most of his clients' tastes, but she might just be perfect for the fringe element of his clientele: The ones who could spend money to scratch the one itch they could not otherwise scratch because of societal standards.

And such a call had come today, offering nearly triple what Mookie would normally charge.

The girl in front of him would be unrecognizable when his client was through with her. She would also be dead if she was lucky. Mookie shook his head and sighed. He had long ago stopped being amazed at such depravity.

Who could have guessed that the young boy with so much promise -- the first child in his family to go to college and actually earn a degree -- would be the so-called criminal he was today.

He did not care. At least he was in charge of his own destiny this way. He did not have to rely on white, corporate America to do the right thing. Instead, he got to make a lot of money by exploiting the corruption in white, corporate America, while, at the same time, pointing out the hypocrisy in white, corporate America.

Not a bad deal.

After all, it wasn't he who was depraved. He was merely providing a service.

OK, maybe he was a little depraved.

The skinny, white girl looked away and went back to work, making coffee. Mookie looked back down at his paper and thought about what to do next. He would send her away now, of course, but he had to figure out the details first. He really did not want her in the same place as her old buddy.

That fucking asshole.

Mookie knew the first time he laid eyes on him what he was … or, rather, what he wasn't. He wasn't an addict, and he wasn't homeless.

Mookie thought at first he might be a cop, but the dumbass was too careless for that: His loud manner, the cocky way he treated others, and the way he made jokes only middle-class, white people would understand.

And his teeth … his teeth were much too clean and straight to be that of his usual employees. Nonetheless, Mookie kept the dumbass around mostly so he could keep an eye on him. Now, though, he was being kept somewhere safe until Mookie could figure out what to do with him. He did not necessarily want to kill the dumbass. He did not know how deeply he was connected or if he could be used in some other sort of way.

He just knew he had to get him out of the way. He was getting too close.

Mookie did not want to send the girl to where the dumbass was, but he knew he might not have a choice.

Mookie could feel the heat coming down on him. The pressure was palpable. The phone calls from the politicians and other highly situated government officials were not as frequent as they had been.

He had already made the decision he was going to have to quiet things down a bit, and he definitely could not risk everything falling apart over two assholes. He would keep the man where he was until he could figure out what to do with him, and he would be done with her once she was in the stream of commerce.

That was the plan, and now he had to put it into action.

The "request," the service which the white bitch would be providing, had been a consistent one from his long-time client. The client would pay a lot of money, but as detached as he had taught himself to be, even Mookie's stomach turned at what this sick motherfucker liked to do.

Oh, to be rich, powerful, and white.

But this was the world in which he lived. He realized early in life he would not be able to change the world, so he might as well exploit it. Yes, as a young man, he was the first from his family to go to college, and not just some small traditionally black college either. He actually attended a large state university and, not only that, was one of the first minorities to enroll there.

Both his parents had been proud, but especially his father. Escaping a life of poverty by joining the Air Force, his father was nonetheless intent on his son becoming an educated man. It had been drilled in Mookie's head for as long as he could remember. Not only was the way to make it in the world to be educated, but it was also the way to be a complete person.

An educated person. It had seemed so foreign to Mookie at the time -- like some mythical creature that existed only in the outer stratospheres of space. And while most fathers dreamed of their sons becoming world-class athletes, Mookie knew his father dreamed of a son in a tweed coat, smoking a pipe while pontificating on the literary greats. His father had seen horrendous things in the war and wanted a life of intellectual ease for his son. If he could have perched Mookie in an Ivory Tower himself, he would have.

His mother, on the other hand, had seen the other side of the war: that of the abandoned spouse, who, in the years after her husband left familiar shores to fight in a foreign land, struggled just to get by. Eventually, she had taken a job as a maid to make the ends barely meet.

She wanted nothing less for her son than to be beholden to no one but himself. She told him this late at night in hushed tones as if anyone could hear her outside their small living quarters.

"Don't you dare ever put yourself in a position where you have to rely on another person. They will always let you down. Always."

On Mookie's first day at college, he had arrived in his father's image: Starched white shirt, short hair. He went to class every day and read late into the night. As one of the few minorities in a large university, it wasn't like he had anything else to do anyway. He was a good boy.

But it didn't last.

He soon grew tired of his professors, even the occasional black ones. The whole college system, even then, seemed so boresome and archaic. Mookie remembered wondering if this was really the way people were supposed to learn. This was the way people were supposed to become educated?

He saw almost immediately how the students who kissed the most ass got the best grades. He saw how the most original thinkers threatened the power dynamic his professors maintained in the classroom and, as a result, were often ridiculed or made to feel less than.

It was not how his father had idealized it to be. It was not a petri dish of free-thinking radicals. Rather, it was a cold, stifling jar of old thought with no room for growth or creativity. Whenever Mookie thought of his good ole college days, he thought of an attic filled with cobwebs and old, dust-covered things that once served a purpose, but about which no one cared anymore.

He did learn a lot from his college days, though -- just not from the books or his professors' formal teachings. For the first time, he realized that he had a certain penchant for seeing the game, understanding the game, and winning the game. The game consisted of whatever it took to get what he wanted. He also saw how others were not willing to do what it took to get what they wanted.

He learned quickly how to get the best grade in the most efficient way in each class. Sometimes it was simply studying, writing, and doing the necessary work in a disciplined, structured manner.

Other times, well, sometimes white, liberal professors got just a little too much pleasure in servicing one of the few black students at their large university. Even after all these years, Mookie still laughed at how pathetic those so-called bastions of enlightenment looked with their pants around their ankles in front of their dusty bookshelves inside their dark, cramped offices.

He had always been in control, though. Always.

He instinctively knew who was the most vulnerable. He initiated the first conversation. He stayed after class to ask questions. He went to office hours. And, when he made his move, there was never any resistance at all. When he would leave their offices, more than once, they were still wearing their tweed coats.

Easy A.

Mookie grinned at how easy it all had been and, at the same time, knew it had set the tone for the rest of his life.

Control. Doing what no one else had the balls to do. Success.

His mother had been right, and his father had been wrong.

There was no Ivory Tower. There was no true intellectual life. In the university setting, there was no pontificating about life and life's issues. There was only bitterness and pettiness, the same pathetic tug of wars that existed in state legislatures, law firms, churches, community theaters, and homeless shelters. The tweed jackets and dusty bookshelves were just lies to cover up who they really were, but Mookie knew. Mookie definitely knew.

He knew there was no art, literature, or religion. There were only fears and wants and, then, what people would do to placate those fears and satisfy those wants. Now, for a price, Mookie could satisfy the most perverted wants and placate the most unfounded fears. As a result, he was rich and powerful, but, more importantly, he was not exposed. He lived his life on his own terms and did not have to rely on anyone else.

His mother would be, oh, so proud.

"Mookie."

Well, yes, maybe he did have to rely on a few dumbasses here and there.

"Yes."

"We gotta make a decision soon."

Mookie took a long look at the dumb, bearded man in front of him: former drug addict, undisciplined, unhygienic, and worst of all, no sense of responsibility. He just did what he was told and blamed others when he fucked up. However, so far, he was loyal. He was also strong and had a certain craziness that scared the shit out of most people.

"Yes, OK," Mookie said, knowing he needed to make a decision and a decisive one at that.

"OK," Mookie said again looking straight into the man's eyes. "Take her out. Tonight."

5.

Cadel thought about his mother. He used to long for her attention. He would tell funny jokes to make her laugh. He liked to see her smile, even though her eyes were always sad. His earliest memory was of a woman changing his diaper and his wondering why it wasn't his mother.

Where was his mother now?

Where was he now?

What is that smell?

Cadel settled back into the darkness, where it was warm and safe. He already knew that he did not want to be . . . where? Where did he not want to be?

OK, let's wake up. Let's figure out what's going on.

No, not yet. It's warm and safe here. I don't want to leave quite yet. I'm not ready for the pain.

Pain?

Cadel felt the pain, running all the way up his leg, through his spine. He felt it mostly, though, in his head.

C'mon, wake up.

Cadel saw the edge of lightness in his head. He felt the pain even more acutely. He could not feel his arms or his legs, but he knew they were there. He did not feel like opening his eyes yet, so he just sank back in the darkness again. One last time, he told himself.

OK, here it comes.

Cadel opened his eyes.

The light seared through his brain and stuck in the back of his skull. He made himself keep his eyes open for as long as he could.

He could not tell where he was other than somewhere dark with light spilling from somewhere. A light? No, it was a crack in the wall. No, not the wall. A door: Light from underneath a door.

He felt around him. Concrete?

He tried to prop himself up, and an unexpected pain in his leg overwhelmed him. He threw up all over the floor beside him, but did manage not to get it on him.

Small victories.

Warmness.

No pain.

Cadel looked at his mother again. She always seemed to visit him in his dreams, even though she had been dead for over two decades now.

She was young, not the old, dried-up version he normally encountered.

And she was smiling.

And she was looking at him with love and compassion.

And he was in her arms.

No doubt this was a dream.

Cadel rolled over into his throw up and made himself roll over again. He felt a chain on his leg that prevented him from rolling all the way over a third time. He felt the wall with his foot and moved himself as close to the wall as the chain would allow.

It felt comforting to feel the wall. He felt stable. He tried to prop himself up into a sitting position, but felt the pain again and let himself throw up some more.

Cadel opened his eyes again, but the pain was too much and so he let himself close his eyes just one more time.

Cadel woke and tasted the dirt in his mouth. He puked what was left in his stomach and dry heaved for good measure. He smelled the musty smells of what had to be an animal shelter of some kind. A stable? His throat was dry, and he could barely open his eyes. He could taste old, crusty blood in the back of his throat. He tried to lift his neck, and an acute pain shot down his right side.

That's not good, he told himself.

He felt his hands tied up in front of him. He tried to open his eyes again. He heard the distant sounds of insects, but that was it.

Insects.

For the first time, Cadel realized he was not in San Francisco anymore. Not good, Cadel tried to say out loud.

He vaguely remembered a brief conversation with someone. An old hippie? Cadel had no idea who the man was. He certainly did not look the part of a kidnapper. The only law he guessed the man had ever broken was smoking lots and lots of weed ... and possibly listening to the Moody Blues.

He looked at a milk jug full of water in front of him and imagined the billions of bacteria screaming his name in unison, wanting to enter his body and eat him from the inside out.

He grabbed the jug of water and gulped down half of it.

He knew he was ill prepared for the country life, so he might as well go with it. If the water was going to make him sick, then so be it. He'll be in overalls and slingin' hay bales before too long. He knew, though, that there was no way he was going to escape if it meant having to spend more than a day in the wilderness. He would have to find another way. In the meantime ...

"Peel the onion and survive another day," he repeated his mantra, lamenting for the first time in his life that he quit the Boy Scouts.

Locks on the outside of a door started turning and clicking. As the door opened, he was momentarily blinded by the sunlight and had to look away, but quickly looked back. The outlined figure eased closer and closer.

Oh, goodie, the hippie. At least, maybe he was bringing him some food. The man was indeed carrying a tray of fruit and bread. Even though he had spent the last few minutes throwing up, Cadel's stomach growled at the sight of apple slices, banana pieces, and a loaf of French bread.

"Good morning," said the man as if he were an innkeeper at a Vermont Bed & Breakfast. He leaned down and put the tray of food in front of Cadel.

Cadel saw the man was smiling.

It took him off guard, so he did what he normally did in uncomfortable situations: He attacked.

"You sure are friendly for a kidnapper. I guess hippie kidnappers are all about peace, love, and hammers upside people's heads. What are you going to do now? Play the Grateful Dead music while you slice my dick in half?"

It wasn't his best, but, hey, he was tired.

The man stopped and dramatically sighed, rubbing his graying goatee.

"Well, technically, I did not kidnap you. We do have to keep you here, though. Do you remember anything about the last time I was in here?"

Cadel shrugged. All of a sudden, he did not feel like engaging in any cute banter.

"Yeah, I guess," Cadel said.

"Well, as I said before, you're safe. We're going to do our best to heal you. We'll even feed and clothe you, if you don't try and run every time we untie you."

Cadel vaguely remembered his pathetic attempt to escape before. His brain was still in a fog, so he willed himself to concentrate. What had they discussed before? He couldn't remember. He just knew that nothing made sense.

He decided to play nice.

"I don't understand what's happened. Why am I here? Why do you have to keep me here?"

"You don't have to understand anything quite yet. Let's just say you got a little too close to the sun."

Oh, great, an intellectual, Cadel thought to himself. He could already tell this guy was way too full of himself. He was a Baby Boomer, though, so what more could he expect?

"But you didn't die," the man continued, "so there's that."

"If you didn't kidnap me, then why I am here? What's your role in this?"

"Let's just say I'm kind of a holding station."

"I don't know what that means. Are the people who kidnapped me coming back for me?"

"Maybe. The important thing for them, though, was getting you out of the picture and keeping you away. I don't think they really have an interest in you beyond that."

"Well, they certainly seemed to be interested in me when they were beating the shit out of me."

"OK, that may be true, but in your case, I think beating the shit out of you was just an extra benefit."

"Yay for them!"

"I'm sure you didn't say anything smartass to provoke them either."

"How dare you besmirch me, sir!"

The man half smiled.

Cadel looked the man over. He was definitely a hippie. Hemp shirt, cargo shorts, sandals -- check, check, check. At least he didn't smell like patchouli. It always bugged Cadel that the people who held themselves out as nonconformists always looked exactly the same. The hippie was no different.

And he was in his what? Late 50s? Early 60s? It was hard to tell.

"Well, if you know me so well, why don't you tell me about yourself? What's YOUR name? What's YOUR story? How did you end up being a non-kidnapper?"

"I don't know anything about you at all really. My name is Alexander. Yours?"

"Joshua."

"Your real name?"

Cadel told him because he knew there was no point in lying … at least about this.

Alexander put the tray of food down before Cadel and sat down against a wooden post out of Cadel's reach.

"So, Alex …"

"Alexander."

"OK, then. Alexander. So, Alexander, what exactly is it you do here? This is some sort of farm, right? If I had to guess, from the look of you, you have a pretty good crop of marijuana."

The look on Alexander's face changed slightly, and Cadel knew he was right … but not quite on the nose either.

"We have a wide range of crops. Now, tell me what you do and why you were posing as a recovering addict at a work/release facility? Not that well, I would guess, by the way."

"I'm a cop."

Alexander's face busted out in a smile, and the deep wrinkles in the corners of his eyes sprang outward. "No, you're not."

"Why not?"

"You're not the type."

"What does that mean?"

Alexander shrugged. Cadel realized he was slightly offended by his deduction.

"OK, I'm not a cop. You got me. I'm actually looking for someone. I was hired by a family to find their kid after the cops decided they wouldn't help."

"A bounty hunter, huh?" Alexander pushed himself up to his feet. "OK, keep lying to me, and we'll keep playing this game for as long as you want."

It was a pretty lousy lie, Cadel admitted. However, he was not quite ready to tell his whole story. He would have to keep it hidden as long as he could. He knew he could very well die, but now, even in his vulnerable state, he was not quite ready to let months of research and writing go down the tubes.

Besides it was not a total lie. He was looking for Mookie. He was looking for who Mookie actually was and what he was doing.

Yeah, OK, that was stretching it, but, hey, he could live with it.

Alexander was still staring at him.

"It's the truth. You can believe me or not." He decided to double down.

"OK," Alexander sighed. "I'll believe your story for now. You do understand, though, that the men coming back for you do not care one way or the other. If you want me to help you at all, you're going to have to trust me."

"Help me? Trust you? What are you talking about? You kidnap me, beat me, hold me against my will, and you want me to trust you? You've got to be fucking kidding me."

Cadel felt the anger rising in him and, then, slowly let it leak out of his body.

"OK, I know you did not kidnap me, but you did have a part in all this. Would I be here if not? Why should I ever trust you?"

Alexander kneeled down beside him and put a hand on the shoulder. "Because, what choice do you have?"

Touché.

"So, have you had any luck?"

"What?"

"Finding this person?"

He's fucking with me now, Cadel thought. Great.

"Nope."

"Male or female?"

"Female," OK, now it was a lie. "I'm done talking until you answer some questions yourself."

Alexander sat down and leaned back on his hands. "OK, what do you want to know?"

"Why, again, am I here?"

"I don't know. You got too close to Mookie's business affairs, or he felt you were a threat."

Cadel's face relaxed. The hippie said Mookie's name. He was taking a chance with him. For what, though? Cadel had to be careful here. He did not want to lead on about how much he knew, but he still wanted some information. He knew, though, that the aging hippie might actually be saying all he knew. He decided to leave it alone for now.

"OK. Where am I? What is this place?"

"I guess you could call this somewhat of a halfway house, where addicts, runaways, and the otherwise homeless get a chance to get clean, learn a skill, and maybe start their lives over. It is, of course, up to them. We lay out certain steps, and if they meet them, they can stay."

"And eventually they can get back into the world? The real world?"

"In a manner of speaking. They can always leave if they want, but they can also stay. Most choose to stay."

Cadel examined Alexander's face to see any trace of a wink wink nod nod.

He wanted to see if there was any chance Alexander was going to let him look further behind the curtain. Alexander's face remained unchanged. Cadel could not get a read on him at all, even though they both knew that they both knew this was a cover story and nothing more.

What Cadel did not know yet, although he was beginning to have strong suspicions, is for what this was supposed to cover.

"Not much of a halfway house, then, is it?"

"I give them a choice. From where they have been in their previous lives, I can't blame them for wanting to stay. There's no danger -- no predators. They get three square meals a day. They work hard, and at the end of the day they have a clean, safe place to sleep. This is a healthy environment for them. For some, it is the first time they've ever been in a healthy environment."

Good, Cadel thought, he is justifying himself. In his experience, that is when people slipped. Also, it deflected the attention away from him. The less he talked about himself the better. He decided to coax the hippie a little more.

"So what do you get out of it? Kickbacks?"

"I do get money to run the place, of course. I'm providing a service after all. But not as much as you'd think."

Alexander stretched his legs out in front of him and leaned farther back onto his elbows. He had visibly relaxed. He had the look of someone completely comfortable with his surroundings and place in the world.

It was disturbing.

"So tell me, please, who are you looking for?"

"A runaway. She ran away from home a year or so ago. I traced her to San Francisco and have been looking for her in various shelters around town."

God, it was a bad lie.

He had no choice now, though, but to see it through. He was just going to try to keep it simple and not volunteer any extra information from which anyone could hang him later.

"OK, then," Alexander said while looking down at the tray of food in front of Cadel. "Go ahead and eat what you can. I'll come back later today."

Alexander got to his feet and looked down at Cadel.

"At some point, you're going to have to tell me the truth. I want you to understand that. There's no reason for you to lie. I'm not going to hurt you. In fact, I'm helping you. You want me on your side."

Alexander turned to walk away. He then stopped and turned back around to face Cadel.

"You don't want to be helped do you?"

The question struck Cadel as odd and totally out of character for this person who he thought he'd pegged. It also completely resonated with him. It struck a chord deep inside him, and so he took the bait willingly.

"Nope."

"You would rather die than ask for a hand up or a handout?"

"Yep."

"I think you might like it here, then."

What a pompous asshole, Cadel thought, as he watched the hippie strut towards the barn door.

6.

Junie woke up and, for a moment, felt the pleasant aura of morning.

Then, she felt the ties around her ankles and wrists and realized she could not move at all. The panic struck her body as she struggled to get free.

She had no idea where she was. She had no idea how she got here. It was dark. It was cramped. It smelled like mildew and dirt. She did not want to be here.

She realized she was also moving. She could feel and hear the hum of the road. She must be in a vehicle. She assumed she was in the trunk of a car.

She felt herself, then, grow calm. This is one thing she knew about herself from her childhood and from her police training. She had the superpower of being calm almost to the point of numbness when she found herself in extreme conditions. Things moved in slow motion, and she was able to think of solutions while others were either panicking or spinning their wheels faster and faster.

She loved this feeling of calm and reveled in it. She wished she also felt it in non-extreme conditions, instead of yelling at herself when she forgot to put the milk back in the fridge.

She slowly and methodically felt around her confines and discovered she was most definitely in the trunk of the car. She felt the dimensions of the car with her bound feet and the rough indoor carpet with her hands. She knew in the newer models of cars there was a latch to open trunks. However, this did not feel or smell like a newer model car, not that she had spent much time in a trunk of any type before now. She decided to check anyway. She swung her socked feet around and felt for some sort of latch. There was none.

Her socks ... no shoes.

Damn.

She was wearing a big T-shirt and pajama bottoms.

They got her while she was asleep?

From the shelter?

How were they able to pull that off?

She calmly pieced together her last memories.

Coffee Shop.

Closing up.

Walk back to the shelter.

Shelter.

She could not remember going to bed or even getting ready for bed.

Some sort of trauma maybe.

She felt sore all over, but her head, other than a mild headache, seemed to be OK.

They must have got her while she was getting ready for bed. In the hall bathroom? That would be the only place no one would have seen them.

OK. Good working theory.

But who were "they"?

Mookie. It had to be. Who else? Was she finally going to enter into his prostitution ring or whatever it was?

This thought did not scare her, though. It comforted her because it meant she had been right.

There was no reason to fight or escape. She would go with it. She had to let someone know, though, because now she was in real danger. That would be a priority when she got to wherever she was going. She hoped she would actually not have to have sex with someone, but if that is what it took to save the girls, who were more than likely there against their will, she would.

This was her meaning. This was her purpose. This is why she was alive at this moment.

She felt her body relax with this realization and settled back into the crevices of the trunk, her tiny body becoming part of the car. The hum of the motor and the rhythm of the road comforted her. She would use this time as an opportunity to heal herself, to rest, and to prepare for what lay ahead.

Her mind drifted back into a dreamy shadowiness. She thought of her early childhood: hot summers running barefoot in fields to find frogs in small creek beds, her friends laughing, sweaty ponytails bobbing up and down, and mud squishing between her toes as the sun beat down on her bare shoulders.

These were her magical memories. This is where she would go to remind herself how good life could be.

Oh, how she longed for those days of youthful bliss. In retrospect, she knew things were not that great -- at least not at home. They had no money, and her parents fought. She had been so happy, though, that none of that had really mattered to her.

One of her happiest memories was waking up on her fifth or sixth birthday. Her daddy had written, “Happy Birthday,” on rolls and rolls of butcher paper. He had wrapped the paper all over the house, including around the mounted deer head in their living room.

She had loved it so much. She could barely remember presents, parties, or cakes from other birthdays, but she vividly remembered that deer looking down at her from underneath a paper turban.

She also remembered the bitter disappointment the next year when there was no butcher paper. She had woken up wanting to feel special, the way she had the year before. She woke up wanting to feel the magic, to feel the unconditional love. Instead, she woke up to people going through the motions -- forced smiles and off-key songs. She remembered her gut telling her something was wrong and her pushing it down, way down, ignoring it. Of course, her gut had been right, and she had rarely ignored it since.

The car came to a stop. She heard the gravel crunching under the tires. A door closed, and she heard footsteps. Showtime. She imagined what a frightened animal would look like. She made her eyes as big as they would go and began making frantic, spastic movements. She knew she had to do this with her body, but, in her mind, she had to be calm and observant.

The trunk door open, and she played the part of the feral animal, pushing herself back from the shadowy figure, looking frantic while flaying her head back and forth. She took mental pictures, though, in her head for analysis later. Even though it was still dark outside, she could see the light beginning to break over the tree line. Dawn. It seemed like a rural landscape from what she could see. She could not see the man's face, but his shadow was big. He grabbed the back of her head, and she let the will flow out of her body. He poured water down her throat. He did not say a word as he did, but she felt a strange gentleness from him while she submitted to the act. When he was through, he shut the trunk. She heard him walk a few steps and, gross, start to relieve himself. The splattering of pee on gravel made an unmistakable and unforgettable sound. She even saw in her mind's eye a yellow river snaking back between his legs. She heard him walk slowly to the driver side, open the door, and start the engine.

So what did she learn from this encounter? She pictured herself writing down her observations. She was a reporter, writing frantically on a flip-top reporters' notebook just like in the movies.

Male, obviously. Big. Hairy. Large bladder. No particular odor other than a slight hint of B.O. He did not smell like alcohol. She could not see his face because the trunk light was out. Professional. At the very least, he had done this a few times. Not rough -- probably not due to his character, but because he was not to damage "the goods," so to speak. She was no different than a fragile box of eggs. She was being delivered for something, probably prostitution. Prostitutes, however, were not valuable commodities in her experience. That struck her as odd.

She did a quick inventory of smells, sounds, and whatever else she had seen in the early-morning horizon. Nothing told her anything other than she was in a rural place. She did not know where, though. She had no idea how long they had been traveling or where, but if she had to guess, they had been traveling for several hours and were heading north. It was just a guess, though.

If they were heading north and they were presently in a rural area, could they be heading to Oregon or Washington? Not exactly hotbeds for prostitution. She assumed that if she were going to bust a prostitution ring, it would be in the City of Angels.

No, they were going somewhere else and presumably not a major metropolitan area.

But why?

7.

Alexander walked back to the Big House and could not help but smile to himself.

He got him.

Or at least he thought he had. He had gotten the stranger to buy into his program -- or at least not dismiss it completely out of hand.

Alexander needed someone like this to help him. Someone slightly educated, not the typical addict who wound up on his doorstep. Someone whose judgment he could trust. Alexander hoped this person might be the one.

As he entered the Big House, he saw the cute young thing from before. She was wearing jeans and a loose-fitting men's shirt. When she had first arrived at the Farm, she looked like someone who had been living on the street. After living on the Farm for just a few months, though, she looked like she had never been homeless. Youngsters could lose the street-worn look faster than those even slightly older. Their teeth were usually still in decent shape, and their faces did not have the look of a shrunken head at a souvenir shop.

She came up to him and stood a little too close. Her red hair was right underneath his face, and he caught himself breathing her in. She looked up at him with her blue eyes, and he knew this could easily become a messy situation.

He had rescued her as he had so many others. She had been part of a "shipment," and he had made a deal with Mookie to keep her. Mookie usually did not mind such a request as long as they did not become too common. Mookie made a lot of money from young ones like this, so Alexander knew he could not get too greedy. He just reminded Mookie that this was supposed to be a rehab facility, and most rehab facilities had young people in them. Young people who still had people who cared for them, who would still pay money to help them, who had not been let down so many times they had stopped caring. Mookie usually agreed with this logic. He usually acquiesced to anything that would make this appear as a legitimate rehab facility.

Legitimate.

Alexander scoffed at the word. He was sure Mookie had suspicions as to what Alexander was doing, even though he never directly expressed them. Instead, he would give a slight shake of the head, a sigh, or a quick "all-knowing" glance at one of his minions. Mookie rarely came up here anymore, though.

Alexander knew Mookie assumed this was some sort of a full-blown, 24-hour-sex party. When, in fact, that was the one thing Alexander had strictly forbidden, even for himself. He was not naïve, though: He knew that "it" was probably going on. People could not help themselves. However, if they were going to be the foundation for a new society -- or, hell, even survive -- they would have to be more than mere animals, humping each other's legs and sniffing each other's nether regions.

The pale redhead, though, was exactly his type: thin, long legs, with no need for any sort of make-up whatsoever. She unfortunately would have to be a necessary non-event, no matter how bad he wanted her. But he still liked having her around, so he made sure her duties were close to him. He had even given her more responsibility than he normally would to someone so young. He sensed a little resentment from the others, especially from those who had been here since the beginning, but they would just have to deal with it.

He suddenly realized she had been talking to him the whole time, and he had not heard one single word. She leaned into him, and he felt her small, but nice, breast rubbing against his arm.

Jesus Christ.

"Say what again?"

"Would you like to review the numbers for the crop rotation again?"

"Sure, yes, of course."

He took the notebook she was holding and tried to make some space between them. He did so while trying not to draw too much attention to the fact that he was moving away from her. He did not want to hurt her feelings after all.

"Now what am I looking at again?"

"You asked me to take a look at the amount of unused land and whether we could rotate some of our other crops or new crops there."

"Right. OK."

He did not remember asking her to do that, and he was not sure whether she exactly had the qualifications to do so either. It did not matter, though. Everything he had done since he had arrived here had been by trial and error anyway.

When he first arrived, this was a simple farm previously owned and operated by an older couple. There was the Big House, but that was about it. He had slowly, but surely, built this place up to what it was today.

He admitted to himself he was proud of what he had been able to build here, especially considering from where he had come.

In high school, he had decided that he was going to be a musician, so his studies became more of a formality than anything. Every once in a while a subject, usually a short story in some random English class, would strike a chord inside, and he would do very well in that class. For the most part, though, he was a bad student. He did not even try to go to college, which horrified his parents. Sex, drugs, and rock 'n roll were what he wanted to pursue, so he moved to LA and discovered, as most do when they arrive in California, how untalented he really was and how talented everyone else was. His pursuits became just the sex and drugs. Then, eventually, it became just the drugs.

His sense of shame was still palpable after all these years. He remembered feeling worthless and not caring. He remembered thinking that if people thought he was a piece of shit, then, fuck it, he was going to be a piece of shit and take as many drugs as he possibly could.

His parents tried to help him, but he just used them to get more drugs. He would tell them what they wanted to hear, act like the good son they always wanted, and maybe even come home and stay for a week or so. Then, he would take their money, or something else in the house, and head straight for the gutter.

After a while, they told him to stay away until he cleaned up. The shame from that still burned inside him. He loved them, but the drugs were too much. He did not have the strength at the time to rise above the circumstances, so he convinced himself he hated his parents.

He realized now it had just been a pathetic way to make himself feel better about himself. He would show them! He would really fuck himself up! When he finally realized he did not hate them and began to understand how much they had done for him, it was too late. Regret was too simple a word to explain how he felt now.

He felt the small breast rubbing up against his arm again and realized he, again, had not heard one word she had said for the last few minutes. It was too late to ask her to repeat herself, especially after he had just done so, and even nodding in agreement was not much of an option.

"I don't have time for this right now. Check back with me later this afternoon."

Her expression was as if he had punched a puppy. She slinked away without another word.

"That did not feel good," he told himself.

He watched her walk away and felt his eyes examine her long, pale legs.

"Jesus Christ," he mumbled under his breath.

8.

Mookie drank the last sip of his coffee, put the cup down, and threw his hands down hard on the table before him.

"You did what?" he asked the man in front of him. "You took her from the shelter? Where anyone could've seen you?"

"Yeah, but no one did."

Mookie looked him over. He had to deal with people like this all the time. What this moron lacked in intelligence, he made up for with pure ignorance and the inability to have an original thought.

Mookie would say the person in front of him was also loyal, and that made up for his stupidity, but he was not sure if that was the case. The man was probably too lazy and dumb to go against Mookie. Now, it appeared that he could not even take orders specifically given to him.

"OK, tell me exactly what happened."

"We followed her after she left here like you told us. We followed her to the shelter...."

"OK, stop right there. You just walked into a women's shelter? Two big, white guys: the type of men women had been running from their entire lives? No one said anything?"

"It was just me. I snuck in the side door -- well, broke into the side door -- and hid in a broom closet near her room. When her roommate left to go somewhere in another part of the shelter, I went in and used the stuff you gave us to knock her out."

"Chloroform."

"Right. Then, I dragged her in the closet with me until everything went quiet and dark. Later, I took her outside, and we put her in the trunk. They drove off, and I walked home."

OK, that actually did not sound too bad.

"You sure no one saw you?"

"Yes."

Maybe he was not that dumb after all.

Mookie stopped to consider this possibility for a moment. Maybe he had underestimated this hired piece of meat. Up until now he had only considered him a waste of human flesh. Mookie did not want to underestimate anyone. That was when people failed. That was when kingdoms fell. That was when worlds ended.

People had underestimated him his entire life, but he also considered it the key to his success.

When he was younger, it would bother him. Why would people think he was incapable of doing even the smallest tasks? Was it because of how he looked? Was it because he was black? He had to work harder than anyone else, that was true, in high school, but he always did very well. Still, he was never chosen for the academic honors, advanced classes, or leadership positions that his lesser classmates were. He never could understand it. Maybe it was something about his nature. He preferred hard work with little acclaim to blatant self-promotion. He liked working in the shadows instead of in the limelight. He could always get more done if he did not have to worry about letting everyone know what he was doing.

Of course, this penchant for doing the work without the acclaim worked very well for him once he began his post-graduate "studies." The numerous politicians and businessmen did not see him as a threat, so they did "business" with him.

They looked down on him, but that was OK. He looked down on them as well.

And as those faceless powerful men rose to prominence and then fell back down to earth, Mookie remained. Always there. Always in the shadows. Always on the outskirts, making sure things were running smoothly… for him.

Mookie look back at the lunk in front of him. No, he would not make the same mistake here. Mookie looked him over. Younger guy. T-shirt, jeans, work boots, close-cropped hair. Bulky frame. Clean-shaven. He looked like he was right out of the Marines or maybe …

"Come sit down."

The man looked at him suspiciously. That was a good sign.

"Come. Come. I just want to make sure we are all on the same page."

Mookie patted the seat next to him. He was sitting at the table at The Coffee Shop where he always sat. The man reluctantly eased his way to the seat and carefully sat down. He looked behind him and, then, to his sides as he sat.

Good. He is paranoid, Mookie thought to himself. He should be.

Mookie knew he did not know much about this person other than he was a buddy of one of his other "employees," who had personally vouched for him. He had been with his operation for a few years and did mostly rote work: errands, deliveries, etc. He had not caused any waves and was relatively drama free.

Mookie put his hand on the man's knee, and he did not flinch. Good, Mookie thought to himself: He has his emotions in check.

He moved his hand slightly more up the man's leg and gave his beefy thigh a little squeeze.

Nothing.

Good. Very good.

He put his hand back on the table in front of him.

"Tell me about yourself. I don't believe we've ever had a real conversation."

This, of course, was the test. Mookie would know within minutes whether this man was a cop or not. If he was a cop, though, he would know he was being tested as well.

Mookie had sniffed out other police infiltrators in the past. Sometimes he had been wrong, but he would rather be paranoid and wrong 99 times if it meant he was right just once. He thought about the sadsack at the Farm right now. He was too soft to be a cop, but there was something else off about him. It might have been that Mookie just did not like his sarcastic, asshole-ish nature either.

The meathead in front of him, though, was just too perfect, too nondescript. He listened to his backstory, but more importantly Mookie watched the man's eyes and body language.

He listened to the tone of his voice and his voice patterns. Was it rehearsed? Was it on some index card in his wallet that he practiced every day in front of a mirror?

Mookie interrupted him mid-sentence.

"What was your high school mascot?"

"What?"

"I love school mascots. I have always been intrigued by what they are and how schools choose them."

"Mascot?"

"Yes, mascot."

"You mean the guy on the sideline of a football game?"

"Sure, but it doesn't have to be that necessarily. What did you call yourselves in high school? The Tigers? The Jaguars? The Bulldogs? What?"

The man sat silent. This question clearly took him off guard. Good.

"Uhhhh, the Raiders?" he finally said.

"Did your school have someone dressed up at football games as a Raider?" Mookie asked quickly. He knew he had to get the man to answer without thinking too deeply.

"Yes."

"What did this Raider look like?"

"Uhhhh, kinda like a pirate, I guess."

"Was it always a Raider or did the school change it from something else?"

"I ... I don't know. I don't think so."

"I bet they changed it from something else. It was probably an Indian or a confederate soldier."

The man did not respond, so Mookie continued.

"Did you know the Oakland Raiders were originally called the Oakland Señors? The team had a contest, and the name, 'Señors,' was voted No. 1 by the people of Oakland to be the team mascot. After a year, though, the management thought it was too offensive, so they changed it to the No. 3 choice, the Raiders."

The man looked at him with a blank stare. There was no fear or panic -- just slight confusion.

"It's funny isn't it? A Raider is considered less offensive than a Señor. What do you think a Raider does?"

"Errrr, raid?"

"Exactly. They raid. They pillage. They rape. In our society, a rapist is considered less offensive than a Hispanic man."

Mookie let the moment sit. The man in front of him looked dazed, but that was about it.

Maybe he was just stupid.

"OK. I assume the package has been delivered?"

This question snapped the man out of his daze for a minute.

"What?"

"The girl. She's been delivered, right? "

"No. Not yet. I don't think so at least. He was on the way, but said he had to take care of some business first."

"Say what?"

"He wasn't going straight there."

"You've got to be fucking kidding me."

"No, but he said it would be OK with you. He said you would not mind as long as the girl was delivered today."

This was not like "him" at all. His number one guy had been with him for several years and was as loyal as anyone who had ever worked for him.

If he had to take a detour, he would have said something to Mookie. The only time Mookie had known him not to do exactly as he was told was when he thought he was doing something Mookie wanted. He had never crossed Mookie before, or even disagreed with him before, so Mookie knew, whatever he was up to, it was not for his own personal gain.

So what the hell was he up to?

9.

Cadel woke up from his nap when he heard the barn door open.

Great, another philosophical discussion.

What he really wanted was not to be tied up anymore and to be able to take a shower and maybe even sleep in an actual bed. Granted, lying on a blanket on a dirt floor with his hands tied up was much better than getting the shit kicked out of him.

His head was also not hurting as bad as it had been. He felt like his body was slowly healing. He was sure at one point the thugs had broken at least a couple of his ribs, but now he was not so sure. He was still sore, but the pain was not quite as acute. Had they actually given him painkillers? He could not remember.

As the person walked closer, he saw it was not the hippie. It was a female. He saw the outline of her shoulder-length hair, and he noticed how she walked in a certain feminine, almost feline, way. He automatically straightened up and felt his chest subconsciously poke out.

Good Lord, why did he have to smell so bad?

"Why, hello there," he said in a southern drawl. "You are the best site I have seen in the past 48 hours ... 72 hours.... or however the hell long I've been kidnapped by you people."

She walked into the sunlight from the window above, and he saw just how correct he had been. She was definitely a female, and she was smiling too.

Maybe his time here would not be so bad after all.

She set the tray of food she was carrying down next to him and took away the empty tray he had devoured. "Thank you, sunshine," he said again in a fake southern accent. He was trying, unsuccessfully it would seem, to use as much charm as he had left in his energy-depleted body.

"What I would really like is a shower or a bath … or even a sponge bath if you know someone who could do the sponging," he blinked his eyes with mock affection.

She shook her head, not to say no, but as if to say, I can't believe this dumbass. It was rather ridiculous, his flirting with one of his kidnappers, but, hey, what else was there to do?

She was cute. Didn't the hippie say this was a cult of the homeless and the addicts? In his experience, the homeless did not look like this. This girl had a certain sweetness to her, even if he had not heard one word out of her mouth yet ... or maybe that was just what he wanted to believe.

She turned to leave.

"Wait. Wait. Seriously, can someone at least bring me something to wash my face? I don't care if it is baby wipes, or a towel, or a dog's ass."

She stopped and turned back around, "I'll see what I can do." She turned to go, but before Cadel could say anything else, she stopped, twisted her head around, tossed her shoulder-length red hair back, and smiled at him again. Then, she left.

"What the fuck was that?" Cadel said out loud.

He looked down at the ties on his hands, from which he had been trying to get free, and decided to hold off on that for a while. He did not feel as if he was in any danger at the moment. They were feeding him at least. He looked at the tray of food: more fruit and bread.

Cadel looked down at his feet. Around one leg was a chain that was connected to the wooden post against which he was sitting. He would just have to play along if he wanted to escape. By the looks of his soon-to-be fellow companion, if he was lucky, that might be a good thing too.

He had to find some answers, though, he reminded himself. He was not here just to play grab ass. If he was out of danger, as the hippie previously proclaimed, then he could play along and eventually, hopefully, find out what the hell was going on in this place.

He listened to the noises outside. He heard voices, but could not hear what they were saying. He did not have to, though. Their tone and cadence told him that they were workers, and they were working: instructions, affirmations, and casual conversations.

If this was a farm, what were they growing? He had assumed, as he told the hippie, that it was some sort of marijuana crop. If this was a place of recovery, though, that would not make much sense. Why didn't the hippie just say so when he asked him?

And how was this place connected to Mookie?

Nothing added up.

As he did when he became frustrated while investigating potential stories, he went back to his old analogy of the onion. He was not at the core yet. He would have to keep peeling away the layers and be patient. The times he had made the biggest blunders had been when he went straight for the core. Patience is a virtue, he told himself, and it was the key to investigative journalism, even though the current state of journalism was a bunch of screaming white males on cable television, who did not care about the truth as long as they could win an argument with a simplistic "us vs. them" or "straw man" sound bite.

He was going to do this right, though. The rest of his life could be a complete mess, but he knew he could do this right.

He heard other voices coming closer. He thought he recognized the hippie's voice. Maybe he was going to free him. He had already decided he would not try to run. He would stay at this place as long as he could -- until he broke the entire story or the thugs came back looking for him.

Or he could see the redhead again.

The barn door opened, and, sure enough, there was the hippie. He had even brought some of his minions with him.

Now, these yahoos looked like addicts.

The man next to the hippie had the weathered look of someone who had lived on the street for a very long time. He was probably in his 40s, but the deep-set wrinkles in his face aged him at least another 20 years.

The African-American woman on the other side had long dreadlocks pulled back into a ponytail. Her face had the weathered look of someone had slept many nights outside, whether by choice or not.

Both had a stoic nature about them, but not the aggressive anxiousness with which he had become all too familiar at The Coffee Shop.

"OK, man, it is time to get up and see the rest of this place." Alexander pointed to the woman next to him. "She's going take you to get washed up and give you some clean clothes to wear. She'll also provide you with other daily supplies you'll need. Later she'll take you to where you will be staying and show you around the rest of the place. We won't put you to work just yet, but we will need you to help out around the place until you get well enough to work."

"What makes you think I won't run away?"

"If you haven't noticed, you aren't exactly in the best shape to make a run for it. Also, these folks will make sure you don't. And even if you do get past them, and miraculously overcome your injuries, you still have to get through the woods surrounding this place. There's nothing but miles and miles of it. It would take you a long time to get to any sort of shelter, let alone civilization. And you don't exactly look like the outdoors type."

Cadel let out a long sigh. "Don't worry. I'm not going to run. I just wish my escorts looked more like the one who just brought me food. She even promised to give me a sponge bath."

The hippie raised an eyebrow and instinctively, with one hand, rubbed the back of his neck, while, with the same hand, combed through his greasy strands of hair there.

Ahhhhh got him, Cadel thought to himself and smiled. "Well, she implied she would. I think she likes me."

"Yes, I'm sure she likes you." The hippie bent down with wire-cutters and severed the plastic from Cadel's wrists. Alexander then unlocked the chain from around his foot.

"Can you get up?"

Cadel slowly got to his knees and raised himself to his feet. He stumbled as he did so, but caught himself on the wooden post next to him.

"Good as new," Cadel said.

The hippie looked at his minions, "Let me know once he is cleaned up and fed. I'd like for him to eat with me at the Big House tonight."

"Oh goody," Cadel said. "I get to eat with the big boss man to-night."

He looked at the faces of those in front of him. Nothing. Not even a smile.

"No one has a sense of humor anymore," he said as he limped to the barn door.

10.

Junie was in a safe place, and it felt good. She was on a beach, and the sun felt comforting as its warm embrace enveloped her. She stuck her feet in the sand and listened to the waves.

Only it didn't sound like waves.

No matter. She was going to enjoy this moment as long as she could. There was a feeling of dread somewhere inside her. She knew there was something about which she should be concerned, but, for now, she was not going to think about it.

Yes … sun, warmth, safety, waves.

OK, not waves. What exactly was that sound? It was familiar, but was definitely not waves. Then, the sound changed to something else.

Don't think about it, Junie said to herself. Stay here. Stay where I am. Don't … Don't … Don't …

Wake up.

Junie heard the wheels hit gravel and instantly knew the waves in her dream had been the sound of wheels on pavement. The change in tone and volume as the tires hit the gravel had not woken her, though. It had been the knowledge that they would likely be stopping now. It was the unsettling gut wrench that things were about to kick into high gear.

It was also beginning to be warm in the trunk, not beach warmth but death warmth. She could see cracks of daylight peeking through her darkness.

"Midmorning?" she wondered.

She felt the car beginning to slow down. They were on a gravel road, but now were turning onto another road. She felt the centrifugal force push her even further into the corner of the car's trunk. She heard the tires sinking further into the gravel.

Driveway.

From her childhood, she knew all these sounds by heart. She could even picture a cheap, plastic mailbox on a decrepit, wooden frame as they turned into an overgrown yard that led to a rust-covered mobile home in the middle of nowhere.

She felt the car coming to a stop and heard the engine shut off. She braced herself for what was next.

She heard his footsteps walk around to the trunk. Then, it was open. The sunlight was blinding, and it disoriented her to the point of nausea. He grabbed her by her hair and lifted her easily out of the trunk. He threw her on the ground. She hit the soft gravel and tried to get up, but could not get her feet to plant and fell back down onto her back.

She felt a hard kick to her side as she tried to get back up onto her knees. Her face fell down into the loose rocks and dry dirt.

"Stay down," she heard his voice for the first time. It sounded vaguely familiar, but she could not quite place it.

She decided to heed his advice and kept her face buried. She slowly lifted up her hands as if to say she was surrendering. She turned on her side.

"OK, OK, just don't kick me anymore," her voice sounded pathetically weak, which surprised her. Her disorientation meant she was not longer in "cop mode," acting like a victim. She realized in a panic she was now, in fact, one.

"If you try and run, I will," he said.

Oh no, Junie said to herself.

She felt the already-present panic rise up inside her as she realized who this was: the asshole from The Coffee Shop. She started to scramble to get away by rolling unto her side. She felt another kick -- this time to the side of her face. She felt him grab the hair on the back of her head. He pulled her up onto her feet.

"What the fuck did I just say?"

"Get away from me!" she screamed as she struggled with all her strength to escape his grasp.

He threw her hard onto the ground, not the driveway gravel, and she felt the air escape her lungs suddenly and hard. She grasped for breath. As she scrambled to her knees, she felt the man's boot meet the upper part of her hip bone.

The pain was much more than she expected -- so much so that she barely felt his dragging her across the ground by her hair.

"Now, you're going to shut your fucking mouth and do what I tell you. If you don't, I'll break your other hip. You understand?"

Damn, he is a professional, she thought in a brief lucid moment, before the bright stars on the outside of her consciousness formed an electric "V" inside her head.

Then, all was quiet again, and she was back on the beach. She would not listen to the undertone of dread this time -- at least not for a while.

11.

Alexander watched his newest citizen walk away. He wondered if the man would try to run away, even though it did not matter. Mookie did not seem to care whether he stayed or not. Mookie just wanted him out of the picture for the time being and had no plans for him as far as Alexander can tell, which was not the case with most of Mookie's shipments. Most had very specific instructions like the one to be delivered later today, which was even more of a "special case." And there had already been a fuck up on that one. He was just glad it wasn't because of anything he did. It should have been delivered this morning, but there had been a delay for some reason. He didn't know why and didn't care. He just had to make sure everything on his end still went smoothly, which meant making sure no one else on the Farm saw the "delivery" or the later "pick up." He wasn't that worried about it, though. Most of the folks here had been in hellish situations way before they arrived here and, as a result, had learned the fine art of select blindness.

Alexander also believed that most everyone here was just grateful to be off the streets and did not want to do anything to disturb their peaceful existence. They were smart enough to realize there was some dark shit going down here, so they left it alone and concentrated on the things for which they were grateful.

And they had a lot for which to be grateful. They were learning how to take care of themselves for first time in their lives. They were learning how to take care of each other as well. They were also learning how to live without electricity, gasoline, or diesel.

Well ... not quite, but at least they were getting there.

They, of course, still had a pick-up truck, mostly for errands. Alexander had a generator hooked up to the Big House. He had no TV, though, and he did most of his reading by flashlight at night. He was not ready to make the switch to lanterns or candles, although he knew at some point he might have to.

He had a disposable phone, that Mookie didn't know he had, which allowed him to communicate with the outside world. He got text messages from various news organizations that told him just enough about what was going on in the "real world" that he knew he was glad not to be a part of it.

Alexander's bookkeeping records were kept in old accordion-like folders, and he got his mail the old-fashioned way. Alexander knew he was not completely off the grid, but he was getting pretty close. And he got closer every day.

"I am coming. Don't hurry me." Alexander heard his newest guest say. Alexander was walking towards the Big House, but turned back to watch his guest limping to the outdoor showers. Alexander decided to follow his newest citizen to see if he could get a better feel for this fellow. Also, he liked to see the place through new eyes -- it gave him a fresh perspective and allowed him to see what he needed to change or improve.

He stayed at a close enough distance, so he could hear what they were saying. He stayed far enough away, though, so they would not know he was there.

"If you haven't guessed it yet, self-reliance is what we strive for here," his female escort said as she led him to the outdoor showers. "Part of that, of course, is basic hygiene. Everyone has their own bar of soap, clean towel, and work clothes. Here's yours." She handed him his bundle of necessities.

"You have to keep up with your bar of soap, but, at the end of the day, you get the next day's clothes and towel, and, at the same time, you turn in that day's clothes and towel."

"What about dental hygiene?"

Here we go, Alexander thought to himself. Although he used toothpaste, and, upon request, several others did too, one of the first decisions he made when he got here, as his first citizens arrived, was to deemphasize dental hygiene. Most of the citizens, because of their drug habits and street lifestyles, did not have many of their teeth left.

He knew it was a source of shame for several of them, the way they covered their smiles with their hands or avoided smiling altogether. By deemphasizing teeth and eliminating this source of shame, he saw their individual confidences go through the roof. They were experimenting with a type of baking soda they could make and use, but it was pretty nasty. Some of the younger citizens insisted on brand-name toothpaste, and Alexander gave it to them with little fanfare. In contrast, he noticed that some of the older citizens took pride in not having teeth. For them, it had become a badge of honor, living here as productive human beings after surviving their previous lives.

"We will get you a toothbrush and some toothpaste if you want."

"Yes, please," Cadel responded with mock eagerness.

Thank God he did not ask for deodorant.

"The outdoor showers are over there. We will wait for you over here. Go ahead. You have your towel and your soap."

Alexander watched as his newest citizen limped to the outdoor showers, which were basically two cinderblocks structures, one for men and one for females. There were partitions to allow for some privacy, but the longer people were here the more modesty became less of an issue.

"Heavens to Murgatroyd!" Cadel screamed from inside.

No hot water.

"Seriously, no hot water?!"

Nope, no hot water. The shower was hooked up to a well, and the water came out more cold than anyone expected -- even now, every morning, it always took his breath away. Alexander did not have to preach on the environmental concerns of using too much water for bathing. People could not wait to get out of these showers. He knew there'd be no California water shortage if there were no hot water heaters.

"You didn't tell me you were the goddamned Amish!"

Funny. Actually, a lot of what Alexander learned when he first arrived here was from what he read about groups like the Amish -- how they were able to live without electricity -- but that was it. Religion was a no-no here. That was a clear line of demarcation. He would not control his citizens through fear. They had to choose this lifestyle

-- not because it was God's will or plan, but because it was their own will, their own plan.

For the first time in their lives, they were in control of their own destinies. They were the architects of their own dreams. They were not reliant on the government, their dealers, or their pimps. They were finally home.

Maybe the cure to homelessness was simply providing a home.

The asshole politicians would never understand such a simple concept, though. It would upset their false self-concept of masculine strength. They were so tough. Why couldn't everyone else be tough? Addicts and the homeless were weak. Plain and simple. Why couldn't they pick themselves up from the bootstraps and be as good and pure as the politicians? All they needed was willpower. So to bolster their false-strength personas, the politicians put in place false steps to "help" addicts. All they had to do was act a certain way, and they would get the help they need. This false bravado was destroying the country the same way it was destroying all other man-made power structures, including, of course, religion and, even more specific, Christianity. The religion based on grace and forgiveness had been highjacked by those who falsely believed in their own willpower. If you decided you wanted to get into heaven, then you had to be strong enough to do it yourself. When, in actuality, Christ's message was about accepting the weak and the dispossessed. It was the realization that you couldn't save yourself, and it was this realization that ultimately saved you.

But it was the same in all political, religious, and social structures. The need to be seen as "tough" ultimately would destroy everything. The systems put in place by intellectuals to protect the population from this innate human flaw would eventually fail too. That is why the closest-to-perfect document created by humans to ensure equality had been hijacked by those who only cared about their guns. What's more "tough" than a gun after all? Much more tough than equality, free speech, and a fair judicial system.

Alexander knew he was weak. But he knew that everyone else was weak too. He just had to make sure his citizens knew that inside them there was also a certain kind of strength. They just had to strip away all the bullshit to get there. If they believed in themselves, in this strength, while still knowing they were weak, then there would be no need for the fake machismo he saw everywhere.

Maybe the meek really were supposed to inherit the earth. There would be no need for self-important blowhards with no true skillset in the post-apocalyptic world. They would die off pretty quickly. No, the true survivors would be the ones who knew their weaknesses and thus believed in the strength of the group. At the same time, they would also come to know their true individual value.

Alexander believed this as strongly as he believed anything in his life. It was the greatest of paradoxes: You only became strong once you knew you were weak.

Alexander watched the newest citizen limp out of the showers in his new clothes and join the others. Once reaching them, he looked over and spotted Alexander. He gave a big, fake smile and waved enthusiastically.

Yeah, this one was probably not going to make it.

12.

Mookie hung up The Coffee Shop phone and felt the blood rush to his face. He was pissed. He had no idea where his employee, his most trusted employee, was. He was supposed to make a delivery hours ago, but no one had heard from him. No one knew where he was. No one knew what his plans were.

This was not funny. Mookie was playing with fire, and his ass was about to get burned to a crisp all because one of his supposedly most loyal employees decided to go rogue. As in all international businesses, if one cog in the machine fails, the whole engine breaks apart. In his line of work, though, if a cog breaks, his whole livelihood could fall apart, and he would wind up behind bars.

It was very risky dealing with the type of client he had in this situation. The delivery was supposed to have been made early this morning. This afternoon the package was supposed to be picked up by his client. The exchange of money, a substantial amount of money, had already occurred. If this particular client meant to pick up this package, after paying what he had paid, and it was not there, things would get real ugly real fast.

The bastard did not even have a cell phone with him. That, of course, was Mookie's fault. He did not like there to be any sort of communication other than face-to-face, which is why he always put the people he trusted in charge of the most delicate situations. In the past, this bastard had always come through for him with no drama. He was professional in every sense of the word. Not this time, though. Not when Mookie needed him the most. He knew that time was now of the essence. If the delivery did not take place in the next two hours, all hell would break loose.

Mookie, as he had so many times before in his life, started to weigh his options. He would have to change once again and adapt. He hated to lose everything he had worked for over the years, but if this delivery did not happen … if this person showed up to pick up his new toy, and it was not there, he would have no choice but to end it all. It was the price he had to pay for doing business with someone so rich, so powerful, so crazy, and so vindictive.

Yes, the money was good. Real good. And the risk, as a result, was all too real. Mookie shuddered at the thought of having to face that horrible face. He would rather pack a small suitcase and disappear forever. There were only a few people of whom he was truly scared. For most people, Mookie usually found a way to manipulate them or at least find some angle to get the upper hand. If he could determine what motivated a person, that was even better.

This, though … this was a whole different ballgame. This was, well, just … evil. Mookie knew most people would consider him evil, but most people had never seen what he had seen. They would not even have a frame of reference for it. To be able to do that to another human … well, Mookie did not want to think too much about it. He just provided a service after all.

Yes, that was all he did: provide a service.

No matter how many times he told himself that, though, sometimes he still had a hard time swallowing it. He provided a service no one else would touch, which is why he got paid as much as he did. Mookie knew he was justifying all this to himself, though, and had a sense that in the end he would have to pay some sort of penance. He was surprised he had not yet.

"Excuse me," Mookie had walked outside to get some fresh air and had not seen the bum sitting on the street corner in front of him.

"I need some money to fill my prescriptions, please sir. Could you give me just a little change? Every little bit helps." The unkempt man had two empty, orange plastic pill bottles and held them up for Mookie to see.

Mookie was sure that if he closely looked at the bottles they would have two different names. If this man really was on any sort of medicine, it would not be in these bottles and it would not be legal. The bottles were props, and, just like lazy comedians, props only played to a simpleminded audience.

Mookie, as most people, usually ignored such begging with a certain nonchalant obliviousness. Today, however, at this very moment, he felt like playing the game.

"What is the medicine for?"

The man looked at him blankly and then nervously began to shake and twitch as he tried to get up from where he was sitting.

"No, stay seated," Mookie said. "I just want to know why you need medicine."

"Awww, man. Ya know, I got everything. Everything. Depression. Tourette's. Diabetes. Sickle cell. You name it. I got it."

Mookie knew that, more than likely, he really did need medication, but the man, at some point, decided he did not want to take it or, paradoxically, the medicine made him feel like he did not need to take it anymore.

The man was, as 90 percent of the people on the street, mentally ill. Anyone who had ever done any sort of work with the homeless came to realize quickly that this country did not have a homeless problem. This country had a mental health problem. Yes, the street did have its share of con artists and straight-up drug addicts, but Mookie knew that most of the homeless did drugs to deal with their mental illnesses. They were not homeless because of their drug problems; they were homeless because of their mental illnesses. The drugs, for the most part, were just a part of the equation.

Mookie usually did not send the mentally ill to his "Recovery Farm." He would send the candidates who could actually recover. He did not want to house those who needed real medical help, even though he was aware they would not get any help on the street either. It was just the cost of doing business. He needed the politicians to see real progress. He did not need them to see people walking around talking to themselves.

When they first started the Recovery Farm, and they were struck with how well it worked with getting people off the street, they tried sending those who were not ideal candidates as well, i.e., those who, mentally, were not all there. It did not turn out great. They could not take care of themselves and did not contribute as the others did. Mookie was stubborn at first and insisted they stay there until they showed some sort of improvement. However, after a few "incidents," he had no choice but to realize that the mentally ill were, well, ill. There was no magical cure.

Sure, they were self-medicating with street drugs, but taking those drugs away did not take the mental illness away. Unfortunately, Mookie realized, for some people, the only way to treat mental illness was to have them institutionalized, not having them work on a farm. And, because the government decided in the 1970s that it was not in the mental health business, American streets would always be chocked-full of people who were mentally incapable of living healthy lives.

And because Mookie could not further his own agenda by having the mentally ill around, he long ago decided he would not be in the mental health business either.

As for the bum in front of him, Mookie, like every other person in the world, ignored him and went about his merry way.

13.

Cadel was not expecting the water to be that cold. It was such a shock to his system that he almost forgot the pain in his leg. Almost.

As he limped out of the shower, he saw the hippie spying on him from behind some sort of structure. He could not mistake that skinny, wiry frame and greasy long hair.

"What an asshole," Cadel thought to himself. "Like I'm going to corrupt his little crackhead escorts."

He put on the biggest smile he could muster and waved with a fervor that could not be mistaken for anything but a "fuck you." The African-American woman turned around to see why he was waving, turned back to Cadel, and grimaced. He erased any trace of a smile from his face in response. She turned to leave, and he followed.

He felt clean at the very least. He did not think any of his wounds were infected either. His right leg really hurt, yes, but he could at least put some weight on it. At the very worst, it was a stress fracture. He had on clean clothes as well. How about that for a luxury? It was not quite a uniform, but it was not quite meant for individualism either.

The woman he was following was wearing a variation of the theme as well. Cadel looked at her more closely. She was a stocky woman, who looked like she could beat the shit out of anyone she wanted, even though she was probably in her early 50s. She had that hard look that told you not to mess with her.

So, of course, Cadel did.

"When is movie night? I'm thinking, 'One Flew Over the Cuckoo's Nest,' is right up this place's alley. Or maybe a little 'Shawshank' action."

He tried to walk fast in order to get next to her, so he could see her facial expressions, or lack thereof. His leg, though, was not cooperating. Nonetheless, from the back of her head, and the way the dreadlocked ponytail continued to bob up and down, he knew her facial expressions, or lack thereof, had remained ever flaccid.

His entourage reached another facility. It looked like a cabin one would see at any state park.

"This is where you will be staying for now," the woman turned to look at him.

"What is this, summer camp? Cabins and outdoor showers. Are there bathrooms in there at least?" Cadel pointed to the wooden structure.

"Why don't you go inside and put your things up? Then, I can show you where you will work tomorrow. Because you are injured you won't be doing much manual labor, but you still have to know where to go or you'll get lost pretty quick. You'll be taking water to the others … that sort of thing."

"Oh goody. Will I get to be the House Massah too?"

Yeah, she obviously did not like that. The way her mouth turned slightly downward in what could be considered a frown told him that maybe he had overplayed his hand.

"Please go ahead and take your things inside."

OK. OK. He was not going to rattle her. Not today at least.

Cadel took his things up the front steps and walked inside. There were several bunks, as he had suspected beforehand. Ten single bunks lined up in two rows of five.

"Just like camp," he said out loud.

Cadel saw there was one area with empty shelves and a bunk with no sheets. He assumed this was his and moved his way toward it.

"Hey, what's up?"

Cadel was startled by the voice. He did not know anyone else was in the cabin with him. He turned around and saw a younger man lying on a bunk next to the door.

"Hello there. Nothing at all. Just putting my stuff down, becoming assimilated. You know, everyday stuff."

"Yeah, well, get used to it, my brother."

Cadel tossed his new possessions on the bunk and turned around to take a look at his new bunkmate. He was younger then Cadel, yes, but he could not tell by how much. He seemed to have a wiry strength, which Cadel always admired, that no amount of running or weight training could provide. He had tattoos on both his forearms. His sleeves were rolled up to the elbows, and Cadel assumed the tattoos did not stop there. He had one on his neck as well -- some sort of snake it looked like.

"Why aren't you out with the other field hands?" Cadel asked his new friend.

"I took the day off," he said. "We can do that if we want to every once in a while." He looked Cadel once over. "You must be new here."

"Yep. I'm getting my tour now. Looks like I'll be sleeping over there."

"Good deal. Welcome to our little slice of heaven."

"Hmmmm, do you seriously believe that?" Cadel turned to look around the cabin some more.

"No, but it sure beats where I was before by a long shot."

"Gotcha," Cadel looked back at him and started towards the door. It was really not that bad. No electricity, but it was brightly lit from the screened-in windows and, because it was under some trees, it was oddly cool inside. Nothing was painted. Just natural wood everywhere. Cadel had a feeling that the whole thing could be torn down and rebuilt in a day. He turned and saw a door in the back of the cabin.

"Where does that go?"

The man looked to where Cadel was pointing and shrugged.

"Outside."

Great. Another smartass. There was only room in this town for one of us, buster.

"And what, pray tell, is outside?"

"Well, there is a porch out back where you can hang your wet stuff. That is also the easiest way to go to the bathroom. Number one of course."

"Let me guess. At night, you sit around, sing songs, play banjo, and hold hands -- a real hootenanny!"

The young man grinned in spite of himself. “No, but I will tell you that the stars, man, the stars here at night are fucking amazing. I’ve never seen anything like it.”

That stopped Cadel in his tracks. Stars.

Cadel always loved looking at the stars as a child, especially on camping trips he would go on with his father. The beauty of it all sometimes was too much for his young heart to take. His father would point out the different star systems and try to get him to see different animals or ancient warriors. That never interested Cadel, though. He was more concerned with the vastness and overall grandeur of what was above him. There was no need to try to find patterns or any other man-made constructs up there. He just tried to take it all in and more than once he found himself floating in the midst of the universe’s water and timelessness, and even as a young kid, Cadel remembered thinking that his brain just could not comprehend it all. At the same time, the glimpses of eternity seemed just barely out of his reach.

“Yeah, stars, man,” the tattooed freak said again. “I like to look up at them every night. All my problems, my past, my shame, all the things that I couldn’t forgive myself for -- no matter how hard I try. I forget all that bullshit when I look up at them at night.”

Cadel was mildly surprised that such a deep sentiment had come from someone like his young friend. He realized maybe he had wrongly judged him based solely on his appearance. He initial gut reaction about people was usually right, but this time he realized he was probably wrong.

“Right. OK, I guess I gotta get going and finish my tour. I’ll see you around.”

“Alrighty. See ya.”

Cadel walked outside and saw his posse. He looked around to see where the old hippie was hiding. He could not see him, but he knew he was lurking around somewhere. He could feel it.

As he limped down the steps, he felt a tug on his shirt. He looked around and saw his tattooed friend, who had a look of concern in his eyes he did not have just a few minutes ago.

"Hey, man," he said. Even though they were in earshot of his escort service, Cadel noticed that the man spoke in a hushed tone, so that no one else could hear him.

"Hey," Cadel said and turned, so no one would hear him.

"Umm, this sounds strange now that I'm saying it out loud, but is the world outside really ending? Is it all falling apart? I mean, is it really happening? Are we going to be the only survivors? I thought for a long time that all of it was bullshit, but now I'm not so sure. I mean, maybe I am losing my mind, or this talk has finally gotten to me. I just don't know anymore ..."

Cadel looked at him closely. The man's cool facade from before had melted into a childlike fear.

"No, no, everything is fine. There are a lot of problems, sure, like there always have been I guess, but everything is OK as far as I can tell."

"They keep saying civilization is crumbling. That it's all ending. Now. If that's true, I just wanted to say goodbye to my sister. We haven't spoken in a long time, but I'd like to see her one more time or at least talk to her."

"Don't worry," Cadel said. "You'll be able to see her again. The world isn't ending tomorrow." He knocked on the wood banister as a joke, but it did not relieve the tension on his bunkmate's face. Good Lord, these people are scared to death, he thought to himself. They really believe the world is ending. Not only that the world was ending, but that it could be any second. That it was imminent.

Cadel knew the danger with such scare tactics. He had been raised in a conservative Baptist Church. When he was 12, he went to his youth group's first "lock-in," which consisted of a bunch of junior and high schoolers "locked in" the church overnight. He remembered it starting out as the most fun he had ever had. Food, candy, girls, games, and a lot of laughing and playing. Kids being kids. Innocence. Holiness even.

Then, around midnight, as kids began to claim gym mats and dark corners in which to fall asleep, the youth minister announced they would be showing a movie, a trilogy even, like Star Wars, to everyone.

Cadel loved movies, even as a kid, and found his way to the classroom where a projector had been set up.

Cadel had never heard of "The Rapture," but for the next six hours he became an expert, watching the movies along with the other sinners. He became intimately familiar with the Antichrist, the number of the beast, and how he would not be swept up into heaven if he had even a smidgen of doubt regarding the son of God. The trilogy ended with people, who refused to get the number of the beast tattooed on their forehead, having their heads chopped off at a guillotine. It was not quite as horrifying as Ewoks' singing, but it still did the trick.

Unlike other scary movies Cadel had seen in his life at that point, which made him jump in his seat, laugh, and then continue eating popcorn, this trilogy of movies not only scared him, it had a profound impact on him. This was real. This was going to happen. At least, that was what he believed as a 12-year-old kid. That was what his church was telling him would happen. Why would he have a reason to believe otherwise? It was not until much later Cadel learned the Rapture was just a bullshit scare tactic from a few evangelicals in the early 20th century, who had culled random passages from different books of the Bible to spin a fabulous weave to explain how the world would end, somehow leaving out the part of the Bible where Jesus himself said no one knew, or would ever know, how the world would end, except for God.

But the scare tactic worked, and, Lordy, how it worked on Cadel … at least, for a while.

It had such a profound impact on him when he was young, it became his obsession. When would the world end? Would he get swooped up into heaven if the Rapture occurred while he was masturbating? What if his parents got swooped up, and he did not? Where would he live? Would he still be able to go to camp? Would there still be school? And, of course, the killer question he could never answer: Why would a loving God create the world only to destroy it and torture its inhabitants in the process? It was the cosmic equivalent of building a Lego Death Star only to throw it against the wall once finished. Was God some petulant child merely throwing a temper tantrum?

As a 12-year-old, though, these thoughts and questions did nothing but cause Cadel even more stress, anguish, and guilt. It meant he had no faith. No matter what he did -- prayers, fasting, self-denial -- the questions and doubts were still there. He still lacked faith. He still came up short. After a few years, he just quit trying. Then he rebelled. If he could not be who God wanted him to be, then he would go to hell in a blaze of glory.

His parents thought, naturally, that he was the spawn of Satan. Soon enough they eventually treated him that way too. He did not help things by wearing black Ozzy Osbourne t-shirts to school every day and listening to Eddie Murphy comedy records at full blast from his room.

His parents tried everything to turn him from his evil ways: praying, yelling, and, finally, petty attempts at manipulation. If he told them, for example, he was going to a concert instead of a church youth group function, his mother would give him the silent treatment for a whole week. It worked to an extent. It did make him feel bad. However, it was still not enough for him to change his evil ways. When his parents split up, it did not make things better either. His mother blamed him for his father's not wanting to be a part of the family anymore. That, through him, Satan had infiltrated their happy home and, like toxic waste, had corrupted the family unit to its core.

When his mother was not spending her days in silent, self-pitying stupors, she would lash out at him in almost-violent, hysterical tirades. His father at first would come around and try to play the paternal role. Such visits, though, would always end in his parents' fighting and his father's storming out.

Through it all, though, his mother continued to go to church, even as her former "couple friends" from her Sunday School class ostracized her. She eventually landed in a pathetic "Singles Again" Sunday School class, which consisted of lonely, damaged women and soft, leering men, who finally found the easy prey that had escaped them their entire pitiful lives.

His mother forced him to go to some of the social functions for her new class, where he met fellow hollow-eyed compadres. No one said much, but there was a bond. They would even laugh together after one of the feminine men would lecture them on how Satan was waiting behind every corner and, then, attempt to prove his manhood by unaffectedly hitting on their mothers.

Cadel did find some solace with those friends, though. He discovered that grace was there in the dark and often times in the places where most people would assume God was absent. He saw more glimpses of grace at those outings, laughing at the soft men, listening to heavy metal, and telling dirty jokes, than in any sanctuary door he ever darkened.

To say, then, that manipulation did not work on Cadel would be an understatement. Now, if he felt like someone was trying to manipulate him -- through scare tactics, shame, or puffery -- it triggered something deep inside him that made him want to destroy the person.

It made him horrible as a relationship partner, but a damn good journalist, in his humble opinion. Because not only could he not stand to be manipulated, he could not stand to see others manipulated either. And the poor sap in front of him just might as well have been his 12-year-old self at a church lock-in, in a supposed safe place, watching bloody heads rolling into a basket. This man was scared shitless.

Cadel looked behind him at the people who were his supposed caretakers. He realized they were scared too. Everyone here had been taken to a place where, in their heads, they were willing and grateful prisoners. The outside world was collapsing, and they had all lucked into finding a place where they could survive. And all they had to do was exactly what their fearless leader told them, and they would survive.

"What a crock of horseshit," Cadel said under his breath.

He looked around for the hippie Jesus/Hitler/Antichrist and did not see his weasely little face anywhere. Good. Cadel decided he would play this stupid little game for now. He would lay low, and he would act like a scared little grateful soldier too.

But he was going to bring this place to its fucking knees.

14.

Junie woke up, and she hurt. She knew from the pain in her side that she had at least one broken rib. Her head was foggy too, so she guessed she was probably suffering from a concussion as well. But she was no longer in the trunk of the car. That was a good thing, but where was she? What happened? She recalled the man dragging her out of the truck, but beyond that her brain would not let her remember. She let her training kick in.

She was inside. It was somewhat dark, but she could see. Air conditioning? Not central. She heard a window unit. Her eyes adjusted to the dim room, and she saw she was in a bedroom. She was in the corner of the room, curled up in the fetal position. She struggled to prop herself up. Her hands were still tied, so it took longer than it should have, not to mention the pain. Her mouth was gagged. Was she gagged before? She didn't remember.

When she finally got herself in a sitting position, she looked around the room. She was not in any position to run, physically or mentally. She was close to accepting her impending death.

The thought that made her the saddest was the realization that she would no longer be able to save those girls. She tried not to think about it, but she could not help it. She had seen many prostitutes in her time as a cop, and, yes, it was the world's oldest profession -- ha ha -- but kidnapping young girls and holding them against their will to have nonconsensual sex with gross, fat, hairy middle-aged man was the image in her head that sickened her the most. And sex trafficking was getting even worse. An age of mass communication and mass transit could have led to so much good, but, of course, it led to the proliferation of the most heinous of all crimes: the kidnapping of young girls to sell as sex slaves. It was so disturbing that most people simply did not think about it. They would rather spend all their energies combatting an easy enemy, whether it was gay marriage, the confederate flag, or abortion.

They could feel good about themselves, while a real evil was slipping by right under their noses. The media and the politicians would not say anything because it did not buy advertising or votes. Churches did not speak out about it because 14-year-old girls in the back of nondescript vans would not be funding capital campaigns any time soon. And, frankly, it was not a priority for the police either. Drug busts were where it was at. Those sorts of arrests made the headlines and were easy to do. Just bust up a house in a poor, black neighborhood, and, boom, you had plenty of headlines and promotions to go around.

Junie considered herself different, though. She told herself she did not care about the headlines or promotions. She wanted to stop this evil. Even though her becoming an undercover detective was a gift from heaven, she knew it would be difficult. She saw the sideway glances and smirks from her fellow officers when they found out she was going to pose as an underage prostitute. She had no doubt they were more turned on than inspired. She suspected that some of them might actually be in it for the sex themselves, whether it was the occasional blowjob or side deals with those doing the trafficking. She was sickened by it all. Why were men so gross?

She sometimes wished she was a lesbian.

It would not be that hard to make the transition since everyone already assumed she was one. After all, she was a cop, she was athletic, and she did not wear much makeup. She guessed her being a lesbian was a natural assumption. She kept her girly self to herself. She knew she could not show any sign of weakness (i.e., being female) in her male-dominated field. So she laughed at the sexist jokes, drank a beer with the guys after work, and even belched really loud every once in a while. But she always felt she was betraying some part deep inside her. She did not necessarily long for Chantilly lace or makeup or China dolls, but she always felt she was not being authentic when she played to her male audience. It was all so disgusting.

Maybe that was why she thought she felt this deep connection to those girls being trafficked. Maybe by saving them she was saving some long-forgotten part of herself. She did not even know who they were, but she felt more connected to those girls than any person she actually knew.

Those girls.

The phrase stuck in her mind and did not leave.

At first, she had an image in her head of a pack of young, feral girls in the back of a 1970s Scooby Doo Mystery Van, being carted around from town to town, having sex with sweaty, bald guys with extreme amounts of body hair and gold chains.

In reality, at first, there was barely any evidence of a prostitution ring in the area. She would hang out in homeless shelters, houses for battered women, and walk around in the normal areas, where streetwalkers staked their claims. She was even propositioned a few times. She also met a few handlers, who never really tried to employ her.

That was all expected, but she could not get wind of any grander scheme or pattern of sex trafficking.

However, the more subtle signs and whispers did eventually lead her to The Coffee Shop and Mookie. As luck would have it, when she reported to her superiors that Mookie might be the door to this world, it turned out that they already knew it. According to them, he had been on their radar for years, but they had never come close to cracking his organization. So she poured over the files on him and discovered they were right: Every leak, every "in," was met with resistance or a dead end or a judo chop that suggested Mookie was not only smart enough to insulate himself, but had some mighty powerful friends to help as well. When she got the green light to go after him, it was only with the condition that she not do anything to alert Mookie or disrupt the organization. She understood that years of observation and investigation would go down the tubes if she got too close. She was to infiltrate his organization just enough to observe and gather information. Under no circumstances was she to make any arrests or "save" any of the young women caught up in his system.

And that is what she had done now for months. It had been easy to get a job at The Coffee Shop, yes, but it had been difficult to get close to Mookie to gather any sort of concrete evidence. The evidence she had gathered had been minimal, but she had done her job. She had taken copious notes on the comings and goings of everyone. She mailed these notes to her desk at the police station, so they would not get lost and no one would see them. When she got the rare chance to go back to her desk, she would open the envelopes and categorize the notes with action items to follow up on later.

She had been professional. She had been detached. She had been careful not to disrupt the process. Mostly, though, she had been patient.

But she was frustrated.

Unfortunately for her, though, her wish had finally come true. Here she was now with a broken rib and probably a concussion. She felt completely helpless and worthless. She actually thought she would be able to bring down this network. Now, she would be lucky to escape with her life.

She wondered what she had done to tip off Mookie.

She had been under the assumption that he was going to put her in the same network as the other girls, but now she could only assume she had been made. If he was going to kill her, though, why hadn't he already?

Junie tried to clear her brain and think through her predicament. She had actually thought, as she was in the trunk, that she would soon be with these other girls. She would get to see the operation from the inside. She would then explore her options on how to crack open the network or at least save some of the girls in the process.

Instead, she had been beaten and left alone. Why? This was not at all what she had expected. This could not be the way Mookie treated his girls. Damaged goods would not sell, after all, and this sort of delivery was not the most efficient way either. It did not make any sense. She came back to her original thought. She must have been made, but why again wasn't she dead?

The door to the small bedroom opened, and the awful man appeared. His appearance again struck some sort of primal-fear button deep inside her, and she found herself, even with her injuries, trying to run, crawl, or roll away from him.

"Calm down, bitch. I'm not going to do anything."

Junie did not hear him. She was flaying herself against the wall behind her as if she could bash in the wall herself.

He walked to her and grabbed her by the hair on the back of her head.

"I said calm down. I ain't gonna to hurt you no more, unless you make me. If you just calm down and sit still, you'll be OK."

She had no choice but to listen. His bulk and overwhelming strength were too much for her. Even though she really had no choice in the matter, some part of her actually believed him. She let her body go slack and tried to speak, which came out in a marbled gurgle.

Right, her mouth was gagged.

She looked at him, and he looked back at her. He nodded.

"OK, then," he said and let go of her hair. He straightened up and sat down on the bed.

"We don't have much time. I'm supposed to have you delivered already, and I am sure Mookie is starting to get restless. It won't take him long to figure out where I am."

Great, Junie thought to herself. This idiot is going rogue, and I am stuck in his stupid plot. Not only am I probably going to die, but I will not even get the chance to do any good in the process.

"Now, look," he continued with his now all-too familiar intensity. "You do this for me, and I will let you go."

She did not believe him, and the look on her face must've told him the same.

"I don't give a shit if you believe me or not. I'll let you go. I don't care anymore. After today you'll never see me again. Either Mookie will track me down and kill me, or I'll get away, far away from here.

"Besides, what choice do you have? You can either do this for me and live, or you can die. It ain't like you're some precious cargo that can't be damaged. You were dead already. You've got no idea what he'd signed you up for."

The look on her face must have betrayed her once again.

"What? Did you think you were going to get out alive or something? You're damaged goods. You're nothing. But that's the point. Hey, I'm no saint. I know that, but this shit. I've seen it before, and it ain't nothing I want to see again. Ever.

"But that ain't what this is about."

The door squeaked open, and Junie's eyes instinctively traced an imaginary line from the horrid face in front of her to the unexpected sound. She saw an older man with a walker and an oxygen tank easing his way through the door. He was wearing a clean, pressed collared shirt with too-large khaki pants. His thin, gray hair had been slicked back and carefully combed.

He stopped and looked at Junie and the man in front of her. He smiled at her, not in a leering way, but in an almost, well, charming manner. It was as if he thought he was 40 years younger and was seeing her across the room in a black-and-white movie from the '50s.

"You were right. She does look like her. Why did you have to beat her? She's so beautiful."

The horrid man in front of her kept looking at Junie intensely. He bent down and whispered in her ear. His breath smell like mothballs and decaying flesh, and little specs of spit splattered on her cheek.

"You know what to do. He doesn't have much time left. Do this and I'll let you go. You don't want to know what Mookie had in store for your dumb ass."

Junie did not understand exactly what she was supposed to do, but her gut told her she better do it. She assumed it was something sexual, although she had no idea how the old man would be able to perform in such a manner.

She nodded.

He got up and pointed at her as if to say she made a deal, and he was going to make sure she stuck to it. He backed away and turned to the elderly man.

"Well, here you go. I will probably end up dead for this, but this is it."

"Oh, stop being so dramatic, you pussy," the old man said with a sudden fierceness that shocked Junie to the extent she still had the capacity to be shocked.

"Why don't you untie her first and then leave the room. If you're so scared, why don't you just go ahead and leave entirely. Go ahead and run."

"You've no fucking idea what you're talking about, you stupid old man. It's a different world out there than you remember. People do shit now they used to couldn't, and, if they got the money, they get away with it. All of it."

"You think that's new? That's the way it's always been, and that's the way it always will be."

"The worst people now are the ones with the money."

"Well, you're pretty horrible, and you got nothing."

The younger one looked at the old man for a brief second, and then he turned to Junie and bent down. He pulled out a knife and cut the ties from her hands and her feet, and he removed the rag from her mouth. He stood up, turned around, and walked to the door. As he walked by the old man, he did not look at him, but as he got to the doorway, he stopped and turned his head around, still not making eye contact with the old man.

"Yeah, I wonder why I'm so horrible?"

Without another word he left the room and shut the door.

Junie's eyes looked at the closed door, and she felt the tension leave her body. He was gone now, her base instincts were telling her. The man, who had kidnapped her, drugged her, put her in the trunk of a car, and beaten her, was finally not a threat, at least not for the minute. She did not care what he had just said about letting her go.

She did not believe him.

She would have to find some way to escape. She had the sense that he was listening to the door or waiting for her to try and escape, and then he could really do her in. Yes, she had to escape, but for now she decided to allow herself to stay in this relatively safe place for the time being. She closed her eyes and let out a long breath of relief. She remembered, though, almost as an afterthought, that she was not alone. She opened her eyes and looked at the man in front of her.

He was looking right at her. He had a strange confidence for a man in obviously poor health. He looked her over with hungry eyes the way she imagined a teenage boy looks at porn when no one else is around. It was almost endearing.

"Well, it's just you and me, beautiful," he said as he continued to look her over. He smiled, and she saw he had some mighty impressive dental work. She scanned the room, trying to discover clues on where she was and why she was here.

It looked like some sort of old ranch house. The floors were wooden, and there was one window. She guessed it was a conventional foundation. The bed in front of her looked old too. The frame looked hand built, and there was no box spring: just one rather pitiful mattress. It looked like it had not been used in a while. The dust floating through the sunbeams from the window told her this room probably had not been used in a while either. The hum of the window unit was the only sound she could hear. No cars. No people talking.

The man shuffled towards her and set the walker to the side. He sat on the side of the bed. He pushed himself back so his legs dangled over the side. He did not seem as frail as he had before. Was it an act?

"You feeling OK?"

She shrugged her shoulders, "I'll live." The sentiment struck her as funny, and she could not help but attempt to smile.

He smiled too, getting the joke.

"Well, I'm glad you think so. I'm certainly not going to hurt you. Not that I would if I could."

"What are you going to do? I don't understand what's going on here."

He closed his eyes, took a deep breath, and let it out slowly.

"I don't know myself… exactly. I don't have much time left. I really just want some female companionship for old time's sake. I want time with someone like you. You're young, pretty, and you remind me of someone I used to know. Someone I used to love. As pitiful as it sounds, I want to feel young again. I want to feel the way I used to feel when I thought I'd feel that way forever. That's the beauty of youth. You're too stupid to know you're young, but that stupidity is what makes you so beautiful and appealing. You only know you're naked after you eat from the tree of good and evil."

"Youth is wasted on the young, right?"

"No, it's youth precisely because it is wasted. When you begin conserving your energy, that's when you're no longer young."

She did not know what the hell he was talking about, but she guessed that was the point he was trying to make. She thought so at least.

They looked at each other for a minute without saying anything at all. He patted the bed next to him.

"Do you feel well enough to come sit beside me? I won't bite."

Something inside of her resisted. It did not feel right to her.

"What do you want? A hand job or something? Is that it?"

He sighed, "Oh, please, don't be so vulgar. Just come sit beside me. Please."

She tried to get up, but the pain in her side was too much. She plopped back down to a seated position.

"I think I need medical attention more than anything."

"Would you rather be dead because that is the choice. All I have to do is call dumbass back in here, and you'll be a shallow grave's best friend."

He smiled as he said this, as if it was the most charming thing in the world, but she recognized the meanness behind the smile. He was old, yes, but that did not mean he was nice.

She pushed herself up to her knees and, with her hands, pulled herself up to the edge of the bed. Using her upper body, careful not to strain her ribs, she lifted herself on top of the bed, rolled over, and sat up, propping herself upright by locking her elbows behind her.

"See, now, that wasn't too hard, was it?"

She was beginning not to like this person at all.

15.

Alexander knew his new citizen knew he was watching him.

Nonetheless, he still decided to hide and eavesdrop.

Why? Did he really care this much about what this man thought? Why was he seeking approval still at the age of … damn, almost 60 now? His parents had long been out of the picture. He knew they were still alive somewhere -- probably in some Midwest nursing home, eating Jell-O and doing wheelchair aerobics -- but as far as being a part of his life, they were not now and had not been in a long time. And he knew that was his fault. He did not blame them.

He just wondered what deep-rooted psychosis still lay dormant, waiting to destroy him. As far as he had come, he still knew he could destroy it all. His self-destructive tendencies were all too real.

So what was it about this guy that made Alexander want his approval? He felt like the little dog in the old Warner Bros. cartoons, jumping up and down around the big dog, yapping, "Wanna play ball, Spike? Wanna play ball? Let's play ball. Whaddya say?"

It made him mad at himself that he was still so needy. No matter what barrier or safeguard he put up, he still had that raw nerve exposed. Anyone, if they knew this, could get to him. Anyone could exploit him. At least he knew it, and he supposed that was a good thing.

It still really pissed him off, though.

The group left the bunkhouse and headed towards several of the work areas. He followed them, but was careful to remain out of sight.

"Excuse me." He jumped at the voice. He had been so preoccupied with not being seen by the group that he did not realize he was being followed himself.

The redhead.

"Yes, sorry, what is it?"

"There's a car -- a black SUV -- that has stopped right inside the front gate. It's just sitting there."

Shit, Alexander said to himself. The delivery. The package is still not here. What the fuck was he going to do? There was no time to think. He had to go and at least let this person know the delivery would be delayed.

He did not know much about this person other than he was the only person who seemed to intimidate Mookie. And that was saying something. Mookie had faced down every kind of drug dealer, pimp, politician, and police officer with a sense of calm and confidence one could only admire.

Mookie's attitude when it came to this … person … was different, though. Mookie was twitchy, anxious, and even panicky. Everything always had to be perfect with these transactions to the point where Mookie himself would arrange all the details, leaving nothing to chance. What Mookie could not do himself he had his most trusted guys handle. Alexander knew the package was supposed to be delivered this morning, and when it was not, he had some concern. He had just assumed, though, that with this being such a priority, Mookie would have it covered.

The package had not been delivered, though. Now, he had to face someone, who he had never met, who Mookie made sure he never met, who Mookie was scared of, and do it all while maintaining the façade that everything was OK. Damn Mookie and his no cell phone policy, Alexander thought to himself. If Mookie just had a burner, Alexander could at least touch base with him to see what to do. Alexander jogged in the direction of where the car should be.

In the past, the car would pull up, pick the package up, and go. He never saw who was in the car. He did not know why this delivery was more special than any of the others. After all, it was not like sex trafficking was an innocent walk in the park. He just assumed it was something he did not want to know much about, so, as he had so many other times before, he tried to stay above the fray and not think about it. He had a higher purpose, after all.

He saw the car as he walked up. It sat idling on the gravel road close to the storage shed where the package was usually located. It was the typical black SUV with tinted windows and chrome hubcaps one would see milling around Beverly Hills, Manhattan, or Washington DC. The immaculate detail of how clean it was connoted the power it was supposed to emulate.

In other words, you did not want to fuck with it.

"Well, this is going to suck," Alexander said out loud.

As he came closer to the vehicle, his instinct started to tell him something was way wrong. He felt it deep inside: Run the hell away from this. Just go. Leave and never, ever come back.

He stopped where he was.

Why was he so scared all of a sudden? Was it because of Mookie's attitude toward the person inside the car? Was there just something off about the whole operation that was registering with his deep subconscious? Were the cosmic elements of the universe sending him a warning? Was God finally waking up from his deep slumber to help out a homie for the first time in countless generations?

Or was he just being a pussy?

He looked at the car, and he swore that it was staring right back at him, piercing his soul. He did not make a move. It reminded him of the old westerns, when two gunslingers stared each other down before shooting each other up.

Except, here, he had no gun.

Not with him anyway.

He stood still for a few more seconds, waiting for something to happen. Anything. A bird chirping, a frog croaking, an asteroid crashing to earth. Nope. Nothing.

"Well, shit," Alexander said and, just as he was starting to make a move towards the car, he saw a door open, but could not see who was getting out. The door remained open, and the person walked behind the car.

He wanted to run. He had a feeling that his life was about to be over. He had given it a good run. He had mostly squandered his earlier life, but now, in the later part of his life, now that he knew his calling and discovered what he was finally good at -- not to mention the good he was finally doing -- it was all about to be over.

"Typical," Alexander again said out loud. "Well, let's get this shit over with."

He started walking towards the car, and he heard the sound of crunching gravel coming from the back of the vehicle.

16.

Mookie looked at his watch. No word yet.

He could not call or text anyone at the Recovery Farm because of his no cell policy. He could call the landline, though. It was his operation after all. But he knew in the overall scheme of things, it was better not to make any sort of calls -- from either a cell phone or a landline -- or send text messages or have any sort of communication that gave the police an opportunity to snoop.

It was much easier for the cops to do so after the Patriot Act, at least that is one of his law-enforcement clients told him. Mookie did not know if it was true or not, but it was better to be safe than sorry, especially in his line of business. He also, simply, did not like the look of a charity worker, who had given his life to helping the homeless, walking around constantly talking or texting on a cell phone -- or constantly buying burners. It was unsavory.

He also liked the simplicity of face-to-face meetings.

Still … it sure would be nice to know what the hell was going on.

He definitely should have heard by now if the delivery had occurred. The driver should have called The Coffee Shop almost two hours ago. He was really cutting it close.

At least he had not heard from … him. If he had heard from "him," things would be slightly different than they were now. He would not be casually looking at his watch, taking strolls, or wondering about the next day's deliveries. He would be thinking of ways to get the hell out of town.

The phone behind the counter rang.

Mookie jumped up from his table and waved off one of his workers.

"I'll get it," he said to the employee, who looked shocked Mookie was doing any sort of menial labor.

Mookie lifted the phone from behind the counter and picked up the receiver. The caller ID said it was a private number.

"Hello, Coffee Shop," he said in as a nonchalant voice as he could muster.

Nothing. No voice, but no dial tone either. He waited for some sign or something to tell him that this was an actual call and not a telemarketer or a robocall. And for the first time in his life, he prayed that it actually was a telemarketer or a robocall.

"Hello?" he said again in a voice more pitiful than he ever would have intended.

Again, nothing. He listened hard to determine whether there was any background noise or anything that would tip him off as to who it was or hopefully who it was not.

A click and then a dial tone.

Mookie hung the phone up. He knew who it was, and it was not good.

He looked at his watch again. He looked around the Shop to see whether anyone was noticing his panic.

"Fuck it," he said out loud and picked the phone back up.

He dialed the number of the farmhouse -- the Big House or whatever Alexander called it -- even though he knew the line was probably tapped. It rang for a long time, but Mookie knew that it sometimes took a while for someone to get to the phone. At this time of the day, they were outside working, and there was no answer machine. He let it ring, and just as he was about to hang up, someone picked up.

"Hello?"

"Yes," Mookie said, picturing the 10,000 FBI agents listening. "Who is this?"

"This is the Recovery Farm. How may I help you?"

"No, no, no. I mean who is literally talking on the phone with me right now? God damnit, never mind. Where's Alexander?"

"He is unavailable at the moment. May I take a message?"

Mookie hung up the phone.

Incompetence. He could not stand it and had no patience for it, which was funny because it was his chosen line of work.

It was how he made money, by exploiting others' incompetences and weaknesses. Weakness and incompetence. Peas in a pod. He knew if someone was weak in one area, it would lead to incompetency in other areas. He knew, then, if, say, a certain white, family values, conservative state legislator had a penchant for young, black transvestites, all his energy would go towards scratching that itch and, even more so, towards covering it up when he actually got to scratch that hard-to-reach place.

As a result, said politician would forget to fulfill certain responsibilities, such as charitable contributions or diversity quotas he had to meet. Mookie, in addition to helping said politician scratch that certain itch, would also help him satisfy those forgotten obligations, giving him the photo opportunities and fulfillments he needed in order to continue to be re-elected. In exchange, Mookie would get certain favors in return.

It was a never-ending cycle, but one that benefited Mookie far more so than the pathetic individuals he "helped." It was how Mookie had remained untouched for so long. Whenever he saw weakness in the so-called powerful individual, he would exploit the incompetence. As a result, Mookie had become a magnet for the weak-willed powerful over the years.

There was the one exception, of course, and Mookie had a feeling that exception was about to burn down his kingdom.

But not without a fight.

"Fuck it, fuck it, fuck it," Mookie said out loud and loud enough for the people around him to hear.

"You OK, boss?"

Mookie turned around and saw the idiot had returned.

"No, not really. Any word from your buddy?"

"Nope."

"OK, let's go to the Farm ourselves. You drive."

"Yes sir."

"We need to make a stop first. Go ahead and bring your car around front. Let me get my things."

The young, white thug left the shop. Mookie went back to his table and gathered his belongings, put on his jacket, and picked up the newspaper. It was a long drive, and he knew the conversation in the car would be lacking.

As he picked up the paper, a thought occurred to him: By the time he got to the Farm, whatever was going to happen would have already happened. There really was no reason for him to go there. Mookie considered this for a moment. Yes, but he would rather take some sort of action then sit around and wait. Also, he had a feeling that there would be a good bit of "cleaning up" he would have to do. It was better to go ahead and get started on that. He also needed to figure out what happened to his delivery in the first place. And he could not forget the dumbass, who was supposed to be doing the delivery in the first place.

Mookie gritted his teeth.

He would deal with that dumbass, but it would be later. He had to clean up the mess in front of him now. And he would. He just hoped it was not too much of a mess. He had the slightest hope that maybe, just maybe, everything would be OK.

Maybe the person, upon discovering that the package was not there, just left. He paid already, yes, but surely he knew Mookie would give him the money back. He must also know that this business is not an exact science. Sometimes these things happen. Mookie had never failed him before either. He had always delivered the goods. This would afford him a little grace, wouldn't it?

Mookie knew as he was thinking these things that it was just his subconscious giving him false hope. He knew he was in trouble and so was his whole operation.

Who he was dealing with was not a normal person. Who he was dealing with did not go by the same logic and rules as the rest of the world. Yes, Mookie had ascended in the world by exploiting weaknesses and then doing whatever it took to get what he wanted, but he still abided by a certain logic.

This person did not.

Mookie never knew what he was going to do or say at any time. Mookie knew there was something seriously wrong with him based on his desires and what he had hired Mookie to provide to him over the years. Even simple conversations with him would often take a left turn, leaving Mookie to ponder exactly what had just happened.

He was the most unpredictable person Mookie had ever known.

And the most dangerous.

And the most powerful.

"Boss, the car is outside." Mookie looked up to see his employee holding the front door open for him. Mookie grabbed his things and wandered toward the door.

As he got to the door, he turned and looked around at the inside of The Coffee Shop. Sure, it was just a front. Sure, the coffee was bad. But this place was his. He had created it out of nothing, out of a void.

And, just like that, in Mookie's mind, he let it all go ... just as he knew he had to. If he never returned here, then, well, so be it. This is what he had always done: adapt and survive. If he had to do it here, then, he would.

Mookie turned back around, passed through the door, and walked outside.

17.

Cadel sensed something was off. His posse had stopped and were talking amongst themselves outside his earshot.

The African-American woman had gotten a call on her walkie-talkie and had pulled the others to the side. She looked concerned, and the slight panic in her eyes betrayed her nonchalant body language.

Cadel tried to act unconcerned himself while straining to listen to their conversation. He only picked up a few words, such as "unexpected" and "car," but he knew they were not happy words.

Cadel played up his own supposed lack of concern by turning his back on the group and stretching his arms up toward the sky.

The whispering became more frantic, and they began talking over one another. He still could not hear exactly what they were saying, but he knew they were on the verge of making a decision by the tone of their voices. There was silence and then whispers again in agreement.

"You need to go back to your cabin until dinner," the woman said, nervously pulling back her dreadlocked ponytail. "We can finish the tour later. With your leg you won't be able to do any work for the next few days anyhow."

Cadel saw the look on the woman's face: stern and foreboding. He knew she had other things on her mind.

Yeah, he was going to have to figure out what the hell was going on.

"Okee dokee, sounds good to me. Why can't I have a look around, though?"

She sighed. "It just would be better if you went back to your cabin and relaxed. You've been through a lot."

He put his hand to his forehead. "Oh, I do declare. I do feel like I just might faint," he said in a mock southern belle voice (or was it Foghorn Leghorn? Is there a difference?)? The woman looked at him, and he actually saw a flicker of anger. Maybe she had blood in those veins after all.

She pointed in the direction of the cabin.

"You should go there now. When you hear a bell, it's time for dinner. Just follow everyone to where they're going."

She turned back around and started walking at a brisk pace, and the others followed behind her.

He was definitely not going to the cabin. Whatever got these folks' druthers up, he was going to find out. He started walking back towards the cabin, and when he was sure they were not looking, he turned around and walked toward the direction they were heading. He eased around a few structures until he saw what looked like another group of people milling about, talking to one another.

Something was definitely going down.

Without warning he heard a loud, wild clap, almost as if it came from up in the trees. People began running about in a disciplined and organized manner, yet it still seemed oddly chaotic. It reminded Cadel of the fire drills he had in elementary school. Kids' running about with a nervous energy, following a usually haggard-looking teacher, who could not believe his or her coffee/smoke break had been replaced by leading a bunch of brats to the football field, where they would all bake in the sun for 30 minutes.

In this scenario, Cadel was the kid in the bathroom when the alarm went off, who ended up extending the drill while teachers looked for him. As he was admiring the inaccurate precision of the worker bees taking their pre-ordained positions, he saw the redhead from earlier.

"Hey, hey," he could not remember her name or whether she even told him her name. She did not look his way.

"Hey, sexy mama redhead!" She did look his way this time, Cadel noting that yelling "sexy" actually made her acknowledge him.

She looked at him quizzically, and then a flicker of recognition spread across her face. She jogged over to him.

"What are you doing out here?" she asked as she got close to him.

"I was being given a tour, and they just left me without telling me what was going on. I don't know what's happening here, but I really need some help."

"Don't worry. This is just a drill we run from time to time in case of an emergency."

"I don't know where to go."

She looked around calmly at the people running/jogging/walking about. He realized she was not nervous at all. It was something else.

Annoyance.

She was annoyed at the interruption to her day. Was it a drill, and, if so, what kind of drill was it? It was not a fire or tornado drill. People were not walking in single-file lines to a wide-open space or some sort of shelter/bunker. They were all going to specific places with intention.

"Wait. Is this some sort of military drill? What exactly are you people doing here? I thought this was some sort of peace-loving commune."

She looked at him with even more annoyance.

"We prepare for all sorts of things, and this is just one of them."

More and more people began spilling out of structures, and even more began appearing out of nowhere. Cadel guessed they were leaving their jobs to participate in whatever was going on.

"Yeah, well, that still doesn't answer my question. What the hell are you doing? What are you preparing for?"

She looked at him with an intensity he was not expecting. The mask of indifference and condescension melted off her pretty, little face.

"The end of the world."

The buzz of the beehive people around them increased, and it all started to make sense to him. This was a cult. This was an apocalyptic cult. They were preparing for the end of the world. He did not know whether that meant that they would literally be drinking the Kool-Aid or whether they would be going down in a flame of Janet Reno-inspired glory.

"OK, well, not cool," he said with a flare of anger himself.

She looked him over. "We have to prepare, and if we do not take it seriously, we will not be ready. Now, excuse me, I have to go to my station."

"Wait, wait," Cadel reached for her arm. She was just out of reach, though, and his gimpy leg betrayed him. He stumbled and fell down to one knee.

"What about me? What am I supposed to do?"

She looked down at him without offering even so much as a hand to help him to his feet.

"You can help or you can get the hell out of the way."

He did not know what to say as she turned and walked away at a brisk pace. What was that? Is the end of the world happening now, according to them?

Gunshots rang out, echoing across the grounds and, also, through the top of the trees. Cadel instinctively spread himself flat on the ground. He felt himself quit breathing, and he shut his eyes as tight as they would go. It was at times like these, no matter his false bravado and smart mouth, he realized that, at his core, he was nothing more than a sniveling coward. He did not care, though. If his cowardly instincts meant that he would not get hurt, or worse, killed, then he was fine with it.

He stuck his face far down in the grass until his lips touched the earth. For a moment, he was struck with an oddly pleasant feeling. The grass was so cool, and the dirt felt reassuring against his face. He could stay here for a long time, if it was not for that whole life-being-in-danger thingee. He waited in anticipation for more gunshots, but none came. The tension in his body relaxed, and he sensed him coming back to himself.

So much for "Fight or Flight," he thought. For him it was flight or crapping your pants.

He listened for anything that would cause him not to open his eyes and keep him from playing dead, if this was what he was doing. He did not hear anything, not even a bird or a frog or a humanoid.

He slowly opened one eye, but could only see the blurry green of the grass pressed up against his face. He lifted his head and opened both of his eyes. He was alone. It was obviously not a drill, but wherever everyone was supposed to be, they were there now. It was too quiet.

He pushed himself up to a kneeling position and looked around. He could not believe his redheaded girlfriend had left him alone like this. So much for his overwhelming charm. OK, Cadel thought to himself: let's figure out what the hell is going on. Apocalyptic cult. Check. Some sort of illegal activity by Mookie. Check. Kidnapped and beaten. Check. Hippie leader with a Jesus complex. Check. Gunshots out of nowhere. Check.

Yep, he had no idea what was happening.

He got to his feet and limped over to the nearest building. He peeked around the corner and still did not see anyone. He thought his posse had moved this way. He assumed they would be at the epicenter of whatever was happening.

He eased around the side of the building until he got to the corner. He peeked around again. Still nothing. Where the hell was everyone?

He started to move around to the other side, when he heard yelling. He could not tell exactly from where it was coming, but it sounded close. He was headed in the right direction at least.

He peeked around the corner again, and this time he saw a group of people, fellow communites, jogging toward the now-silent yelling with each carrying some sort of gun. Cadel now had confirmation that they were not so peace lovin' after all.

The group jogged behind another structure, and Cadel limped afterwards. He could not help himself. Yes, he realized at his core he was nothing more than a coward, but his curiosity always overrode any lack of moral fiber he had. When he got to the next building, shots rang out again. He did not stick his head in the sand this time, though. Maybe it was just the shock that got him last time.

He did jump, though, and he felt his heart racing. He realized, almost as an afterthought, that it probably would have been in his best interest if he had, in fact, gone back to his cabin.

He kept moving forward, though. He was going to find out what was going on. He reached another building and looked around its corner. He saw a black SUV with a body slumped over the hood. He scanned the horizon and saw several groups of people. Some were pointing their guns at the car and others were milling about in a cautious urgency.

Cadel realized he was witnessing some sort of standoff.

He could not see, though, with whom exactly the standoff was. Was someone else in the car? There had to be, right? Cadel looked closer and saw that indeed, yes, someone else was in the car. Two people maybe? Someone was definitely in the front passenger side seat, and it looked as if someone else was in the back of the car. It was hard to tell, though, with the way the sunlight shined on the car. It was dark in there, and there were also the tinted windows with which to contend. He just could not tell.

Cadel scanned the groups of people for anyone he might recognize. The hippie leader with the Jesus complex? Nope. The dreadlocked, African-American lady? He did not see her either.

His soon-to-be redheaded girlfriend, who was obviously playing hard to get? No sir.

"What the fuck you doin' out here?"

Cadel jumped at the voice.

He turned to see the tattooed youngster from his cabin.

"Just chillin,' yo. You?"

The youngster tried to play it cool, but his anxiety was obvious.

"I was asleep in the cabin when I heard the alarm. I thought it was just another drill and was going to sleep through it, but when I heard the gunshots, I ran over here."

"I assume, then, that this is not a regular drill."

"No, no, hell no. Our drills are mostly going to bunkers, checking supplies, cleaning guns, and other stuff."

"Wait. Bunkers? Guns?"

His roommate looked at him with a sudden suspicion that made Cadel reevaluate his tone.

"I mean, yes, sure I understand," Cadel said. "Soooooo, do you know exactly what is going on here? This doesn't look good."

"No, it doesn't look good."

His roomie gestured toward the hills surrounding the driveway, "We have people lined up on the perimeter in case it gets nasty."

Right. Lined up on the perimeter. This guy had obviously watched a lot of Law & Orders in his lifetime.

Cadel scanned the scene again. He looked for anything that would give him a clue as to what was happening. He looked closely at the car. It was a black SUV. It looked expensive and not very environmentally friendly. It was likely, then, not of this place with its hippie/commune/apocalyptic ideals.

He looked at the body. It was male, he thought. It appeared as if he was wearing a black suit. He imagined an FBI-type bodyguard running around with sunglasses and talking into his wrist.

He looked at the hippies on the other side of the clearing. Well, they did not necessarily look like hippies, he supposed. In fact, if they were not camped out at a commune, he would have thought they were just your typical gun-toting dumbasses with no sense of self-awareness.

He was not much of a gun guy, but he recognized that most were not carrying assault rifles. They looked more like hunting rifles. Maybe that is how they would kill their food once the zombie apocalypse destroyed civilization.

They were obviously not police or military trained either. Of course, neither was Cadel, but he had seen enough police actions over the years to know that whatever these guys were doing here it was not anything remotely related.

They had surrounded the vehicle by about 100 yards. Most were hiding behind some sort of shelter: trees, tree stumps, garbage cans, etc. Others were lying down on their bellies holding their guns in front of them as if they were snipers in some overseas war.

Cadel wondered why the car did not leave or at least try to drive away.

Sure, there were more hippie warriors behind the vehicle, but it looked like the SUV probably could barrel its way out. Just as he was thinking that, though, a few of the minions shut the gate that led to the road. Cadel wondered why they did that too. Wouldn't they want the car to leave their paradise? With that thought, he finally realized what was happening: This was a hostage situation, and these hippie freaks had no idea how to handle it.

Cadel was somewhat confident this place's drills were geared towards keeping intruders out. They had never prepared for what would happen if an intruder was trapped inside with them.

Well, in their defense, Cadel thought, what rational, middle-of-the-road apocalyptic cult would prepare for such a scenario?

It was not going to end well. If Cadel did not have the sense that his life was still very much in jeopardy, he might have enjoyed munching on a proverbial tub of popcorn and watching it all play out.

18.

Junie decided that the old man must have downed a whole vat of Viagra. His boner poking up in the middle of his Walmart-pleated khakis was one of the most unnatural things she had ever seen in her life. Hey, he just wanted to talk. Riiiiiight.

She was no longer in immediate danger, so that was a good thing, of course. Of course. But maybe, just maybe, being stuck as a hostage with a vulgar old man in a musty room with the Washington Monument poking out at her, beckoning her to please, pretty please, take a gander, was not the most ideal situation either.

But she would take it over getting her jaw kicked in again. He had also given her some pretty good pain meds. Definitely opium based, she thought, as the gentle, warmness spread up and down her spine.

She was feeling so good that she was even entertaining the idea of giving this old decrepit bag of flesh one last ride. Other than the tent pole in his khakis, though, he had shown no interest in making any sexual advances. He had been more concerned with her well being, giving her meds and even washing her face. He had even found an old shirt for her to wear rather than the nasty thing she had been wearing.

In return, all she had to do was sit on the bed and try not to escape. She knew the other, horrible, man was lurking about somewhere, whether it was outside the house or somewhere inside. She knew he was somehow watching them, keeping tabs on them. She just did not know how.

She looked at the old man, who was currently taking his own medication. The tree trunk in his pants was still poking out at no one. She had always heard tales of boys in middle school, going through the first throws of puberty, who did everything they could to hide their unexpected erections. She never noticed, but did recall wondering why all the boys at her school started untucking their shirts at the same time. She thought it was very unflattering and, in her own girl puberty mind, assumed they did so because they thought they were fat -- that untucking their shirts would hide their own bloated bellies.

This guy, though, was not hiding anything. He was out there and loving every minute of it.

Junie laid back on the bed and put her hands behind her head.

"So what exactly is going on here? I mean do you live here? Does your friend outside take care of you?"

The medicine had given her a little more confidence than she thought possible. She was beginning to understand why so many people were addicted to prescription drugs.

He looked at her and smiled with a tiny bit of condescension behind the happy facade.

"Well, aren't you the curious one? I don't really feel like answering any of those questions. I might later. It depends on how I, well, feel."

She propped herself up on her elbows. She did not feel threatened by him at all, even though he did seem to possess a certain strength. He was probably a badass back in his day with the way he carried himself, even now, with a walker, oxygen tank, and boner.

She was not scared of him now, though.

"Let me ask you one simple question: Am I your prisoner?"

He sat back on the bed next to her. He put his hand on her knee, "That is kind of relative, isn't it? You aren't tied up, are ya? But at the same time, it's pretty clear you can't leave, for the time being at least. Maybe later, we'll see. Not to get too deep, but aren't we all prisoners? It's just a matter of perspective. I am a prisoner in this horrible, broken-down body. I would give anything to run outside and roll around in the grass, soaking in the sun. Instead, I stumble around with this walker and oxygen tank."

"I don't think they're the same thing," she said. "I mean, I'm sorry your health isn't good, but isn't that part of life? Everyone, if they live long enough, gets old. For me, someone took away my freedom. It wasn't just because I lived a long time."

"I think you're missing the point," he said. "It's OK, though. I don't expect you to understand. No one does it seems. The answer to your question is, 'Yes,' you are my prisoner, in that, for the time being, you can't leave. But I am not cruel. I am not going to torture you or kill you. Let's just see where this goes," he said with a grin.

No one understands? Ugh. Really? Even when they are at death's door, men have to be so goddamned condescending. She felt the blood rush to her face. Her laid-back confidence gave way to an annoyed anger.

"You want to have sex? Is that it? Fine then."

She started taking off her pants and violently wriggled her jeans halfway down to her knees. He again put his hand on her knee.

"Stop. Just stop. Let's not make this situation bad for both of us."

She obeyed. Her little temper tantrum did not have the desired effect. He was also clearly still aroused. What was this? When no answer came to her, she realized she had become too upset. She took a deep breath and tried to regain control.

She wriggled her pants back up and put her hand on his.

"Thank you for being so nice to me. I'm sorry for getting upset."

He looked at her and took a deep breath.

"Well, there is one thing I would like to do with your permission, of course. "

She looked at him suspiciously, "OK, what is it?"

He leaned over and stuck his face in her hair. He breathed in deeply. She felt him shuttering against her shoulder as he took another deep breath.

She got the sense as she continued to hear and feel him take breath after breath that he thought she was some sort of fountain of youth -- that if he could stuff her in a blender and concoct a youth smoothie, he would.

In contrast, she could not help but smell his oldness. The mothball smell from his breath was so repugnant she intentionally breathed through her mouth. He also reeked of urine, and by looking at his khakis, without being distracted by his boner, she noticed the stains of food from that which had dropped in his lap from a shaking hand.

She would give anything, instead, to smell the manly smell of B.O., scrotum sweat, and sperm she so strongly associated with the sex she used to dread.

He put his hand over her ear and pulled her even closer. She wondered what it was about her that was getting him so off. She did not smell so great herself. She had been locked in a car trunk for goodness sakes. It wasn't like she had been hanging out at the spa. Maybe she was the first living female he had seen in a while.

There had to be something about her specifically, though, that meant something to him. She recalled the ape earlier saying something to that effect. She reminded him of someone from his past, right? The old man released her and sat up straight. He had a strange look on his face -- not one of satisfaction, which she assumed he would have, but one of, well, confidence.

"That is what I miss most of all: the intoxicating smell of youth. I can do without the sex. I don't really mind the wrinkles, gray hair, or even flabby body. I do wish I had taken better care of myself, and I wish I'd flossed a little more. That isn't here nor there, though. I just miss that vigor. That smell. That sheen."

He sighed, and she saw that confidence, or whatever was, slowly seep out of his body.

She actually felt sorry for him.

"I'm sure you had a good life, though, right? I know your health isn't all that great, but your mind still seems to be sharp. That's something, isn't it?"

He turned to look in her eyes, and she saw the coldness.

He put his hand behind her head.

She thought for a second he was going to lean over and start smelling her hair again. Instead, she felt the tension in his arm as he brought her head toward his own. She then felt him pushing her down -- down to the still erect Leaning Tower of Pisa straining beneath the cheap fabric.

Oh, she thought. Gross.

19.

Alexander looked at the barrel of the gun pointing at him. This was not the way he saw things playing out. He thought he could speak rationally and logically to this person, and they could reach some sort of understanding. Instead, he was in the back of an SUV with a gun pointing at his face. He could tell his brain was trying desperately to make sense of the situation, and it could not. It was all beyond his comprehension, what had happened. Now, he was just a lump of flesh with no emotion. He did not know what to do, and he did not care he did not know what to do. He had completely given up.

If this was a movie, one of two things would happen: First, he would calmly talk his way out of the situation or just enough to get to a point where he could escape. Second, he would grab the gun and do some sort of kung fu move where he acquired the gun for himself and possibly even broke the other person's arm in the process.

Alas, he was going to do neither in this situation. He had completely melted down.

He looked at the barrel of the gun. It was beautiful in a way. The black steel had a way of deflecting the light that was elegant, yet strong. He thought for a moment that it would not be so bad to die this way. He probably would not feel any pain. The gun was too close to his head for the bullet to miss. He would likely just hear a loud noise, and then his brain would take over. It would release enough chemicals, so he would not feel any pain. He might even see the bright light with long-lost relatives floating all around him. He read in an article the brain had evolved over the years to evoke such hallucinations, so that the last thing one feels before dying is calmness.

Then, there would be nothing, sweet nothingness. That would not be so bad, Alexander thought.

He could not remember how exactly he found himself in the back of this car. He knew he had tried to talk rationally. He had tried to take control of the situation. Instead, there had been no talk. There had been no control. The situation had devolved so fast Alexander had no time to react. He had gone from being a king to a pawn in a matter of moments, and the illusion of control had vaporized right before his eyes. The dead body next to him was nothing more than a prop in this horrible, surreal world in which Alexander had suddenly found himself.

He looked at the lifeless face on the body next to him.

Whatever life-force had been in the person's body was now gone. He wondered if the man had a family. He wondered if the man was making plans with his parents to visit this Christmas. Maybe he had a daughter, and this morning they hugged before he sent her off to school. Maybe he had promised he would make it to her basketball game tonight. Now, his face was a bag of formless matter. His mouth was wide open, and his eyes stared at the car's ceiling. There was no color in his cheeks.

Once you had seen a dead man's face you never forget it. It is never peaceful. It is always horrifying. Morticians make their money by sewing the mouth together, putting makeup on the cheeks, and making sure the eyes stay closed. There would be no open caskets if people had to look at the true face of a dead man.

As a reflex, Alexander without warning kicked the dead body out of the car with a violence he did not know was still in him, especially given the circumstances, and shut the door. He had been told not to move, but nothing happened to him when he decided to kick the flesh sack outside. The gun remained steady. Its one eye stared him down, making sure Alexander knew that no matter what little temper tantrums he might throw, he was not in control here. His actions had no effect on the situation.

He heard some scurrying around outside. He looked through the dark, tinted windows and saw his colleagues lining up alongside the road. They did not know what they were doing. Some had hunting rifles, and a few had assault guns, all of which were donated by Mookie. Alexander was positive no one outside had ever handled such firepower outside of a target range. He had been more concerned with their learning how to hunt than how to handle combat, let alone a hostage situation. It was all rather pathetic. If he did not die from the gun staring him down, he would get blown away by those outside the car. Once the shooting began everyone would join in. He was not going to escape this situation.

And that was OK. He was resigned to it now. He had led an interesting life, at least. He tried to turn things around and make a difference at the end, but it had been too late.

He knew he had been messing with a rough crowd, but considering where he had been -- the street -- there really had been no other option to get where he wanted to be or do what he wanted to do other than to align himself with the shady element of life. What other options were there? Politicians and corporate interests had gutted out the country long ago to make it near impossible for anyone living in poverty -- let alone anyone who had stumbled in life from addiction, homelessness, or mental health issues -- to make a decent living without doing something illegal. It was funny that the politicians who were so against crime were also against programs that would eliminate crime.

He had gotten the opportunity to get off the street, lead an easier life, and help some people in the process, so, sick of living the way he had been living, he took it, even though he knew part of what he would be contributing to was, well, bad. Bad stuff.

And now that badness had come back to collect its investment, and it was going to cost Alexander everything, including his life.

He sighed. He was fine with it, he supposed. There really was not anything he would have done differently. No, that is not entirely correct. He wished he had treated his parents better. They had not deserved the heartache he had brought upon them. He respected them in a way for cutting him off the way they did. He deserved it.

He had resented them for so long after they had finally decided that enough was enough. Even when he started getting clean, he would daydream of showing up on their doorstep, letting them see how he had turned his life around and, then, before they could say a word, shoot them the bird and ride off in the sunset. That image had motivated him in some pretty dark times, especially when he found himself on the tightrope of recovery, where he could easily have fallen back into the cycle of shame, self-loathing, and abuse. Instead, he had forged on with the image of his middle finger stuck up to the heavens in marvelous glory emblazoned on his brain.

Even when it came time in his recovery to forgive them and make amends, he lied. He had so much hatred in his heart, when all his parents did was love him until they could not anymore. He was sure they would have welcomed him with open arms, if he had gone to them, but his pride and hatred would not let him. When he started the Recovery Farm, and began preaching what he could not practice -- forgiveness, loving your neighbor -- he would always imagine them sitting in the kitchen waiting for him, waiting for him to come back, waiting to welcome him back into their fold.

And, yet, he could not. He could not go back.

Now, it was too late.

He wondered why he had been so intent on hurting the ones who loved him, while seeking approval from the ones who only wanted to hurt him? The thought stabbed at his heart.

It is probably the same reason why he could never believe in God. He hated himself so much, and was so ashamed of everything he had done, he simply could never accept he was loved. To him the thought that someone or something, whether it be a parent or a deity floating around in space, actually did love him was simply not true. It was a lie, and it filled him with rage.

His attention wandered back to the gun barrel. It really was a beautiful piece of machinery. The "O" at the end of the barrel was a perfect circle. He wondered how long it took to make a gun so perfect. He guessed the machinery, which made the gun, was also flawless. They were both perfect little machines. He thought about the machine that made the machine that made the gun. He imagined it was perfect as well. And what about the machine that made that machine? At what point did the imperfect human stick his or her greasy thumb in the middle of the pie? The quest for perfection, of course, was to take out the human element.

That was the purpose of the machine in front of him: to take out the human element. In a way, then, it was the most perfect of all machines. The less humans in the world, Alexander thought, the more perfect the world.

Just a short time ago he thought he could be a part of a more-perfect world. His little slice of heaven would be the opportunity, the second chance, for humanity to do it right. He thought if he could infuse a small group of humans with the right ideals and morals at the outset, those seeds would sprout, and humanity could take its rightful place alongside nature, not dominate it, but be a symbiotic part of it.

He always knew deep down he was being a little too naïve, a little too unrealistic, a little too idealistic. Humanity would never figure it out. There would always be the selfish gene inside that would not let us succeed as a race. A human would never let another succeed if it meant he or she could not succeed as well.

None of it made any sense, and Alexander could not take it anymore. He was done.

And, yet, the perfect machine kept staring at him, saying nothing. The eye was piercing through his soul, his very essence. It was a perfect circle, yes, but it was more. It was a perfect creation. It was so much better, so much more perfect, than anything that could be said about humanity. There was certainly nothing perfect at all about himself. He had never achieved anything close to perfection. His whole life had just been one disaster after another. He knew perfection would always be out of his reach. He was not capable of it. He would never be close to the plane of perfection on which the eye looking at him was.

Alexander was struck with a very simple thought: This was not an eye looking at him. It was a mouth.

It was a mouth screaming at him, but not in an angry way. It was a scream of jubilation, a scream of domination, a scream of power, a scream of control. He imagined the same scream coming from a Neanderthal after he had killed his dinner. It was primal, yes, that was for sure, but it was something else. It was a scream for meaning, for relevance. It was a scream for everything that Alexander's life lacked. It was a scream for the masculinity that society was constantly trying to downplay or eliminate altogether.

Suddenly, the perfect mouth was no longer screaming, but rather it was singing. It was singing a siren's song, beckoning him to drop his previous messy life in favor of a life of perfection.

Without thinking, Alexander said out loud, "Yes, I will. I want that."

Not being able to resist the siren song, Alexander bent down, grabbed the barrel of the gun gently, and pressed his lips to the cool, steel mouth. Feeling the perfection spread through his body, he stuck his tongue inside the gun's mouth.

20.

Mookie knew he might not ever go back to The Coffee Shop, but deep down he didn't really believe it. Oh, he would leave it all behind in a heartbeat. He just had a feeling everything would resolve itself before he had to insert himself into the picture and, consequently, take himself completely out of the picture. Whatever happened, though, he would adapt. He would not only survive -- he would prosper. He would win. He knew that about himself.

First, though, he had to get a handle on what was actually occurring. He had to gather all the facts -- firsthand -- and then take action.

His first thought had been to go straight to the Farm and attempt to resolve the situation. He knew, though, that if he went there he would more than likely find himself in the middle of a shit storm. He knew the players involved, and he knew it would not be pretty. He thought it would be better to let that situation resolve itself. Instead, first, he would find the girl, as well as the dumbass who was supposed to take her to the Farm. He could have easily gotten another girl, yes, but he had not had a shipment in a while, and the most readily available ones were definitely not the "type" his client preferred. They would be tatted up and would look, well, used. No, his client likes them clean, pure, and natural. He shuddered to think what came next for the nature goddesses.

And he had scoped this one out for a while.

She had stumbled into his shop one day and asked for a job, the way so many drug addicts and homeless folks do. She said she was staying at the nearby women's shelter, and the volunteers there had told her about him and his willingness to give people like her a chance to get back on their feet.

He had told her to come back in a couple of days. In the meantime, he had a few of his "contacts" at the shelter check her out. They confirmed her story. She had wandered into the shelter asking for help. She kept mostly to herself, but had asked around for ways to get a job. Mookie had her belongings searched and nothing suspicious had turned up: just T-shirts, paper-thin panties, raggedy jeans, and Wal-Mart brand sneakers.

Apparently, she had a journal too, but wrote in some sort of childish gibberish. No one at the shelter could interpret it, which had initially caused Mookie some concern. He assumed, though, that most girls probably wrote in some sort of code, so snooping parents and siblings could not read what they were confessing. She was a runaway too, so she had likely been hiding plenty from her previous nuclear family unit.

Mookie had almost put her in the stream of commerce before, but she had to go and strike up a friendship with the resident smartass. Mookie preferred for his product to disappear without any drama. He liked for no one to blink an eye. He knew the smartass would wonder where his friend went and would probably start asking questions. Mookie did not want that.

Of course, that part of the equation was now somewhat resolved.

And, even though he still had to deal with "him," Mookie would deal with this situation first. He had invested too much time and effort in the girl. He knew she was exactly what was needed to assuage the situation. He knew things would go to hell first -- he already resolved himself to that -- but he believed his best chance at salvaging his operation, before chunking at all, was to offer her up. If that did not work, he was gone.

He had a vague idea of where she might be. His former most loyal subject had no ties to the outside world, other than one -- his boss before Mookie, who also happened to be the man's stepfather, i.e., the guy who started banging his mom after his real father died.

Mookie only knew this because he happened to know the old man. In fact, it was the old man who asked Mookie to employ his stepson and show him the ropes. Mookie had done business with the old man for years, and he felt as if he owed him something. Mookie took the kid in and brought him up from the ground floor. The kid did everything Mookie asked him to do without nary a question. He had survived all of Mookie's tests of loyalty to the point where he trusted his underling as much as anyone.

The one chink in his armor, though, was the old man. Whenever Mookie brought the old man up, he saw the look in his eyes: fear. The old man must have really done a number on him when he was young. He also understood his employee mistook that fear for some sort of perverted sense of loyalty. The old man probably knew that too and exploited it, even now. How else could an old man in his presumably last days control someone half his age and twice his size other than to mindfuck him completely. Mookie, in a way, admired the ability to control another, which he possessed to an extent. His rational, calm pragmatism, though, lacked the cruel exploitation of the old man.

As a result, Mookie suspected that if his employee betrayed him or went against his wishes, it would have to be because of the old man.

So that is where they were going: the old man's place. Mookie knew where the old man now lived, or at least the proximity of where he lived. He remembered when his employee bought the cabin and set the old man up. At the time, Mookie thought it was somewhat noble.

But what the hell did this girl have to do with the old man? Why would he risk everything, including his own life, for this? Mookie did not have an answer, but knew, just knew, it had something to do with the old man, which is why they were going to find him.

"I might know where the house is."

Mookie looked at his driver. He was turning out to be much more useful than Mookie had anticipated. They had been discussing possibilities of where to look, and Mookie suggested they should start with the old man. He did not mention anything other than giving general directions to the area where he thought the old man lived.

"Why's that?"

"We talked about going hunting a while back. We were going to go deer hunting last fall, but I had to back out at the last minute. He gave me directions."

"A year later and you can still remember the directions?"

"Yes sir. I remember because it was near a place I went camping as a kid."

"Camping?"

"My friend's grandfather would take a group of us camping every year. I think there's a national park nearby. I had not thought about it in years until we began planning that hunting trip."

"You know how to get there?"

"Pretty sure."

"OK, let's try that place first."

"I'm not sure it's the same place. I just know it is in the same direction we are going."

Mookie did not let on, but his antennae were up. How the hell did this idiot know where to go? He suddenly felt like something else was going on between these two. Were the two working together to take him out? That seemed to be the most logical explanation: use the girl as bait to get him all the way out in the boonies and kill him.

Well, this was certainly an interesting development, and one that he did not have the time to deal with right now. He weighed the different dangers. Did the concrete danger the maniac at the Farm pose outweigh the potential danger of a double-cross from these two idiots?

Shit, Mookie said to himself.

"OK, then, let's find this old camping place of yours."

21.

Nothingness. That is what he felt. Nothingness. Pues y nada. But it would not last long. Eventually it would feel good to him. He was going to kill the person in front of him, and he would do it with cold precision. Then, he was going to kill every single person who got in his way. There would be plenty of dead people left in his wake today.

No one would know he had been here -- no one left alive that is. He liked to kill. It did not necessarily give him any pleasure, but he liked to exert his power over others. He liked to lord his exactness and control over others. It felt good to him. It felt natural. It felt clean.

The low people wandering outside the car with their little guns were nothing more to him than little mice scurrying around. They did not realize they were in the presence of something glorious, something wonderful: a god, a true ethereal being that could not be killed by anything in this world. Those outside were truly the proverbial ants beside the superhighway -- completely oblivious.

They had no concept or frame of reference for his nature. If they truly knew, they would drop to their knees and praise him as he slit each and every one of their throats. He wished he had the otherworldly powers he had in his previous lives on other worlds and in other dimensions. He often dreamed of those times when he could merely look at another being, and it would die and be grateful. To have one's lifeforce taken from you by a god was a privilege. That was understood in his more cultured and sophisticated existences.

In this archaic and savage place, though, where its simpleminded inhabitants only knew fear and lust, where he had to take their lives by hand or barbaric weapons, they would not know or understand the cosmic privilege with which they had been graced. It was a shame really. He did not know why he had been chosen to inhabit this world, and, frankly, he could not wait to transcend into his next existence. He hoped in that place he could exude his powers rightfully, and its creatures would understand what he was and be grateful to be in his presence.

These creatures, though, were just pathetic. When you live in a world with no powers, you could get used to living in the muck, he supposed. He never lost sight, though, that he came from a different plane of existence than these worthless creatures, even if his powers did not work here. He could still feel those powers, even if he could not use them. He could feel the lightning bolts behind his eyes, struggling to get free. He could feel the ability to wish things into being just itching at his fingertips.

Most of all he missed the undying awe of his subjects. Even just a little gratitude would be nice in this place.

When he was born into this low world, he remembered the bleakness of it all. He was a baby, yes, but he still remembered the dullness in the nurses' eyes. Even the embrace of his mother lacked the love and awe he fell from the lowliest person on one of the other worlds on which he had lived previously. He did not understand why he had to be here. He often communed with his, well, father, for lack of a better human word, at night, as well as other ethereal beings. They would lift his inner self so high that he would be reminded of what he was and from where he came. It was during these times he would get all the answers. He would instantly understand the nature of things and why he was here. But when he awoke, it all slipped away. This little world of density and ignorance sapped all his powers away.

The only thing that made him feel close to his true nature were the sacrifices.

In his other existences, his subjects would gladly and gratefully hand over living sacrifices to him. In this world, he had to purchase them. It was all so vulgar.

When his body was younger, and he realized he would not enjoy the benefits he enjoyed in other worlds, he would capture small animals and do the rituals that connected him to his true inner being and to the glory of his ethereal brethren. He remembered the first time his birthmother saw his bloody face and the carcass of the recently given Easter bunny. She was horrified, and he thought it was funny. He laughed out loud because he knew her stupid brain could never comprehend what he was doing and why.

Of course, as a result, he had to go to countless psychiatrists and take many mind-numbing drugs. He remembered the way the drugs made him feel: stupid, ordinary, and dull. The facilities in which he took them were drab, bland, and run by blunt objects. He understood what his spirit brother must have felt talking to the Romans and corrupt Jewish leaders of his day. And, just as his brother had learned at the temples as a youth, and especially after the clay pigeon incident, he would have to bide his time as a youth, learning the ways of this low world until he was an adult. Then, his real ministry would begin.

One of the facilities where he stayed as a youth gave him a good feel for what it was like to live as a regular inhabitant in this low world. The drugs, yes, made him dull, but also the conversations he would have and the food he had to eat were all pure torture. He finally realized it was all a test … no, not a test. A school. A school on how to live in a low world and, ultimately, how to conquer it. When he was finally released, he never forgot the lessons he learned, especially as the drugs wore off. He continued to act as if he took the drugs every morning, dumping them in the toilet and smiling with a heavy-lidded nod to his birthparents. Inside his mind, though, the lightning crackled. To the outside world he acted as if he was moving through maple syrup, and he was amazed at how much people liked him when they thought he was stupid.

Even his brother confessed to him, in one of his dream states, that the reason he was killed was not because he was a god, but because of his intelligence. Caiaphas thought his brother was just a little too uppity, and Pilate, well, he actually enjoyed their philosophical banter -- that is until his brother had to go and one up him.

Of course, his brother was not the only god killed in this world. They had been coming here throughout history to try and uplift the species, and they had all been killed.

His ministry would be different than theirs. He would show them the way of meekness by showing them how weak they really were. Once these inhabitants understood their insignificance, they would be free. Once they saw how powerful he was, they would have no choice but to accept their utterly powerless lives. There would be no reason, then, for them to search for some sort of meaning in their lives. There was none. They could put aside their bitching and moaning, their tweets, and their Facebook posts. The men could burn their scarves and skinny jeans. The women could stop injecting their faces with poison and scorching their insides by lying in ovens. There was nothing special about them. There was nothing to hold onto. They were just meaningless organisms floating in a petri dish.

His counterparts had made the mistake of trying to rise up the so-called lowliest in this world to show them how equal they were to the rest. He would do the opposite. He would show them all how unspecial they all were, especially those who considered themselves powerful. He would do so by showing them his true power, his true beauty. Then, it would not matter what sports teams they cheered for or what neighborhoods they lived in or what schools their children went to.

For example, the person before him just a few minutes ago thought was really something. He had his little caste system all worked out. He was the big cheese in this little operation, and everyone else served him. He strolled right up to the car with an all-knowing smirk, as if he was calling the shots. No no no. That is not the way things are. In his defense, the man obviously had never been in the presence of a god, of true greatness. The man's importance had melted off his face in mere seconds when he discovered what his true nature was. Now, he was truly free.

The people outside the car would know soon too, or they would be dead. Either way they would be free. He did more in his ministry than any of his ethereal brethren had ever done in that regard. His way was the correct way. This low world did not deserve his love or his compassion. They hated themselves so much that they could not even begin to accept a godly love anyway. They would continue to prop themselves up in this world of muck only to knock each other back down. The cycle would continue and continue. They would lead low lives in a low world and then die and be put back in the unseen vortex surrounding this dimension. They would never comprehend true holiness, and, so, he was determined to give them all just a taste of his glory.

He had been driven to this place in order to feel his own essence again, to tap into the true nature of the universe. It was ridiculous that he had to purchase his own living sacrifices, and, yes, he understood they were not really sacrifices if he had to purchase them. It was just one more way he had found to adapt to this world. He had been longing for this for a while now. It had been almost a year since his last, and he had been growing increasingly restless and disconnected. When he got the call, it was all he could think about. The call was only a short time ago, and yet it felt like a whole lifetime before he could get here.

When the time finally arrived, and he traveled all the way out to this place, things were not the way they were supposed to be. And he had let his wrath be known.

He had paid a lot of money for this, which he did not mind because he had a lot of money to spend. Just the audacity not to know with whom they were dealing was enough to set him off. No, you cannot just stroll out and reason with him. They would know him now, and if they remained in this world, they would never forget him either.

Of course, he was in a bit of a predicament. His driver/bodyguard was dead. He had been a good subject and would be missed.

But the person in front of him, yes, he was going to die. Or not. It depended on how he felt. It might be better for this human to see those killed on the outside and know how lucky he was, in case he ever had to come back here again. One thing was certain: If he could not have his sacrifice, then everyone here would understand why he or she had not done the right thing, including the one in front of him.

He had to make sure, first, that his sacrifice really was not here. Maybe the person sitting before him was trying some ill-advised, last-minute negotiations. Maybe he was trying to be a hero. He had to make sure because it would be a long time before he would have another sacrifice -- at least the kind he needed to continue maintaining a pure connection to his ethereal self.

He looked at the person in front of him, who was staring at the gun in an odd way. Was he going to try and take it from him? What a horrible decision if so. No, he had another sort of look to him, as if he was, well, enamored with the gun in his hand. He should, in fact, be enamored with the person holding the gun. This world and its things.

Everybody was so in love with things. If one had never seen true glory, he supposed one would look for it in "things" too. This little world and its absence of power, glory, magic, would of course lend itself to false power, false glory, and false magic. The thing in his hands was false power for sure.

The man in front of him slowly bent down, put his mouth around the barrel of the gun, and began sticking his tongue in and out of the end of the barrel. The look on his face was one of joy, as if he was a teenage boy, making out with a pillow in his bedroom.

Of course, this low person would have such a love for a false object, he told himself, as he contemplated whether to pull the trigger now or later or not at all.

20.

Mookie felt a sense of dread as they pulled off the interstate. The more he thought about it the more he was convinced he was walking into a trap. The guy driving next to him all of a sudden blurts out he knows exactly where Mookie wants to go. It did not make any sense at all. But why in the world would these two want to take him out? It was not like they could take over his operation. Maybe they thought that they could, in their tiny little brains. Maybe they thought they could take over just a little part of it. Maybe they thought they could just get some girls. Who the hell knows? But he knew something was going down between these two.

This was going to take some balancing on his part.

On the one hand, he was going to have to figure out what the hell was going on with these two. Then, he was going to have to get the girl. Then, he was going to have to deal with the old man. And he was going to have to do all this probably at the same time, probably within a few seconds. If he could get the girl unharmed, he might be able to salvage the situation at the Farm. That was way down on his priority list now, though. He always prided himself on being cold, detached, and pragmatic. Now, though, he could feel the angry and vengeful side of himself creeping back to life.

These dumb fucks really thought they could take him out? Well, let's see them try, Mookie thought to himself.

No, No, No, he reminded himself. He was not going to be angry and vengeful. He let his calm side rise to the surface. No, he would do this in his practical way: quick and precise, but rational.

The road they were on now was a two-lane highway, and there were signs for various camping sites. They were close to where he thought the old man lived. He wondered if they were actually going there, or if that was a ruse as well.

Mookie fingered the safety on the gun inside his jacket. The thought popped into his head that it might be a good idea just to take out the dumbass right now. If he killed him, though, Mookie might not be able to find where the old man lived. And, oh yeah, the dumbass was driving.

Damn. Damn. Damn.

There really was not an easy way out of this one. As usual, there was no fucking magic solution that would easily solve everything. He was just going to have to suck it up and do it.

After a few minutes of driving, they turned onto a side road. The road was paved, but just barely. They drove past the occasional trailer and garbage dump. They really were out in the middle of nowhere.

Maybe this is just what redneck, white people like to do in their free time, Mookie thought to himself. It was all so foreign to him. This preoccupation with being out in the woods and killing creatures for no reason. He had killed enough in his life. He did not need to kill animals to feel like a man. Instead, he felt the presence of those people whose lives he had taken, and it did not make him feel like a man. It made him feel something less than human. More than anything it made him tired, carrying the dead on his back. It would be too simple to say he had no regrets. Of course, he did. Yes, he had been justified in most of those killings, and, yes, those he killed were not the greatest of people. He just felt deep down it was not his place to take the life of another.

But he did. Several times. And he would continue to if necessary, starting with these two bastards.

They pulled onto a gravel road, and Mookie braced himself for what would come next. They passed a couple trailers and yet another garbage dump. Mookie looked at his driver. He did not look concerned at all. He had no stress on his face.

"I think it is up this road just a little more. I thought he said it was past some trailers and the only cabin around."

"And you've never been to this place before?"

"No. Like I said: I used to go camping at the state park back on the highway, but I've never been back here. I just remember the directions from when we were supposed to go hunting last year."

Mookie was still not buying it.

They drove into a clearing and, sure enough, there was a cabin. It looked like one of the pre-manufactured cabins one would see advertised from time to time on late-night TV or in the back of a magazine. Mookie supposed it was better than a trailer. There were two cars out front. Of course, he recognized one as belonging to his so-called loyal employee, and the other was a much older car: boxy, unwashed, with bald tires.

"Stop here," Mookie said. "Put the car in park."

This driver did as Mookie said. The car sat about 50 yards away from the cabin, idling. Mookie did not see any movement, but that meant nothing if he was walking into a trap.

Mookie wanted to do something. He hated just sitting here waiting, but he knew that was what was required. Yes, that was what made him different: doing the things no one else wanted to do.

But this was torture.

His driver calmly tapped the steering wheel. He did not seem to have a care in the world.

Mookie looked outside the car at the rough natural landscape. Most people considered any sort of nature as beautiful, but not Mookie. When he looked at nature, any nature, all he saw was messiness, pain, and brokenness. The only type of natural "beauty" he enjoyed was that which was maintained. He hated golf, but he admired the controlled beauty of a high-end golf course. He liked the fluffed pine straw. He found comfort in the green, green grass and the scorn placed on the places where there was none.

That was not nature, of course, that he admired. That was man taking something inherently flawed and making it better. He was sure there were weeds on golf courses somewhere, but they were either in a constant state of being poisoned or cut down to where no one could see them.

Mookie again looked out his window. He looked at the broken tree limbs and the mounds of leaves covering the ground. All the trees were different types. There was no grass, and there were no flowers anywhere to be seen. The only green he saw were the tall weeds on the side of the gravel road. Nature. Give me a parking lot any fucking day of the week, Mookie thought.

Mookie looked toward the cabin and saw his employee walking in front of the rundown cabin. The man did not see the car at first. He was busy with, what, rolling up a hose? Feeding a blue tick hound? Picking a banjo? God, even in California there were hillbilly rednecks.

He looked up and saw them. He saw the car. He straightened up and looked right through them. Mookie clicked the safety of his gun off with his thumb.

Here we go, he thought, and braced for whatever madness would come next.

19.

Alexander had his tongue inside the barrel of a gun.

At least that was the last thing he remembered before the cool darkness. He did not know where he was now. He also remembered not caring whether he lived or died. He did not know where his mind had gone when he thought he was going to die, but it was not pretty. He smelled shit, so that happened. He was not quite as mentally tough as he thought. Now that he had a shot at living, his mind had shifted into overdrive, searching for ways to get out of this predicament.

He just had to remember what had actually happened, and then he could figure out what to do next.

And where the hell was he?

He was facedown in the dirt. The shit smell permeated all around him. He heard the sounds of the rural: birds screaming, sticks snapping from unknown animals, and leaves being pushed around by those same unknowns.

He did not hear any human sounds -- no talking, no coughing, no cars humming. He picked his head up and looked around. He was in a ditch by the side of a gravel road. It looked familiar to him, but he could not quite place where he was.

His head was killing him, and his mouth was dry. He tried moving his arms and felt pain shoot up and down his right side. He laid his body back down.

He wanted to rest, but his brain would not let him. His mind was racing. Random objects, faces, and places that seemingly had no relation to his situation popped into his head: parents, high school, old girlfriends, the redhead back at the Farm, throwing dirt clods at childhood friends, workers at rehab facilities. They all flew in front of his face and did not let him stop to think about any one in particular. They just kept going, this roulette wheel of memories.

He buried his face deeper in the random pile of leaves, sticks, and dirt.

He did not want to die, but he did not want to get up either. He found himself in a strange position of being extremely tired and extremely wired at the same time.

He decided to do one thing at a time. He slowly rolled onto his back. The pain again ripped up and down his right side. He looked up into the sky. He saw the road just barely above his vision. He saw the tree line and realized he was more than likely on the road outside the Farm.

The gun.

Right, the gun. That was the last thing he remembered. What happened after? He tried to focus.

Had he been shot?

He felt around on his torso. He did not feel anything that would indicate he had been shot. He lifted his head and looked down. He did not see any blood. He slowly sat up in the mound of leaves and loose dirt.

Yes, he was definitely on the road outside the Farm. There was not much traffic -- one of the reasons they had chosen this place -- so in order to get some sort of medical attention, he was going to have to walk back to the Farm.

He could not tell how long it was back to the Farm, though. The landmarks on this stretch of road all looked the same, but he thought he was not that far.

He eased himself to his knees and tried to stabilize his head when the pain shot up his neck. This was not going to be fun, but what other choice did he have? He could not just lie on the side of the road all day.

OK, here we go, he said to himself and got to his feet. He immediately felt nauseated, and the earth rocked back-and-forth beneath his feet. He stumbled and fell back into a pile of leaves.

How pathetic, Alexander thought to himself, but at least he knew he could get to his feet, even if he could not stay there.

Alexander let out a long sigh. It was just this morning he had been in charge of something that was making a difference in the world, something that could change and shape the world to come. Now, he was lying in a ditch by a gravel road with shit in his pants.

No, it was not going to be this way. He had worked too hard to fall back into his old patterns of self-pity and self-destruction. He was going to do this thing. He was going to get back to the Farm. He would not let it slip away this easily.

He got back to his feet much easier this time. He slowly climbed out of the ditch and onto the gravel road. He started limping in the direction of the Farm. He found that, once he started moving, the pain was not as severe. As he hobbled down the road -- there really was no other way to describe it -- he tried to remember again what had happened. His mind was slowly starting to calm itself, and he hoped that would bring some clarity

OK, he remembered the car. He remembered approaching the car. He remembered being inside the car. He remembered thinking he was going to die. He remembered thinking it was somehow a good idea to suck a gun's innards. Other than these memories, and they were vague at best, he only had fleeting images and feelings. He tried not to force them.

After no more than a second, though, Alexander gave up trying to remember.

Ah, hell, what does it matter anyway, he conceded to himself and felt the relief of such a concession infiltrate his body. All that mattered was that he was alive and headed home.

18.

Junie look at the bloody mess before her. She had probably blown her cover and had probably killed herself in the process.

However, she decided, as she saw the gray pubic hairs, shriveled balls, and unnaturally erect member making their merry way toward her face, that she had had enough of the disgusting men in her life, even if it meant sacrificing her own.

When the old man had started to yelp after the initial shock, she stuck the wad of cloth that had been in her mouth into his. She had done it all with a certain automatic quickness and relative ease. The strength the old man had shown when he thought he was going to get a blowjob from a young, sexual nymph had dissipated when he realized he was not the one in control of the situation. Now, he lay on the bed whimpering. She felt adrenaline pumping through her body. Her vision was clear, and her mind was completely engaged. She now had to decide how to deal with the ape outside the door.

No, she knew what she was going to do: She was going to kill him. She was not doing this shit anymore. Yes, she realized it meant she would no longer have the opportunity to save those girls, or anyone, but she could not worry about them now. She was not going to subject herself to the debasement of men, even if it was in the name of the greater good. Fuck the bigger picture. She was sick of it all. She was sick of this world. She had tried to play the game, but learned she could not. Now, she was going to end it, and possibly her life in the process, but she was going to do it all on her own terms.

First things first: the old man. He was in shock, gasping for air through the rag while snot went in and of his nostrils. Junie looked at his pathetic old face. He had been used to dominating women his whole life, she guessed. Hell, he had probably been used to dominating men too, including the poor sap wandering outside. He was not making much noise now, but Junie knew the old man would begin moaning loudly once he snapped out of it. His hands were desperately padding around his groin, looking for something that was no longer there.

Phantom limb, indeed.

She took the belt from the khakis still hanging below his knees. She wrapped it around his neck and pulled it tight through the metal loop before he knew what was happening. She watched what little life was left in his face explode into bulbous purple. The gasping ceased. He did not put up much of a fight after all.

Chalk one up for the girls, she said to herself as she let go of the belt.

Junie knew it would be not be long before the ape outside bashed his way into the room. She was still injured, but at least the old man's drugs had taken away the pain. She looked around for any sort of weapon. The old man's walker? If she had time, she could have broken it down, but of course she did not have that luxury. She scuttled around to the other side of the bed and began looking through the chest of drawers. The smell of old people hit her senses as she opened the top drawer.

"Gross," she said.

There was nothing but old, yellowing clothes from decades of non-use. She was getting nowhere, and she sensed she was running out of time.

She searched the small, bedside table and only found "knick-knacks" and spare change. She looked under the bed and saw nothing useful there either.

OK, she was screwed, she thought, if she stayed in this room. She did not know where the gorilla was, but she realized she would have to get outside of these four walls if she was going to survive.

She walked over to the window to see if she could catch a glimpse of him. If he was not actually in the house and heard the yelping, she might have a chance. She did not see him. She looked around the room again. The old piece of shit must have some sort of weapon in here. He looked the type to have stashes of guns and knives hidden in random crevices.

She looked out the window again. She did not see the lump of a man anywhere. She scanned the landscape. She really was out in the middle of nowhere. It did not even look like California, but she knew she had not been in the car long enough to be anywhere else.

Her view was to the side of the house, but if she pressed her face to the glass, she could see some of what was in front of the house and what appeared to be a gravel driveway.

She thought she saw a car just out of her view at the very edge of the tree line. She knew a car by itself would not be that big a deal, but she did not remember this one when she was getting the shit kicked out of her. It was definitely not the one in which she had been trapped.

She looked closer.

Closer.

Yes, she thought she saw the outlines of two people in the front seat of the car.

She pressed her face harder into the cool class, so she could get a better glimpse. It was all just out of her vision. The distortions in the window glass made the car, what she could see, wavy and out of focus.

Without warning the ape passed underneath the window. It startled her so much, she fell backwards and knocked over the bedside table. She landed in the bed by the bloody, cold mess that used to be an old man.

She waited for any repercussions from the ape. She braced herself for the sound of a door closing, yelling … anything. But nothing came.

He must not have seen her, Junie guessed. She eased her way back to the window and looked outside again. She could not see him anymore. She pressed her face to the glass again to see if she could see the car. She could see it barely, but she also saw movement. The ape was walking towards the car with a fierceness she knew all too well. She also saw some movement inside the car, but could not tell exactly.

The old man grasped for air suddenly, and she screamed in spite of herself. Not being able to control her surprise and anger, she turned around and, before she knew what she was doing, was hitting the old man in the face. She hit him over and over and over again. Then, she grabbed a bedside lamp, ripped the lampshade off, and brought down blow after blow upon his face.

Well, there's your weapon, stupid, she said to herself.

Gunshots rang out, and she found herself screaming out loud once again. She instinctively dropped to the ground and rolled under the bed. More gunshots. They were definitely coming from the direction of the front of the house where the car had been.

In her training, she had, of course, had the opportunity to hear gunshots over and over again. Still, she could never get quite used to the unholy sound of the piercing pops and echoes. And there was always the unnatural silence that followed, as if the world was holding its breath to see what sort of life had been stolen this time.

Junie realized she also had been holding her breath. She reminded herself to breathe and take a logical and rational survey of her predicament.

She listened. Nothing. Silence. No more gunshots. No yelling, wailing, or gnashing of teeth, but slowly, where there had been only silence, she began to hear once again the chirping of birds and random wildlife scurrying about.

She slowly crawled out from underneath the bed. She stopped and listened again. Still nothing. She lifted herself up, made her way to the window, and again pressed her face to the cool glass.

She could not see much. The car was there, even though she could still barely make it out.

She heard the front door open, and any hope that somehow, miraculously, everyone had killed themselves, and she was now free, evaporated in her mind.

Her feral instincts took over, and she fell to the floor with more noise than she intended. She rolled under the bed without thinking and waited.

She listened.

Nothing.

Maybe her mind was playing tricks on her. Maybe a tree limb had hit the roof, and she mistook it for the front door closing. Maybe someone had come in the house, but had decided to leave. Maybe someone came in, but was mortally wounded.

Maybe.

Maybe.

She heard footsteps, and her hope dissipated again as quickly as it appeared. The footsteps and opening and closing of doors throughout the house told her that whoever was in the house was looking for something or someone, maybe herself, so she assumed it was not the ape from outside. He would have come straight back to the room. The footsteps stopped. Whoever was here was right outside the door. She braced herself for whatever would come next.

The door creaked open. She waited for a scream, a gasp, or some sort of reaction from whoever it was seeing the bloody mess on the bed, but she did not hear anything.

She held her breath and waited for something. Anything. She wanted to get this over with, but she would not be the one who made the first move. She had no plan and no strategy for getting out of this mess. She would just have to react to whatever happened.

"OK, come out, come out wherever you are. I don't have time to fuck around."

Mookie. Shit.

"Come on now, I'm not going to search this room. We both know how this is going to end. I have a gun, and if you had one, I'd already be shot, or you'd be trying some sort of half-ass negotiation. We both know what the endgame is, so why don't we just skip the drama? It would make everything a lot easier."

Her mind was racing.

She looked around for the lamp. Maybe she could jump him when he had his back turned. Or maybe when he looked under the bed, she could hit him in the face. Could she make a run for it? Could she get out the window? Break the glass with the lamp? The image of John McClain running over broken glass barefoot replayed in her head on a continuous loop. Die Hard. She never really thought about the title of the movie before. In her head, it had always just been synonymous with action movies of the 80s. The two words immediately conjured up an image of Bruce Willis's slightly bald anti-hero. The title, though, Die Hard: It did not really make much sense did it? How could one die hard? How could one die easy? Isn't death just death -- an absence of life? She thought of other examples: kickass void, extreme nothingness, radical hole.

"Hey, cutie pie, whatcha doin' down there?"

Shit. Mookie.

Junie looked over and saw the outline of Mookie's head peering at her under the bed. She looked straight up at the mattress above her.

"Nothing."

"Nothing? I'm not sure the thing in the bed above you would agree."

Junie shut her eyes and sighed. She was screwed. She could not think of anything to do except give up, tell the truth, and let the chips fall wherever they were going to fall.

"No, probably not," she said with just a little too much resignation than she intended.

"No, probably not," Mookie repeated. "Well, why don't you get up, and we'll get out of here before any other trouble happens."

"I'm not so sure the ape outside is too happy right now. I'm not so sure he'd be crazy about us leaving here either."

The outline of Mookie's face disappeared. All she could see were his feet.

"Let's get up now."

"Why do I have a feeling you aren't exactly my knight in shining armor?"

"Again, I'm going to ask you nicely, and then things won't be so nice anymore. Please get out from underneath that bed and get up. Now."

Junie looked around one last time for any object that could be used as a weapon.

Nothing.

She scanned the mattress right above her face for some sort of secret compartment where the old man may have hid his post-apocalyptic stash of guns and food rations.

Nope. Nothing.

"Come on now. Don't make me drag you out from underneath there. I'm not going to hurt you. We're just going to walk slowly to my car and then leave. Whenever the police decide to make their way here, they won't even know we were here. But we have to go. Now."

Junie sighed and slowly scooted out from underneath the bed. She got to her feet and made the mistake of looking down. The pile of red meat that used to be the old man's face stared right back at her. Wow, she really had wailed on him. She felt the bile coming up her throat before she knew what was happening. What little that had been in her stomach splattered all over the bloody mess, as if the body needed any more desecration, which in turn made her dry heave even more. When she finished, she looked up and, through a teary vision, saw Mookie staring at her with bemusement.

"I guess you should've thought of that before you killed him, huh?"

Junie reached for the lamp still lying on the bed, but before she could get to it, Mookie grabbed it and threw it on the floor behind him.

"No, no, no, we aren't doing any of that. If you want to do this the hard way, then I can oblige, but you need to remember I'm the one holding the gun. Now, I want you to walk slowly over here and keep your hands where I can see them. We have to get going, though."

Junie, still in some sort of shock, tried to clear her head. The drugs, while keeping her pain-free, were obviously keeping her brain from working at its highest level. She could not think of anything to do other than exactly what Mookie was telling her.

"OK, then, let's go," Mookie said, and Junie, completely resigned to the situation for the moment, started toward the door of the bedroom. As she walked through the door, though, she stopped and took one last look at the bloody pulp lying on the bed.

"Fuck him," she said, spitting on the floor in the direction of what was left of the old man.

"OK, then," Mookie said and shut the door behind them.

17.

Cadel limped closer to the scene of the massacre and looked around to see how much carnage there really was.

There was a lot.

He had watched the whole thing play out right before his eyes and still could not believe what he saw. He had seen depictions of standoffs before on movies and television, but they had never looked like this.

The random chaos of it all had been what shocked him. Where three people had been standing, one's face had been blown off, while another dropped to the ground, and the other looked around as if nothing had happened.

Cadel had heard the whistling of a bullet go right over his head and ping the garbage can right behind him. That could have been his face getting blown off too.

He tried not to think about it.

From what he could tell there was only one person in the black SUV who had caused all the carnage. He was not sure how it all happened. All he knew was that the man in the SUV had some serious firepower whereas those outside had mostly shotguns and hunting rifles. He had driven away before incurring any serious damage to himself. It was really miraculous in a way. The man had acted as if there was no way he would ever get shot as he casually strolled from the passenger side to the driver side, unleashing holy hell to anyone who happened to expose themselves. He plopped himself inside, turned the SUV around, and drove away. Cadel could have sworn he saw the man smiling through the front window, the only one not tinted, as he crashed through the gate, which naturally flew open with hardly a scratch.

Cadel looked at the bodies around him as he limped to the middle of the clearing. Just a few minutes ago they were peace-loving hippies in a situation that was way over their heads, doing what they thought they were supposed to do to protect their way of life. The way of life that had gotten them off the streets, off drugs, and gave their lives meaning, a purpose. Now, they were dead and had been killed in a manner that was as violent, if not more so, than anything they had encountered before. He had looked down on them previously, but now his heart was filled with a surprising sense of loss.

He limped to where a small group of people was gathering. They were clearly still in shock and not quite comprehending what had happened. He looked around and saw there were people injured and not getting the medical attention they needed. As he walked up, he listened to their conversations, which did not make sense to him -- and, hey, given what had just occurred who could blame them?

One woman, who appeared to be in some sort of authority role, was trying to take control the situation, but no one was listening to her.

"We have to make sure the gate is closed and locked. We cannot have him come back. We also need to make sure our weapons are categorized and put back in the stockpile."

She might as well have been talking to herself, and she seemed to realize her lack of resonance. Cadel got to where the rest were milling about and scanned the landscape and the injured. He was shocked that no one, except a few, was helping those hurt.

He could not stand it anymore: He was tired of being a passive participant in this situation.

"OK, listen," he said to those around him, including the woman, who seemed to have given up any plan to assert order in the chaos. "We have to help the injured first and foremost. Let's scan the area and take those injured and those who we can move to the infirmary. We also need to call an ambulance and get the seriously injured to the hospital."

"No phone," the woman, who had been giving unheeded words said.

"What?" Cadel could not believe anyone was that gullible. He shook his head. "I guarantee you there's a phone around here somewhere."

"No phone," she said.

"Wait, do you mean there's no phone in this entire place or that you don't want me to use the phone?"

She rolled her eyes and wandered off, Cadel supposed, to help someone.

Cadel looked around at the people standing by him and noticed they were looking back at him, waiting for him to give them some sort of guidance.

Yes, Cadel the leader, said no one ever, he thought to himself. He had always been something of a lone wolf and preferred it that way. In his experience, which was vast at 40 something, people were not to be trusted. He could count on his fingers and toes, and other appendages, the number of people in his life who he had at one time admired, or relied upon, or loved, and who had all either let him down or outright betrayed him.

Yeah, the hippie had been right about him.

His father, who he had adored at the time, left his family after, Cadel found out later, years of screwing around. That had been the first real betrayal Cadel had experienced, and the second had been when his father up and died on him years later. His father had skedaddled away to another state far away, where Cadel never visited. Cadel only heard from him on the odd occasion of a movie's opening or some weird entertainment news: "Have you seen Raiders of the Lost Ark?" "Did you know Johnny Carson was mad at Joan Rivers?" "Did you know Michael Jackson lives with a monkey?"

Cadel originally had assumed such random conversations were just his dad's feeble attempts at appearing hip, or at least relevant, in his son's eyes. As he grew older, though, Cadel realized they were, instead, feeble attempts to have conversations with his son without taking responsibility for, or even coming to terms with, the pain and suffering he had inflicted. His father wanted a relationship only if it meant the good stuff and none of the bad.

Fucking Baby Boomers, Cadel thought. Always cleaning up their shit.

And it still messed with him today -- long after his father died -- even as he stood amongst a pile of dead bodies, injured victims, and meandering zombies still in shock from the day's occurrences. He did not know upon whom he could rely to help, and he knew whoever he did choose would eventually let him down. If he could do it all himself, he would. At least he knew it would be done right, but with his own injuries he knew he could not do what needed to be done by himself.

He looked around at the various groups of people milling about randomly helping those injured and, lo and behold, saw his old friend, the redhead from earlier.

He waved to her, but she either did not see him or completely ignored him. He chose to believe it must have been the former.

"OK, people," he said loud enough, so she could hear. "We have to get our injured to the infirmary and STAT!"

Out of the corner of his eye he thought he saw her looking at him.

Good, good, he thought to himself. It is all going according to plan. Orchestrate a mass killing, so I can get some primo trim.

"OK, you, you, and you," Cadel said, pointing to random stronger looking men. "Go get some plank boards, so we can transport the badly injured without hurting their necks, or backs, or whatever."

To his amazement, they obeyed him.

"And you, you, you," he said pointing to members of the more fairer sex, "errrr, go to the infirmary and begin preparing, uh, places to treat the injured."

To his further amazement, they obeyed him too. And he did not even know there was an infirmary. He just guessed.

He began giving out other orders too, and everyone did exactly as he said without so much as a look. He was beginning to admire his own leadership abilities and wondering why he had not been more of a leader in the past, when he realized these people were used to taking orders. In fact, they preferred it. They would much rather have someone tell them what to do than think for themselves.

They were pretty good at taking orders, though. Cadel was amazed at how thorough, yet quickly, they all did what they were told to do.

The hippie had his little puppies trained very well, Cadel thought to himself.

Oh, yeah, the hippie. Where the hell was he? He was not one of the dead bodies lying around. Cadel knew from his limited interactions with him that he would not like Cadel barking orders like this. He would probably have some groovy reason for why it was better to encourage everybody in a positive way instead of just telling them what the hell to do.

Nonetheless, the hippie was the one in charge around here, and Cadel did not want to usurp his authority. Well, if he was being completely honest with himself, he did not want to have authority over anything. He wanted to leave this place as soon as he could, and not pissing off the Grand Poobah was the first step in getting out of here.

He saw the redhead tending to one of the wounded near him.

"Hey, there," he said and walked towards her. "Where is, what's his name, Alex?"

"Alexander," she said. "You seriously didn't see what happened?"

"No, well, I mean I saw most of what happened as far as the shooting and everything, but I didn't see him, Alexander, anywhere."

Her eyes began filling with tears, and, as was his usual reaction when anyone, especially women, began showing any sort of emotion, he changed the conversation.

"OK, OK, I'm sorry," he said. "I didn't know. Can you tell me where a phone is, then? We have to get some sort of medical attention for these people. We have to get the police here too."

As soon as he said it, he knew he had overplayed his hand. She jumped up and got in his face, wiping her tears away.

"Are you crazy? We can't have the police here."

He was slowly realizing there was something else going on here. He assumed this place had been part of Mookie's drug ring, but even that did not make much sense. It certainly would not have explained her reaction. She could just leave or point her finger at the head hippie. She was not personally invested in whatever criminal enterprise was happening, was she? From his limited time here, he did not think so. It just did not make any sense.

"OK, OK. Well, what about the injured? They need to get to the hospital, right?"

"We can treat them here. We don't need the extra attention."

He looked at her closely. There was definitely something going on she knew about, and the others probably did not. His bullshit detector was going off, and he decided to listen to it.

"OK," he said. "Well, let's do that. Who around here is a doctor or a nurse or whatever?"

She pointed to the group of buildings where the others had been taking the injured. Before he could say anything else she walked off to help some of the others left behind.

This place is sooooooo fucked up, he told himself. He thought about leaving, and now was the perfect opportunity. He needed to. At some point Mookie or one of his henchmen would be back to get him. His life was definitely in danger if he stayed here. All he had to do was walk out the front gate. He could call the authorities and bust this place wide open. He had enough to write a pretty good story, and there would certainly be follow-up stories. He could definitely get some pretty good coin out of it all.

Nah, fuck that shit, he said to himself.

He was going to burn this whole thing down, despite the danger to himself, and then he was going to write about it all on his own terms. No paper. No editor. No deadline. No advertisers or politicians throwing their weight around to change the story or tone it down. And that meant, more than likely, no paycheck.

He was going to tell the story the way it needed to be told. If that meant he would be penniless and, hell, friendless, he would do it. He had to be true to the story and as a consequence that meant he had to be true to himself. No compromises. No shortcuts. No lazy unnamed sources. It would all be meticulously documented and written -- without a concern for word counts or losing the reader. It would be the way journalism was supposed to be. It was not supposed to matter what the public wanted. What they needed was the truth -- whether they hated the messenger or not.

And there was not any amount of sugar that was going to help this medicine go down. This was going to hurt a lot of people, including himself probably, but he was going to tell the truth about what was going on here even if it meant destroying lives in the process. Even if he had not connected all the dots yet, he knew several politicians and prominent businessmen who were involved and would go down. He knew that most of them had families, and he knew that there would be carnage among the innocent, but this is what happens when you tell the truth. The lies and falsehoods on which people build their entire careers and, hell, even personas, at some point have to give way when the truth had its say.

And, with that self-affirming pep talk, he limped off in the direction of what he assumed was the infirmary.

16.

Mookie looked at the girl in the passenger's seat next to him. She was clearly still in shock. He had bound her hands behind her back and her ankles together, even though he did not think it was necessary. She was in another world. He could not blame her. She had been drugged, beaten, and, he assumed, raped -- although from the carnage he had seen in the cabin, she had defended herself rather well.

Mookie certainly did not want his head busted in, though, so he had made sure the ties on her wrists and ankles were tight. He did not see the need to put her in the trunk, though.

He looked at her again. Despite her appearance from the day's events, she was still quite pretty in a nontraditional way. She had a translucent look to her -- ageless -- and when the light struck her face in a certain way, her skin was almost ethereal.

"Do you have any tattoos … well, hidden tattoos?" he asked her. The words were the first spoken between the two of them since they left the old man's abode. Even when they had gotten to where the bodies were, she casually stepped over them as if they were merely stage props in a play. Without saying a word she plopped down in the passenger side and stared straight ahead. She did not put up a fight as he bound her hands and feet.

She turned and looked at him with a blank expression. "No," she said simply and turned her head back to look straight ahead into the nothingness before her.

"Yeah, I didn't think so," he said. His client would not have minded a few tattoos here and there, but he definitely wanted the body to be as pure and non-desecrated as possible. Mookie assumed it made it all the more pleasurable to the maniac when he conducted his, well, business.

Mookie shuddered in spite of himself.

Poor girl, he thought. He realized that while she had worked in The Coffee Shop for not that long, he did not know much about her. Yes, he had done the usual background checks on her from his contacts at the shelter, but he had hardly talked to her at all other than asking for more refills of the black swill passed off as coffee. He never got a good read on her because he never really cared enough to do so.

In his mind, he had filed her under "Poor, white trash, who ran away from home, ended up on meth, prescription drugs, or some combination of both, and found herself living on the street." She had probably not been on the streets long, though. She did not have that "street look" ... yet. It did not take long for the homeless to look homeless, though.

She had been roughed up pretty bad. He could see the new marks on her body that would soon become deep bruises. Her mouth was bloody, but he was not sure if that was her blood or not. Her hair was matted with sweat, mud, and the usual grime. Under different circumstances, he might have made sure she was cleaned up and looked a little fresh. He just did not have that luxury. He knew his client would complain when he first saw her, as he always did, but Mookie knew he would take her, do what he does, and then leave Mookie alone for a few months -- maybe even longer -- before he had to do it all over again.

Even though he was paid very handsomely, Mookie wished he had never met the guy. Mookie wondered why he did not just let this be the opportunity he needed to end the whole thing. He could let the girl out of the car and drive far away. He knew he could be in Mexico by tomorrow, and, from there, he could travel anywhere in the world. He had enough money stashed away to last a few years, and, at least, he would be alive.

Mookie was not ready for that yet, though. Something was telling him he could get out of this situation and salvage the entire operation. Mookie just hoped it was not his ego telling him so. He had always prided himself on the fact that he could give it all up if he had to -- he could just disappear. He had always believed that was one of the things separating him from the others in his business. While they rolled around in huge cars, flashing expensive jewelry and strutting around in designer clothes, he had lived a modest, under-the-radar lifestyle. He did not attach himself to things. Things were what weighed people down. Things were what kept people from being nimble. When things became what identified a person, then he or she was done. It was only a matter of time.

Mookie did not have things, but he had money, lots of it, and he had power. He wondered if he was allowing both to cloud his judgment right now. If he left, he would still have some of the money, but he would not have any of the power. Yes, it may be clouding his judgment, but to him, it was worth it, at least, to try and salvage before bolting because, frankly, he liked having power. He wanted to maintain it.

If he could get to the Farm and deliver the goods, he might be able to keep everything in place. He knew there would be no talking sense to the maniac. Mookie would have to be ready to get out of there as soon as he could and just hope that the exchange of goods would be enough to placate the man. If he was too late, then he would just keep driving. He did not know what he would do with the girl at that point. Maybe he would just drop her off on the side of the road. It would be her lucky day, despite being drugged, kidnapped, beaten, and raped.

If he knew what was actually happening at the Farm, it would make things a lot easier. Damn his no cell phone policy. Worse, he was out in the boonies, and there were no payphones, to the extent there were any payphones left, to call and see what the hell was going on. His plan, then, was to drive to the Farm, assess the damage, and determine whether he could salvage his operation. If it were all beyond repair, he would simply turn this car around and drive away forever. The maniac at that point would not only stop doing business with Mookie, he would do everything in his power, which was considerable given his wealth, prestige, and family connections, to destroy Mookie. Sure, Mookie had the goods on him, as far as the maniac's past sick exploits, but it would never come to that. The maniac knew what Mookie knew and would take no chances.

The key to everything turning out exactly the way he wanted it to, the key to his future, was the little pixie next to him. She could be his salvation.

He glanced over at her. She definitely was resigned to what was about to occur. Of course, she had no idea the full extent of what was about to occur, or she would jump the fuck out of his car. However, she seemed to have some vague understanding that this was the end of the line. She did not ask one single question about where they were going or what was going to happen. She just stared ahead of her as if she was a little girl going to the zoo on a sunny Sunday afternoon. Even though she was in shock, he had been around others in such a state before, and they had at least talked, even if it was nonsense. No, this was different. It was a resignation, an acceptance. He imagined she looked just like a Mayan virgin before being chunked into a volcano.

She did have a certain innocence to her. It would be a shame to see that desecrated, but if it had to happen that way, so be it. If not her, the maniac would find someone else. Yeah, that was a pretty lame justification, Mookie realized, but it was the truth. If there were going to be people in the world like the maniac, then Mookie might as well make a profit off them. And it was more than just money too. The maniac's powerful connections had served Mookie well over the years. Basically anything Mookie wanted from the private sector, or the government realm, he could ask for it and get it. It might take some time, but it would eventually happen. He had no idea how the maniac was able to get whatever he wanted without going through the usual political glad handling, but he did, and all Mookie had to do was keep providing the services for which he was paid handsomely.

Mookie knew, though, deep down at some point his relationship with the maniac would come back to bite him in the ass. You could only play with fire for so long, and this was much more than a little campfire in the backyard. This was a raging inferno scorching the earth, leaving absolutely nothing behind. Mookie felt the anxiety stiffen up his back and neck. He knew he was going against his credo by even going to the Farm. He was trying to make things happen instead of letting them happen. He was not adapting to the situation. He was forcing. He knew he should just turn the car towards Mexico and disappear. He did not know why after all these years he felt the need to do things differently, but he was. He was probably making a huge mistake, but he couldn't help himself.

"Motherfucker!" he screamed and pulled over onto the side of the gravel road. He beat the steering wheel with such ferocity that he thought he might break either his hands or the wheel.

He looked over at the girl, who had turned her face towards him. Apparently, his little hissy fit had awoken her from her slumber. They stared at each other for a few seconds, and then she turned back and stared straight ahead.

Mookie crossed his arms across his chest and looked up at the ceiling of the old car. He did not like losing his cool, and he certainly did not like doing it in front of another person. He closed his eyes and felt the frustration run through his body. Then, slowly, he felt it all ease away.

No, he was not going to let his whole operation go up in smoke. He had worked too hard to let it all go. He felt certain he could work his way out of this.

And, if he was being honest with himself, he would have to admit that he was just too old to start all over again. He did not have the energy -- let alone time and patience -- to start over from scratch. No, he would have to try and salvage this whole thing all by himself.

He could feel her looking at him again. He looked over at her. He felt the hate and pain coming from her eyes, but he had felt that before. It was nothing new. People always hated him, and it was mostly because he had, in fact, caused them some sort of pain. It was the only way to get ahead in this life, though. In order to win, someone else had to lose. The shots on television of the losing team on the bench with the towels over their heads and the sad fans in the stands with their hands on top of their heads, it all just meant that someone else had won.

The winning team did not feel sorry for the losing team. They had the trophy. They did not have time to wonder if scoring the winning basket would make the mama of one of the other team's players sad. They had to spend all their energy and focus on winning -- not worry about the consequences. Later, they might feel a twinge of guilt when they hear the story of so-and-so's grandfather who raised his grandson and had to sacrifice so much only to see his grandson's team lose after traveling over 500 miles to see him play. But that was life. And the winning team would soon forget the sad grandfather and only remember the trophy.

He was going to win, like he always did, and that meant this little pixie would lose. It meant that several other people would lose too. He would win, and it was his choice to be a winner and not worry about the losers.

He stared back into her eyes. He let her feel the uncaring, the apathy, he had for her hate and pain. She wanted a rise out of him, but she was not going to get it.

He looked ahead. It was time to get going. He put the car in drive and eased back onto the road. He felt the gravel underneath the tires and could almost taste the chalky dust that popped up as he upset the dormant, gray pebbles.

15.

Alexander knew he was close when he saw the odd tree formation. It was near the turnoff that led to the dirt road that led to the Farm. He had seen it so many times he had forgotten it was there: two huge trees intertwined like a pretzel that suddenly separated into two. He had never seen trees do that, and he wondered how it had happened. It was almost as if the trees were attracted to one another in their infancies. They could not get enough of one another. They had to be together. They had no choice, but to be one. There was no way to tell where one started and the other ended. Then, just like that, it was over. They were apart, and each stretched to the sky on different trajectories.

Nature has a strange way of putting things in perspective, Alexander thought to himself. Here he was in the midst of a total freefall with his dreams crashing down all around him, and the random chaos of nature was there to remind him of the path upward. The world was so much bigger than he. The world was so much bigger than his dreams. He looked deeper in the woods for some other sort of insight. Maybe God, or Jesus, or Mohammed, or Buddha, or Yoda was trying to tell him something from outside this world's measly parameters.

Nothing -- just trees and fallen leaves and dirt and dead bushes.

But, to him, it was beautiful. He remembered as a kid going to Disneyland on a school trip. The bushes had been cut down to resemble characters in the Disney canon: Snow White, Tinkerbell, and the like. The teachers on the bus "oohed and ahhed" upon sight of the bushes and pondered out loud as to the work and care that went into maintaining these living sculptures. All the while, Alexander felt sick to his stomach. It had seemed so grotesque and unnatural to him. As he wandered through the park that day, as his friends were riding rides, eating junk, and spending copious amounts of money, he found himself obsessing over the rows and rows of flowers throughout the park. They were all so carefully planted and maintained. At one point, he took his hands and measured the distance between each flower in a particular flowerbed. Each flower was planted a specific distance between each other. Then, he counted the flowers in each row. Each row had the exact number. One of his teachers saw him looking at the flowers, walked over to him, and, with a toothy smile, remarked about how beautiful it all was. He could not believe the words coming out of her mouth. It had been the most disgusting and unnatural thing he had ever seen in his entire life. He could not get his young mind around why anyone would want to do this -- let alone think it was beautiful.

Even as a kid, he knew that if they left those flowerbeds alone, it would not be long before the weeds popped up. It would not be long before the bushes filled in. It would not be long before the flowers wilted and died. At what point does one give up and just let nature run its course? In the end, nature would win. When it was all said and done, no matter how much one kicks and screams and feebly attempts to manipulate nature, he or she will only be left with leaves on the ground and deformed trees reaching for the sky.

As he shuffled past the deformed trees, he realized maybe he had been doing the same thing in his own life. Maybe he had been denying his own nature by trying to be something he was not. Maybe he was attempting to manipulate nature the same way Disney gardeners shaped already beautiful bushes into distorted images of Goofy and Cinderella.

The extraordinary amount of futile energy those gardeners spent planting flowers at the exact same distance was the same amount he was spending on himself, trying to be a good person -- attempting to please or gain approval from … who exactly?

Well, that was obvious, he told himself: his parents, even though he was, in essence, dead to them. There would always be some part of him that would always be trying to please them -- to show them he had turned out alright, that he became a good productive member of society and all their fears about him were unfounded. His father could finally put down his paper, his mother could back away from the stove, and both could look his way and mutter the words that had always eluded him, "We are proud of you."

So what was his true nature? Was he just a weak, pathetic piece of shit? No, he was not that either, but he was who he was. He had desires, and he was selfish. He did not want to go back to snorting coke off the lid of a trash dumpster, but he was going to stop denying himself things he liked for the mere sake of being a good person. It just was not in his nature to be a good person no matter how much he wanted to be seen that way.

Even with his injuries he felt a weight slide off his shoulders and a freedom he had not felt for a long time. He stopped, even though he knew losing his momentum would only mean that much more pain when he started walking again.

Why was he going back to the Farm, he asked himself. He did not know. A sense of obligation perhaps? To finish what he had started?

To create a new world as the old one faded away?

That was what he had been telling himself, but in reality, he knew deep down that it would not work. Today's events further solidified that hidden knowledge. They could not even protect themselves from one mad man. In some future lawless world, there would be more than just one. No, he had to let go of that illusion. He was never really going to create a New World Order. They would disappear along with the rest, violently in some cases, but, more so than not, pathetically silent.

No, he was not going back to the Farm to create a new world. Was he going back to rectify the wrongs in his life by doing good things for others? No, it was not that either. He tried to peel back the layers of deception in his own mind. The things he had been telling himself over and over that he knew deep down were not true -- he had to put those to the side. This was his opportunity to see what his motivations were, to see why he was so drawn to this place, to see who he really was.

Was he really just a pathetic, powerless, no-name druggie?

No, he was more than that. And, with that thought, he knew why he was going back to the Farm.

Alexander knew Mookie was using the Farm as a cover for his activities, and Alexander knew what they were, even if he did not know all the details. OK, so he had helped some of those girls, but that was just to make himself feel better for what he knew deep down was his true selfish motivation: He liked being in control. He liked being in the know. He liked having a secret that only a few powerful people knew. He liked telling people what to do. Even if it was a failure, it would be his failure. It was the only time in his life he had felt important. It was the only time in his life he felt like he meant something.

Yeah, OK, so he was a piece of shit. He was part of a sex trafficking scheme after all -- no matter how much he tried to justify his actions to himself, there was that ugly fact staring him in the face. He could not get around it.

Something deep inside him shifted, and it hurt. He felt the tears burning beneath his eyeballs, and, before he knew it, he was weeping uncontrollably. He felt his knees crumble, and he was on the ground. He wept. He wept for everything. He wept for the people he knew and loved, who he had let down over the years. He wished he had the guts at the time to tell them all he was sorry. He wept for the potential his life had at one point, but that he pissed away. He wept for the missed opportunities to love, to live, to be fulfilled merely because he was too cool to try.

He wept for the health of his body he saw leak out firsthand through needles, papers, and pipes. He wept for the dark places of his soul in which he would find himself again and again, where he would eventually believe he belonged, instead of going towards the light, where he eventually believed he did not belong. He wept for the delusions he held onto as some sort of way to be happy that he would never have: love, God, family. He wept for the empty shell of a man he had become. He wept for the desire to become more than just an empty shell, but not knowing how.

Finally, he wept for the death and destruction of the Farm. The lifeless bodies of his comrades he had seen on the ground as the SUV sped away -- he did not pull the trigger that killed them, but he might as well have. They were dead because of him.

He could tell himself over and over again that it was not his fault, and technically that would be true. Deep down, though, he knew he was culpable. He knew he had led these lambs to their slaughter. In a way, it was crueller than their inevitable deaths on the street. He had given them hope, yes, but it was worse than that. He had helped them believe in themselves for probably the first time in their lives. He had put them in charge of things. He had given them authority. He had made them feel special. And he had done the cruellest thing of all: He had made them feel that even though the world hated them and cast them away, in reality they were something incredible. They were wizards, superheroes, and Jedi, all of them -- and they had not even known it.

And, now, when they had finally started to believe in themselves, he had abandoned them. Now, they were probably realizing what every non-psychopath discovers at some point in their lives: They are not special. They were nothing more than specks of dust floating through the air for a brief time, and then they would disappear forever. Instead of choosing to enjoy their brief time in the sun and be grateful for the chance to feel what it means to be alive they instead chose to be anxious about why they were specks of dust and why they were not flying as high as the other specks and why they had to disappear. Or, worse, they deluded themselves into thinking that if they were really good specks of dust, they would be rewarded in dust heaven with a fatted calf, whole milk, and as many virgin dust specks as they could handle.

Well, he owed it to them at least to go back and clean up his mess. He would take responsibility for the whole thing. Then, he would quit trying to manipulate life. He would let nature take its course, and that meant being true to his own nature. He was a piece of shit. He was not a good person, and any attempt to be one was a worthless endeavor.

He picked himself up off the ground and started walking. Then, he stopped, turned around, and looked at the deformed trees shooting up to the sky. He sighed, turned back around, and pushed himself down the road towards the Farm.

14.

Junie did not know where they were going, but she had a pretty good idea that, wherever they went, it meant she was back in the game. She could not believe her good fortune, but she just could not understand why. Why had Mookie personally come to get her? He always kept himself far removed from anything that could remotely implicate him. She did not have enough evidence to arrest him before, but she had not really cared. She had been more concerned with saving the faceless girls in her dreams and busting the ring wide open than actually bringing down the ringmaster. Yet here he was, and he had plopped right in her lap.

She was amazed at how things had completely turned around for her so fast. She had assumed that she would die at the hands of the ogre, or if she somehow escaped, she assumed she would be relegated to a desk job at the police station and never given the opportunity to go undercover again. All her work would have been for nothing. And all the fat, disgusting men with their potbellies, short ties, and coffee in tiny Styrofoam cups would smirk as they whispered behind her back about how the little girl had blown her chance.

Worse for her, though, was the knowledge that she had failed the faceless girls.

Those girls had haunted her dreams from the time she saw a truckload of them as a rookie cop on a routine traffic stop. The driver pulled over the U-Haul on the side of the road, and her mentor got out of the squad car, mumbling something about how such rentals always had a taillight out. He had planned on just giving the driver a warning. He was going to tell the driver to make sure to notify the rental place about the faulty equipment. However, when he got to the door of the U-Haul, the driver, clearly panicked, opened the door, got out with his hands in the air, and, without warning, ran out in the middle of the interstate only to get flattened by a tractor-trailer.

It had happened so quickly that Junie, still in the car, did not even have time to take her seatbelt off. Her mentor looked at her and, before she could move to get out of the car, motioned for her to stay put. He pulled his gun and walked around to the back of the truck. He opened the back sliding-door slowly, and Junie had a front-row seat as to what was inside: at least 50 girls, standing with their hands bound, all with looks that ranged from fear to panic. However, it was the ones with looks of helplessness -- no, it was a certain sort of neediness -- that stayed with her. The looks of desperation peered straight into Junie's soul, begging for her help. They all were foreign, mostly from Russia or other Eastern European countries. None could speak English, Junie soon learned, as she brought them out of the truck one by one and had them sit down on the little hill next to the shoulder on the side of the road.

Most of them were no older than 18. They smelled like B.O. and urine, and, even though the smell had been repugnant, Junie would give anything to go back in time and bathe in their very essence, hugging them, loving them, taking care of them.

At the time, all she did was remain detached, professional, not because that was what she was supposed to do as an officer of the law, but because she did not want to be judged as weak, or -- gasp -- feminine, by her male colleague. No, she had to remain tough and show no emotion or compassion for these needy little nymphs. She still hated herself for it. She hated she tried to be something she was not in order to impress some man, who probably just wanted to have sex with her and every little girl in the truck -- or at least masturbate to them later that night after his wife and kids had gone to bed.

She had continued to show no emotion as she processed each one later that afternoon at the police station. The department got them food and even some clean clothes from the local shelter. Social workers came in and helped clean them up. The workers, along with Junie, took the girls to the locker rooms below, away from the eyes of the glaring men, and bathed each one down, making sure they had no lice or other hygiene problems. The girls remained in a state of shock and hardly acknowledged what was being done for them. At least that was what Junie told herself. She could not get her head around the way the girls, previously needy, now seemed aloof, almost ungrateful, as the social workers tried to help them. After all that had been done to them, it was no surprise, Junie assumed, they were somewhat reserved and untrusting of the first sign of kindness shown to them in these United States.

Junie helped get the girls clean and made sure they were fed, but in pure Pontius Pilate fashion, washed her hands of them after that. She had seen the stares and snide remarks from her male counterparts and superiors and, again, not wanting to appear weak, went back to regular old police work.

At the time, she was mad: Of course, she thought, just because she was a female she was expected to be doing the feminine-type work of cleaning and feeding and nurturing. Even though she was mad at the time, when she caught a glimpse of the girls being led out of station one by one, the anger fell away. What she saw haunted her in the years since: the looks on their faces. She realized what she mistook for aloofness and ingratitude was actually a deep sorrow. They had lost everything. Their short childhoods, which, at one point, meant love, joy, and excitement had given way to darkness. No matter what happened to them for the rest of their lives they would have the knowledge stuck in the back of their brains of how truly dark and depraved mankind was. They would never feel safe. They would never truly experience joy. They would never trust their loved ones. They would live lives filled with pain. Even in her stubbornness and anger at the time, it filled Junie with an immense sadness she never quite got over.

Unfortunately, it was not the last time she had seen that look. She saw it on the streetwalkers. She saw it in the homeless shelters. She saw it on domestic abuse house calls. She saw it over and over and over and over again.

So when she realized she was back in the game, she knew exactly how to act. It was not hard to incorporate that look onto her face. It was a role she was born to play. She sat in the passenger's side of the car and let her whole face go numb. She let herself become resigned to the situation. She felt what it would be like if she did not care anymore. She felt what it meant to be alone. She felt what it meant to be helpless. She felt what it meant to be hopeless. She felt what it meant to have the whole world crashing down all around, and all she could do was watch and wonder why she was still alive. She felt herself wonder about all the horrible decisions that had gotten her to this dark place -- that if she had done one little thing differently, maybe she would not be here. She let herself believe she was a bad person. She let herself believe she was unlovable. She let herself believe she would never feel joy again. She let herself believe she would never be safe. And she let herself believe that all of it was her fault.

It must have worked because Mookie let her sit in the front seat and, other than bounding her hands and ankles, left her alone. He even looked at her with what one could possibly call empathy. If she continued to play the part, hopefully she could save the faceless girls of her dreams. She could bust the whole thing wide open.

She tried not to get too excited, but she could not help herself. She was back from the dead.

Still, she could not help herself but go back to her original thought: It did not make sense; it did not match up. Why would Mookie drive all the way, expose himself, make himself vulnerable, just for her?

Before she could give it much more thought, Mookie pulled to the side of the road and started beating the steering wheel. Junie found herself breaking character just slightly in order to see what the hell was going on. She turned to look at him. She had never seen him show much emotion at all, and here he was now screaming at the top of his lungs.

No, it did not make much sense. Junie's instinct was to ask what was wrong. She wanted to inquire as to why things were breaking the way they were. As her lips begin to move, though, she stopped herself.

The look.

Those girls would not have cared about Mookie's erratic behavior, so she would not either.

She felt the muscles in her face relax, and she turned her head slowly to face the front of the car once again.

She allowed her brain to go blank. She felt Mookie looking at her, examining every inch of her as if he was suddenly suspicious of who she was. She felt goose bumps pop up on her arms and thought for a brief moment that maybe he could read her thoughts -- maybe he slithered up into her brain and was prodding around until he found what he wanted.

As illogical a thought as it was, she nonetheless felt panic rise up inside her. He knew. He knew she was a cop. He was going to kill her right now and dump her on the side of the road. Panic began to swallow her whole. She began thinking of an exit strategy. Why had she not thought of one before now?

Just as she was about to pull the door handle with bound hands and try to run -- or more likely hop -- into the woods with bound feet, Mookie looked away, put the car in drive, and eased back onto the gravel road.

She again felt her face and body relax. She felt the panic slip away and, for a brief moment, felt the pain from the void left in its place. Her brain hurt, and she felt tired. The wide swing of emotions over the last few minutes, and, well, the whole day, left her exhausted. She suddenly wanted to close her eyes, if only for a few minutes. She felt the fog settle on her brain and could not think her way through it. She needed rest, if only for a few seconds.

Before she drifted off, though, she felt that brief glimmer of hope that made her insides smile.

She was back in the game.

13.

Cadel always knew he was meant for something greater, and this was it.

He had been instructed by the infirmary's doctor/nurse/aide/whatever to clean up the vomit on the floor. Not being able to find a towel he had been reduced to crawling on his knees with a threadbare towel, cleaning up chunks of someone's late breakfast. Yep, those were definitely eggs. Yep, there's some bacon.

Just a few minutes ago he was Patton, barking out orders to those around him, and people actually listened. Ahhhh, the fog of war. Now, the rightful order of this place had come back into being, and he was right back at the bottom.

But that was OK. He guessed it was better to be as anonymous as possible in this situation. He knew that others in leadership would fill the vacuum left by the old hippie, and he hoped business would continue as normal. Then, he could find out where the bodies were buried.

OK, that was a bad analogy, he told himself, especially since people were actually burying dead bodies.

Cadel was still amazed that no police or ambulances had arrived. He assumed someone outside this place would have heard the gunshots -- maybe a random hunter or camper or bird watcher or Unabomber. But, alas, no.

If a mass murder occurs in the forest, and no one is there to see it, did it actually exist? Apparently, in this case, the answer would have to be no.

He was also amazed at how quickly these people went back to their normal jobs, other than, of course, the workers in the infirmary treating the injured. There really were not many people milling about. They were all doing something.

But, of course, they would try to assemble some sort of normal routine. People were hard at work clearing the wreckage in New York on September 12. People were breaking out the chainsaws and cutting up fallen tree limbs the day after Katrina. People were busy shoveling the mud out of their abodes the day after the Japanese tsunami. It went on and on and on. Whenever something tragic happened, humans were hard at work establishing some sort of normalcy the day after.

And here they were, ants busily putting back together their dirt pile the day after some asshole strolled along and kicked it over. What choice did they have but to try and put it back together again?

Cadel had been patiently cleaning up various messes before the current slop of vomit, but really he had been trying to listen to the conversations around him to discover what had happened. The best he could tell was that the person who had wreaked all this havoc was someone no one knew. No one had seen the SUV before today. No one knew why he was at the Farm at all, and everyone seemed distraught that the hippie had gotten in the car. They were all very worried he was now dead.

However, no one seemed to think he was part of the problem. No one seemed to think that maybe, just maybe, the aging hippie had brought all this on himself -- that he was the reason so many people were dead. No, they were not connecting the dots. But that was his job after all. For he is: Super Journalist. OK, well, maybe not super, but he was a journalist, one of a dying breed.

In a way, this event was a microcosm of what happened in the world every day. Something crazy and chaotic and random would happen, and he, as a journalist, would be there to try to explain it and give it some sort of meaning. He would connect the dots, yes, but there were a million dots, and it was up to him to paint a pretty picture out of something horrible and random.

It did not mean it was not true, though. It just meant it would be the truth he decided to tell.

And that truth was that this was mostly the hippie's fault. Sure, Mookie was the mastermind, and Cadel would make sure he got his due too, but the hippie was something different. He needed to be exposed. He had duped these people, who mostly were in recovery and, thus, in Cadel's experience, extremely vulnerable.

The hippie had taken away their drug of choice and supplanted it with another addiction: a cult or, rather, a cult lifestyle. He had taken away their freedom of choice. In order to recover, they had to learn how to live with freedom. They had to learn how to make the right choices and accept the consequences of the wrong ones. The hippie had taken that freedom away, which was the worst crime of all.

Cadel was not an addict, per se, even though he saw the bottom of a bottle more often than not, but he was very familiar with addictive personalities. Too familiar.

He had seen the struggles firsthand. He had seen some of the most intelligent people he knew throw their lives away because they could not accept they were addicts. Family members, best friends, co-workers -- he had seen them all drink, smoke, fuck, cheat, and lie their way to the bottom. Some had found their way back up, but it was only after they had accepted that their so-called freedom had been an illusion. Freedom was not the ability to do whatever the hell you wanted. Freedom was understanding what you could and could not handle.

Yeah, Cadel agreed with himself, we have freedom of religion in this country, but it does not mean that we could all go around taking peyote or throwing virgins into volcanoes. Yeah, we have freedom of the press, but it does not mean that he could go around writing stories without sources. Yeah, we have the Second Amendment, but it does not mean that some psychopath can go around stockpiling weapons at his own little apocalyptic cult place. As humans, we just could not handle unfettered freedom, but the beauty of true freedom was the right to determine what one could and could not handle.

The old hippie had taken that away from his little culties. He had taken away their freedom to hit rock bottom. He had taken away their desire not to end up there again. He had taken away their ability to determine how not to end up there again.

He had taken away their freedom to choose for themselves not to be an addict -- the choice an addict has to make every day in his or her life.

Now, they were addicted to the cultish lifestyle, and they sucked on it like their previous meth pipes.

It was funny to Cadel to see them continue their addiction in the hippie's absence. Cadel was sure it would break the poor hippie's heart to know he was not missed nearly as much as he thought he would be.

"Hey, you over there!"

Cadel snapped out of his half dream.

"Yup," he answered. He looked towards the voice, even though he already knew who was shouting at him.

The stout-looking African-American woman from his earlier "tour" was staring straight at him.

"You only got here today, right? I mean it was in the middle of the night, but you have only been here a day, right?"

Cadel nodded his head slowly. He did not like where this was going. The other thing people do right after a tragedy, he knew, was look for someone to blame.

"I mean, there's no way that you just get here, and then all this happened. And now you are acting like you are helping out, cleaning up, whatever. I've been watching you. You're just sitting here listening to everyone else. You don't belong here."

Cadel was slightly offended. He had worked hard at his appearance, but now was not the time to argue about his choice of demeanor.

Others in the infirmary area stopped what they were doing and turned to look at him. They were waiting for him to say something. Most were too weary or distracted to care. They just wanted to complete their jobs. They did not want to think about who Cadel was or why he was here. That was good, and Cadel did not want that to change. The last thing he wanted was for this woman to make him into the boogeyman. If others woke up from their haze, Cadel would never find out what was happening here. He would be thrown out or locked up or even worse. At the very least, his anonymity would vanish.

He had to salvage the situation.

"I don't have any idea what you're talking about. Hey, I'm working just as hard as everyone else around here. And, by the way, I was also out there getting shot at -- just like everyone else. Once the shots began I ran over there to help, even though, in case you didn't notice, I'm injured too."

He pointed at his leg in an exaggerated fashion, and he saw the confidence slowly drain from her face.

"If I was in on it," he continued, "don't you think I would've stayed far out of the action?"

He had her on the ropes. Now, he had to go for the knockout.

"And where were you, by the way?"

"I was there too," she snapped back.

"Funny," he said before she could say anything else, "because I didn't see you at all once the shots started firing. Did anyone see her?" he asked those around him.

Oh, this was a gamble, but he could not help overplaying his hand. It might be the only shot he had.

No one said anything. The look on her face told him he struck a nerve. She was ashamed of something. Maybe she got scared and ran away. Maybe she pulled a Platoon and found a dead body as her safety blanket. Maybe she pissed on herself. Maybe she shit in her pants. Maybe she vomited. Maybe she shut her eyes and wished it would all go away. Maybe she responded exactly the way someone should respond when gunfire erupted: do whatever it takes not to get shot. Whatever she did, once the shots rang out, probably revealed something of which she was not exactly proud. She looked down at the floor, sighed, and looked back up at him.

"I was there," she said. "I saw it happen. I saw a lot of my friends die."

She turned to go, but stopped herself and looked back at him. "I don't trust you. Alexander likes to take hard cases and make them whole again. And he was good at it. Look at me. I was as hard as they come, and he turned my life around all by himself. You, though, are something else. You just don't belong here. I don't know what happened earlier exactly, but it can't just be a coincidence you showed up beaten up, tied up, and later all hell breaks loose."

She sighed again loudly and looked at the others around her. No one could offer her support or, for that matter, disagree with her either. They were amoebas floating around in a petri dish with no direction. The weight of it all seemed to hit her at once, and Cadel was no longer a priority to her. It seemed that way at least. Cadel hoped it was that way at least. She turned and left the infirmary area, and everyone went back to their jobs, including Cadel.

Cadel thought about following her and continuing the argument or, maybe, talk to her in a reasonable way -- try and make her see his side of things. She was a well respected figure here, Cadel assumed, and he thought he might need something from her in the future. At the very least, he did not need her against him, constantly fighting him. Either way, there was no point in arguing with her now. And Cadel knew he would not be able to convince her of his innocence when she was probably still in some sort of shock. He decided just to let her, and the argument, go.

And, as much as it hurt Cadel to admit it, she had a point. It was a pretty big coincidence. Maybe he did have something to do with it in some bizarre way.

No, that was not it at all. He had nothing to do with it. The dreadlocked hag did not know what she was talking about. She was way off. She just did not understand how truly corrupt this place was. He felt sorry for her. She was one of those who needed freedom, who needed the truth, who needed to learn how to live by herself, who needed to learn how to control what she could control. It would be hard for her, as it would be for the others, but, in the end, it would be best for her as it would be for the others.

In Cadel's mind, it was always best to know the truth no matter how much it hurt. It was always better to be honest no matter how hard it was. Journalists used to tell the truth or at least make it a priority, Cadel heard the refrain in his head. Now, they were more concerned with meaningless awards and striking book or TV deals.

He noticed that the latest vomit he was cleaning up was sufficiently removed from the floor. It had been harder than he thought, and his injury had limited his mobility to get up and down from his knees.

The wooden flood had also kept him from getting all the semi-digested food out of the cracks and crevices.

He realized his OCD was kicking in, so he made himself decide it was OK not to get every spittle of vomit off the floor. It was time to move on to the next mess. As he struggled to get to his feet, he realized he had not been paying attention to the conversations in the infirmary after the older African American lady had left. His brain was a funny thing. It was one part OCD and another part ADD. He guessed the two parts should, in theory, even each other out, but instead it fostered an intense self-hatred at times when he could not remain focused at the task at hand.

Oh well, I'm a fuck up -- what else is new, he said to himself. People had told him that since, well, forever, and he had never done anything to convince himself or anyone else otherwise. So when he decided to fuck up other people's lives for a living, it was not that huge of a leap. Truth was the ultimate proverbial monkey-wrench thrown into the engine. He was always amazed at the lies and deceits people told each other and themselves in order to keep the machinations of their little lives intact. It was no wonder, then, when the gears of their lives came to a screeching halt they would be upset at the person who exposed their levels of deceit.

It was addicting, though, Cadel admitted, grinding things to a halt, upsetting the mainstream, exposing people as the hypocrites they were. Even better, doing so kept the microscope off himself.

The best of both worlds.

Because he realized deep down he was insecure and would not want the same type of scrutiny on himself that he was so willing to provide for others. By fucking up other people's lives, even if it was under the guise of the search for truth, and even if he did some good along the way, it meant that he was not such a fuck up himself.

"Ouch," he said out loud. See, he told himself, even you do not like to hear the truth, you fucking hypocrite.

"Yeah, well, what are you gonna do?" he again said out loud.

Cadel looked up and realized he was talking to himself louder than he thought. One of the many drawbacks to being a loner: Sometimes his inner dialogue and outer dialogue blended together. He straightened himself up and looked around to see if anyone had heard him. There were a couple of glances his way, but most were busy attending to their tasks at hand.

OK, get your shit together, he told himself, and made sure not to say it out loud this time. He had one shot to get in the good graces of those around him. If he blew it, he knew he would not have the time to recover. He looked up again with a big smile on his face, but no one seemed to notice. Good, he thought, and turned back to the busy task of appearing busy, hoping to avoid any further scrutiny.

12.

Mookie made himself think about where things had gone wrong. As usual, he had tried to get the small details right first and waited for the bigger pieces of the puzzle to fall neatly into place. It usually worked. Here, it had not.

Where had he gone wrong? The obvious answer was that he never should have done business with a maniac, but that was not it entirely. After all, he had to do business with maniacs in order to get the sort of money and power he wanted. It was high-risk, high-reward, maybe, but he believed he was one of the few who could make it work.

No, not doing business with a maniac was not the magic answer for which he was looking.

Where did it go wrong?

Was it his employees? Was it merely that he chose the wrong two people? Should he have screened them better? No, that was also an all-too-easy answer. They were screened as well as they could be. And it was not like he could hire Rhodes Scholars for fuck's sake.

So where did he go wrong?

Was it just the nature of his business? At some point, the random chaosness of it all would be too much, and something would have to give?

Maybe. He sensed he was getting closer to the answer.

Was it because of him? Was he getting too old to do this type of work anymore? If he was perceived as weak or vulnerable, he knew he would open himself up to, well, challenges. He knew he had to be ruthless at times, but, again, that was just part of the business he chose.

No, at some point, he realized, it would all just catch up with him. It was not because of the maniac, or his employees, or the type of business, or him: It was the world itself. No matter what he did -- what precautions he took, how ruthless he was, how adaptable he was, how smart he was -- eventually the world would just win.

He looked over at the girl next to him. The world had done a number on her. She never had a chance. Uneducated, or worse, homeschooled. Rural. Female. Pretty enough to get into trouble. She probably grew up in a household with drinking, abuse, and Fox News on the TV at all hours. She probably was taught that because she was a white Christian the world was rightfully hers.

Nah, she didn't have a chance.

Now, she was a waste of human flesh and would be sacrificed in the name of the true god: money for Mookie.

Well, there were worse ways to die. She could continue to live on the street and die a random death because of her inability to adapt or accept the world on its terms. At least this way, someone would profit, and it would be him.

He caught another glance of her while trying to keep his eyes on the road. She was really out of it. She had that dead fish look to her that so many of her generation had: open mouth, chin down, blank expression. All you have to do was plop a phone in her hands, and she would look like every teenage girl in every outdoor mall in the nation.

Maybe she did deserve to die.

They were getting closer to the Farm. When he and Alexander were looking for places, they at first thought it would be best to try and hide in plain sight. They looked at buildings close to The Coffee Shop -- somewhere Mookie could take the politicians and within minutes have a photo op to put on their website or whatever campaign fund-raiser propaganda they chose. Alexander had convinced him, though, to go bigger. Mookie remembered, at the time, being impressed with Alexander and his vision. He had not thought much of the man before. He had just been another recovering junkie, who had stumbled into Mookie's Coffee Shop, looking for a job. He was smarter than the normal employee, though, and Mookie found himself trusting the man more and more and giving him more and more responsibility.

Eventually, he let Alexander in on some, but not all, of his operations, and the man did not bat an eye. Instead, he came up with ways to make everything appear legitimate -- things Mookie had never considered. Things only a junkie would know.

The Coffee Shop was already a front, but Alexander was who started reaching out to the homeless shelters and addiction centers and who started hiring exclusively from those places. Yes, Mookie would still occasionally take someone from the street, but by hiring directly from shelters, etc., and by putting Mookie's name out there as a way for the distraught to become a part of "normal" society again, Mookie found himself also becoming associated as a legitimate member of society -- and not only legitimate, respected.

As a result, Mookie discovered he liked being respected, and the more he became respected, the more power he garnered. It was a very strange symmetry. The politicians and power brokers, who he had already been serving in the shadows and who could barely look him in the eye after a night of high-priced debauchery, were suddenly shaking his hand in front of cameras in broad daylight.

Alexander, in turn, while not taking any credit for the uptick in business, kept pushing for something bigger. Mookie initially liked the idea of Alexander's to purchase something outside the city limits because he knew it would be cheaper, but he never anticipated what Alexander had in mind.

But it worked perfectly. All the pieces of the puzzle fell into place so well, it made Mookie mad for not thinking of it himself.

They found the old farmhouse way out in the boonies after exploring several other options, including abandoned summer camps, old 60s era "retreats," and various camp houses. The farmhouse was perfect, though. It had been a thriving farm back in the day, but the family that owned it could not keep up with the modern times. They would not take out the loans they knew they would never be able to pay back in order to buy the most expensive, technologically efficient machinery. They also refused to buy the latest in copyrighted seeds. As a result, it was not long before the whole thing fell into a state of disrepair.

At least that was what Alexander told Mookie, who was sure some of the story was tempered by Alexander's bullshit liberalism. It was the same liberalism, though, that had served Mookie well over the years, so he guessed he should not complain all that much. And even though he had to listen to Alexander's rants about "the Man" (like he had any clue, growing up in a white, middle-class household, who "the Man" really was) and the evils of capitalism and the supposed wrongs of every Republican president since Eisenhower and how the Tea Party had finally exposed conservatives to be the race-baiting, hate-filled, Nazis they had always pretended not to be, Alexander turned out to be his most trusted advisor.

Well, for most things, but not all things, of course. Mookie did not like putting all of his eggs in one basket. There were still some things Mookie would only share with one person: himself. Still, for the everyday-type dealings, Alexander had everything running like a finely tuned and well oiled machine.

And, when it was time for Alexander to make the move, he had made sure everything was in place for Mookie to run in his absence.

Frankly, Mookie did not know how it would go once Alexander had moved to the Farm full time. At first, Mookie spent a lot of time there too, trying to oversee direction of the operation, but it became clear quickly that this was Alexander's vision. It was better just to let him do it his way. Of course, because Mookie was supplying the money, he still had the ultimate say, and he would veto some of the more outrageous expenditures from time to time. After Alexander threw the predictable hissy fit, he would eventually calm down and come back with a more reasonable request.

And so it went for months. Mookie would go out to the Farm once a week to see the Farm's progress and go over Alexander's budget and purchases.

Through his recovery program Alexander had found former contractors and builders. Strangely enough, there were an inordinate amount of former contractors, construction workers, painters, and handymen either in recovery or on the street. Once Alexander found one he adopted him or her immediately into his ever-growing family.

Mookie, of course, had contacts in the construction business himself, so he got whatever machinery Alexander needed. Within a year the old, dilapidated farmhouse had been refurbished, and Alexander's minions had built a barn, barracks, an outdoor kitchen, and a dining hall. Since then they had added various other outdoor structures, including smaller cabins and a large gathering area. Mookie barely had to lift a finger. Alexander had done it all.

The farming had been more problematic. Alexander had no idea what he was doing other than what he could look up on the internet or read in the public library. While there were many former builders in recovery, there were absolutely no farmers. Alexander only had himself on whom to rely.

There was a lot of trial and error, but eventually Alexander seemed to have it worked out. At least, Mookie assumed he had. On Mookie's visits to the Farm, which became less and less frequent, there was stuff growing, and people in the fields doing whatever it was that people do when it comes to farming. Mookie had no idea what it was they were growing or how they were growing it. As far as he was concerned, his people had spent thousands of years getting out of the fields, and he was not about to get back in them. He left all of it to Alexander, who seemed to be doing just fine.

The Farm ended up being the perfect place to store Mookie's product. Alexander and his people did not bat an eye. Alexander, for all his self-righteousness, was, like Mookie, at his core: a pragmatist. He did not question why the world worked the way it did, and, in the meantime, he would carve out a little somethin' somethin' for himself. Every so often Alexander would ask to keep a girl, to whom he had taken a shine. And Mookie would acquiesce most of the time just to keep the wheels greased. He was very pleased with what Alexander had built, and he wanted Alexander to be happy. However, in the end, all this was still Mookie's, and he had to remind Alexander of that fact from time to time.

Mookie was not sure what Alexander did with the girls he kept, though. He did not seem to be the sexual deviant with whom Mookie had become all too familiar over the years, but nothing really surprised him anymore. It was always the quiet ones who ended up being the freakiest. Mookie did not believe it was that way for Alexander, though.

Mookie sometimes wondered if Alexander was having sex with anyone, but knew that was crazy. Of course, he was having sex with them. That is what humans do: bone each other into oblivion no matter the consequences, whether it be broken marriages, lost jobs, or, hell, criminal records. It was all quite pathetic to Mookie, but it paid the bills.

But, even if Alexander was not having sex with the girls he kept for himself, Mookie knew Alexander had not bargained to keep them in order to "save" them. Alexander was much too pragmatic for that. Whatever the reason, Mookie knew, even if it was not prurient in nature, it certainly was not virtuous.

In the end, it did not matter, Mookie supposed, but it always aroused his curiosity -- what made people tick, what motivated people to do what they do. He knew it could have even been an occupation for him in some alternate universe. He pictured himself as a psychologist, smoking a pipe in some dusky office, while a bored housewife told him about her daddy.

It had never been hard for him to determine the motivations of others.

For the most part, Mookie realized early in his life, that the world had devolved into a state of "fight or flight." Everyone, for the most part, was in some sort of heightened state of anxiety all the time. Mookie could recognize it almost immediately in a person. Once he saw it, he knew exactly how to play the person. Alexander was not that way, though. He seemed motivated by something else entirely, and Mookie knew he could not play him ... at least not the way he played others.

As Mookie removed himself from the Farm, he did so with a confidence that whatever happened there Alexander would handle it the best way possible. At least, Mookie knew Alexander would not do anything to jeopardize his business. Alexander himself had worked too hard and had too much invested to hightail it and run. He was also too deep into it to give anything to the cops. While not an active participant in Mookie's overall business plan, Alexander was definitely complicit.

Mookie knew that Alexander, even though he was pragmatic, was also the type of person who would go down in flames out of principle rather than cut bait and run.

So maybe that was it. Maybe Alexander had rubbed off on him. Mookie had always been one to walk away and never look back, yet here he was, rushing straight into the lions' den.

He looked over at the girl, who continued to look straight ahead. She was still in shock. It would all be over for her soon ... and it might be for him too ... and it might be for Alexander too.

Chaos always wins.

11.

Alexander trudged along the gravel road. He was almost to the Farm, but the pain throughout his body would not allow him to get there with any ease. As a result, he resigned himself to the familiar pattern of walk, stop, rest. He tried not to think about how much longer he had. Instead, he set little goals for himself: get to the next telephone pole, get to the odd-looking bush, get to the random dead branch jutting out in the middle of the road. The heat and the pain were excruciating, though, and clouded his thoughts. He was almost there, he thought, but it felt like he would never arrive.

He wondered why no one from the Farm had come to look for him. He supposed it was because they thought he was either dead or taken far away. But still … there was more than one type of vehicle at the Farm. Someone could have followed him.

Was he not that important to them after all?

No, no, he was not going there. He was not going to start feeling sorry for himself. Of course, he was important to them. He was their leader after all. No, it was not that. In fact, he realized, it might be they just did not know what to do. They were training for an attack, but they had not trained for what to do after an attack. They certainly had not trained for an abduction, an abduction of their fearless leader at that.

Had they given up that easily, though? Could they not at least have sent one car to look for him?

OK, he was going to feel sorry for himself, but he did not care. He wondered what they would do when they saw him walk through the gate. Would he be heralded as the return of the king? Would they feel ashamed and hide from his sight? Maybe whoever had stepped into the vacuum would feel threatened and order his head offed?

Again, he did not really care. He just wanted to get back. He was getting closer. He thought he had about an hour left of walking at this pace. If he were at full speed, he would have been there in 15 minutes.

Who were these people to whom he was so eager to get back? They had their problems, yes, as does everyone, but they were all so deeply flawed. He had singlehandedly picked each person, not because there was something special about him or her, but because he saw someone who wanted a second chance -- an opportunity to wipe the slate clean. Each had wanted an opportunity to discard the old world and begin a new one. He thought by giving them such an opportunity he would buy their undying loyalty as well.

Maybe they were just losers, always had been and always will be, always making the wrong choices, always living in an anxious state with no desire to think logically or solve real problems. Always the victim.

Crunch, crunch, crunch, crunch.

The sound of gravel underneath his feet became a rhythmic song in his head. The beat of a drum that went on and on and on. He concentrated on the steps he was taking instead of where he was going. He did not know what he would find once he got there. Part of him did not want to go back. He knew there would be carnage, and he knew there would be pain. It was so much easier to avoid pain.

He could hear the old-familiar "fuck it" voice inside his head that made him want to chunk it all. It was still very much a part of him, the instinct to self-destruct and the shame that constantly reminded him he was not worthy of anything good or pure or holy.

He knew, if he was on the streets right now, where it would lead: a dusty hotel room with a girl and enough drugs to last him for days. It was the same pull inside that led people to look at porn or eat 20 pints of Ben & Jerry's Chunky Monkey. No one chooses the good or the pure or the holy because no one thinks they deserve it.

And once he felt the pull there was nothing he could do but let it pull. If he tried to control it or avoid it, it would only become worse.

He just had to go with it. What other choice did he have?

He continued to put one step in front of the other while wishing he could shoot up once again. The nastiness of it all, the dirt and the grime, still appealed to him. The excitement of making a score and knowing he was about to debase himself with another human being was overwhelming, and his brain could not handle it. Thank God he was out in the middle of nowhere.

It was one of the main reasons he begged Mookie to move their operation all the way out here. He had hoped, if he could just get away from the streets, then the pull would just be a pull. It did not change him, but it removed the option to act.

God, he hated himself when he had these glimpses into who he really was. He had built a place far from temptation, for the most part, and he had done a lot of good for a lot of people, but in the end, it was just a world of make believe. He would always be that piece of shit who squandered everything his upbringing, parents, education, opportunity, and privilege had given him.

But he kept walking.

He kept making his way to the place he had built, even with the knowledge that it was as much a façade as he was. He was not going to run away from the pain as he had most of his life. He was not going to let the pull inside him destroy what he had built. He was going back to the Farm, and he would rebuild the whole damn thing by hand if he had to.

He awoke from the monotony of his walk. He heard a car coming up from behind him.

His mind filled with panic. Maybe the maniac was coming back to finish him off. He did not understand why the man had dumped him out of the car to begin with and not killed him -- especially after the way he had finished off so many without batting an eye.

It may have been as simple as Alexander's no longer serving the man's needs. Whatever the reason, if this was his car coming back, the man obviously had second thoughts and was coming back to finish Alexander off after all.

Alexander frantically looked for a place to hide.

The woods were his only option. He limped down the shoulder of the road and made his way to the tree line, but stepped in a hole hidden by dead leaves right before he got to the first tree. He felt a new pain shoot through his body as he fell to the ground. His survival instincts took over, though, and he crawled past the first tree, ignoring the pain, until he thought he was sufficiently out of sight.

The car got closer and closer. He manipulated his body back around, so he could see what was coming. He had another moment of panic with the thought that maybe, just maybe, the car was from the Farm, and he had just ensured that he would not be found.

Now that would be typical, he told himself.

The car got closer and closer. Alexander also realized it might not be the maniac or anyone from the Farm. Maybe it had nothing to do with him. Maybe he had just thrown away his last chance to get some help.

Eh, I think I'll trust my gut on this one, Alexander told the nagging, negative voice in his head. It was worth bypassing help to avoid the risk of ever seeing the maniac again.

The car got closer. He could see the cloud of dry, gravel dust from the car approaching.

Shit.

He knew that car from anywhere.

Mookie.

He started to get up and wave the car down, but something stopped him.

He put his head back down and pressed his body into the leaves and dirt. The car drove by, and Alexander peeked to see if it was Mookie inside or one of the blockheads who did his bidding.

It was definitely Mookie and someone else too. He could not tell, but it looked like a child. That did not make much sense, but with Mookie you never knew what he was up to, and Alexander did not want to know either. This time, though, Alexander could not help but wonder what Mookie was doing up here. He had not been to the Farm in quite a while. Alexander doubted Mookie knew about the massacre. After all, no one on the Farm but Alexander knew how to contact him.

The car passed by, and Alexander watched it leave. Once again he found himself in a pile of leaves and loose dirt. He tried to lie still and just relax for a minute. His body hurt, but if he could be still, the pain would leave him alone for a few seconds.

"Yeah, this sucks," he said out loud. He wondered what Mookie would think once he got to the Farm. He would be furious, that was certain, and more than likely would blame Alexander before he could gather all the facts. That is the way it always was: The most loyal person always got his or her teeth kicked in by the person to whom he or she is most loyal.

"Awww, boo hoo, you pussy," Alexander said out loud and made himself start getting up and back onto the road.

He was not quitting. Not this time. His body and his ego were both bruised and bloody, but he was going to carry on. The stiffness and the newly acquired ankle pain kept him from getting back to the road as quickly as he wanted, but he eventually got there.

He looked up the road towards the Farm. He had thought he was close, but was not so sure now. He saw a telephone pole that did not seem so far away. "Just make it to that pole," he told himself and shuffled towards it, trying not to think about the pain both inside and out.

10.

Junie, now that she was back in the game, felt pretty confident she would come out on top. She always felt this way when she realized people were underestimating her, and it was happening now for sure. The way Mookie glanced her way from time to time somewhat confirmed what she thought: He felt sorry for her, the poor little girl from nowhere who had no one.

She could not wait to take him down.

He disgusted her, the way he strutted around like he was the smartest person in the world. He was definitely smarter than the crew with which he surrounded himself, but he was not smarter than her, and she was going to enjoy seeing him destroyed. She pictured herself in a courtroom, laughing as he's led out in an orange jumpsuit and shackles, with a shocked look on his face, wondering where it all had gone, oh, so wrong.

He had not said one word to her in a while. He just kept driving, looking straight ahead, deep in thought, while letting out a loud sigh every few minutes, with the occasional nervous glance her way. She did not know where they were going, but she knew it would not play out the way Mookie thought it would.

The only thing that made sense to her was that he was putting her in the stream of commerce, which is why he came to get her. She still did not understand why he killed his two thugs, other than it could not have been just for her. It was obviously something personal to him, and she did not have the time to figure out why.

She found herself looking out the front window at the sky. California's skies could be so beautiful. That was one of the first things she noticed when she arrived in the state: the sky that stretched out farther than she had ever seen back home. The colors and hues had seemed so clear and rich and textured. It had been the first time in her life when she had been struck with such awe.

Even now, after everything that happened her, she still felt the awe that comes from being in the presence of something greater than her. The way the sky's blueness embraced the clouds was overwhelming. She felt tears gathering behind her eyes as a sense of gratitude enveloped her. The beauty of it all, this life, this time in history, she believed she was exactly where she needed to be. The pettiness and small-minded nature of life that drove her crazy at times just did not matter. It all washed away in front of her eyes as she experienced true beauty. No matter what happened with Mookie she would consider herself blessed to have been alive and been able to experience love, grace, and beauty.

Who was she after all but a speck of paint in the Creator's grand masterpiece? Yes, she was part of that painting. She had beauty, and she had meaning -- just like girls in the van, all sweaty, grimy, and beautiful. She felt the awe lift her from the car and into the clouds. She had these feelings of being truly connected to the world and to God, or something, only every once in a while.

As a young girl, she remembered the feeling she had one day playing in the backyard of a neighborhood friend: a sense of electricity, voices, in what could only be described as a cloud, not quite there, but on the edge of her senses, telling her that none of this was real, that she was a part of something greater, more wonderful, more powerful than she could ever imagine. At the time, it felt more natural and wonderful than anything she had ever experienced, but her mind could not quite grasp it all. The more she thought about it the more incomprehensible it became. After a while she stopped thinking about it and let it live on the edge of her consciousness -- always there, always reminding her of what was real, what was underneath the canvas of life.

Only a handful of other times in her life had she felt that direct connection again, and it went away as fast it came, leaving her breathless, even scared, at her glimpse of the infinite and eternal, as well as frustrated for not being able to understand or comprehend her experience.

But, if she could just concentrate, she could for a brief time wipe away the levels of reality and time and get to that deep place, where she had felt the electricity, and her heart would fill with joy and gratitude. She would feel unbounded love, but more importantly she would understand, even if only for a moment, that everything was happening exactly the way it was supposed to happen.

And, yet, here she was in this smelly car with this disgusting human, who she hoped was going to sell her to another disgusting human in order to have sex.

None of it was real, though. It was just an exterior that masked what was underneath. Because as humans we could not truly comprehend our reality, we had to make up things to give our brains something we could understand. And there is nothing more simple or understandable than basic fear and anxiety. It was so much easier to live in a state of fear -- whether that resulted in lashing out in anger, judging our neighbor, or being the hipster sarcastic coffeeshop asshole, who never had one original thought in his or her life -- than living in a state of incomprehensible joy.

The sky at which she had been looking started to shrink from her view because of the tree line from the country road on which they had found themselves. She could barely see the clouds anymore, and the sun was almost completely gone from her sight.

So, now, she looked straight ahead and ignored the sky. She would think more about her place in reality later. For now, she had to come back to Earth and concentrate on staying alive and doing her job. She felt the scales reasserting themselves on her eyes and willfully succumbed to her blindness. In a way, it felt more comfortable in the darkness. She felt in control and powerful, even if she was anything but.

She felt Mookie looking at her again. He was driving, of course, but he was looking at her out of the corner of his eye with an occasional glance her way. She could tell he wanted to say something to her. Maybe he wanted her to say something to him. He was, after all, her knight in shining armor. He had rescued her, but they both knew it had nothing to do with her well being. A "thank you" was clearly not in order.

He was at unease about something, though. His usual cool veneer was gone. He was more twitchy than she had ever seen him, and his sighs and nervous glances her way told her he was way outside his comfort zone.

It scared her for moment. If he was not comfortable doing what he was doing, what did it mean for her? Maybe this was worse than she expected.

Wait. Worse than being a sex slave? She tried to calm herself. Of course not. She was just freaking herself out.

She was in control of the situation. She was a police officer. She knew exactly what was going on. She was not in the dark. She had trained for this, and she was not going to let those girls down. She told herself these things over and over until the panic became nothing more than a nagging doubt in the back of her skull.

Maybe that was why Mookie appeared out of sorts. Maybe he could sense her confidence beneath the veneer of her state-of-shock acting job.

Good, then, let him sweat it out. Let him think things were slightly off. She would do nothing to give him a reason to suspect her, but she could watch him struggle with a sense of unease.

She kept waiting for him to say something. He had, after all, just killed two people. Even with the ever-increasing sighing and fidgeting, he was remarkably cool given the circumstances. It was impressive in an odd way. She thought back to her times in The Coffee Shop. He never really moved from his spot at the dirty table in the back corner, but when he had, it was with a methodical exactness. He knew what he wanted, where he was going, and he did so with surgical accuracy.

He certainly never displayed any sort of emotional passion.

She had never seen him be violent either. He was not touchy-feely to be sure, but he never did anything, she had seen at least, to indicate he would kill two people. She was sure he would have no qualms to have someone do the killing for him, but for him to do it with his own two hands was out of character.

In fact, it was one of the reasons he had been able to survive as long as he had, not to mention not be arrested. He was so detached, even though she had worked at The Coffee Shop for over a year, she could not tie him directly to anything. He never used a cell phone. He rarely used a landline. No email. It was as if he communicated through some unknown brain frequency.

And he rarely left his spot at The Coffee Shop.

Yet here he was, driving a car out in the middle of nowhere by himself after killing two people with only her as his passenger.

And he was acting nervous.

No, it did not feel right at all. She looked back up at the sky to help her forget the nagging voice in her head. The trees, though, still blocked her view. She could barely see the blueness, and the clouds moved through the trees like an old movie.

She knew she had to remain calm, but she could feel herself succumbing to the voice. There really was no reason for Mookie to be here. The confidence she had pulsing through her veins minutes before was gone. Instead, she felt paralyzed by that old familiar feeling of self-doubt.

Oh, you idiot, she told herself, completely giving in to the voice. You missed something, didn't you? You stupid, stupid idiot. You don't have any clue what's going on.

She frantically searched her brain for any sort of clue, any detail, that might help her understand what was going on here.

Abort. Abort. Abort.

If she had an ejector seat, she would pull the lever. Her ego had gotten in the way of her evaluation and judgment. She had been trained to stay above the fray, to remain calm and undaunted, when the shit was falling down all around her, but she failed. She missed something.

She tried to calm her mind, but the panic had set in. She frantically tried to think of an exit strategy.

The car turned onto another gravel road, and Junie, for an illogical second, thought that maybe they had ended up back at the old man's cabin. The road, though, was cleaner and more well traveled.

She had to wait. She had no other choice. And she had to make her brain accept that fact. Her training took hold, and the panic slowly subsided. She told herself quietly that it was OK -- that she was part of something greater. Even if she died today, she was OK. None of this was real anyway.

9.

Cadel had finished his chores and had not learned anything new from his fellow culties. All their conversations involved the actual chores at hand. He stumbled outside the infirmary and noticed the same banal activities that had taken place before the massacre. No one seemed all that concerned with what had happened.

Cadel knew, though, it was more than likely the shock of it all. They had gone back to doing what they knew, instead of obsessing over what they did not. He did pick up a few nuggets of info, though.

First, the concept of time was not particularly relevant around here. No one seemed to know what time it was, and simple tasks such as checking the blood pressure of one of the injured was done by counting out loud.

Second, one hand definitely did not know what the other hand was doing. No one seemed to have a concept of the big picture. Apparently, the hippie kept his cards close to his vest and delegated little to no authority.

Cadel noted the classic cult activity that consolidates all the power to one person, who could, then, control everyone. However, usually there was a second level of power, or a second lieutenant, or someone, on whom the Grand Pooba could rely. That just did not seem to be the case here. Sure, the dreadlocked, African-American woman was acting like she had some authority, but no one really seemed to be giving her much attention, let alone deference.

Third, this place was beautiful, and everyone seemed to take pride in maintaining its natural character. He saw several people stop and pick up random pieces of trash or pull up a random weed when they did not have to. The hippie had convinced his culties that this was their place too, and they should take pride in it. How sweet, but how stupid. It was not theirs any more than it was Cadel's.

It would be interesting to see what happens once the realization hit them that things would not go back to normal, that it would not be business as usual.

Of course, it was natural to feel that way after a catastrophe.

Cadel again thought of 9/11 and the news shows and interviews and speeches in its aftermath, where everyone was encouraged to go back to "normal." And he remembered the collective longing to go back to the way it was before. Of course, things never went back to the way they were. The whole world changed. On a smaller scale, it was the same with the death of a loved one. It changes you. The more you long to be the person you were before the loss the worse you make it for yourself. And the people here were not ready for such a brutal truth. He saw it in the way they tried to maintain their routines and, thus, their sanity. If they scrubbed the bedpan just a little harder, maybe their Messiah would come back to life.

Cadel heard a stirring, a rise in the mumblings and background noise from one of the gathering areas, to which he was close. He made his way toward the noise that grew louder as he limped his way there.

As he walked around a cabin, he saw people gathered in a circle. He made his way through the crowd and saw two people wrestling on the ground, throwing random punches at each other. Everyone was standing around yelling random, nonsensical phrases. Cadel looked closer and saw two males in the middle of the circle: one he did not recognize, but the other he actually did know. It was his cabinmate from earlier in the day.

Of course, things would devolve in the chaos once their leader was gone, Cadel thought.

WAIT … Yes!

Cadel smiled. He had his angle. He knew what his story would be now. How many exposes of cults and crazy, Scientology-like religions had he read over the years? No, this would be what happens when the cult falls apart.

Not too shabby, he thought.

The two men fighting must have been engaged for a while because they seemed to be getting more and more tired. Their wrestling was more like a tired embrace on the ground. The man, who was fighting Cadel's young cabin mate, was a little more chunky than the wiry kid and was loudly wheezing through a red face.

"You bastard. You piece of shit," Mr. Red Face gasped between shallow breaths. The wiry, tattooed kid, who was a good bit younger than Red Face, did not say anything in return. In fact, on a closer look, he was not really fighting at all, but, instead, seemed barely attempting to subdue Red Face's halfhearted attacks.

Finally, both stopped completely, mostly because Red Face ran out of steam, and lay next to each other. The crowd slowly dispersed, but Cadel stood there watching the two. He caught the eye of his cabin-mate, who did not seem to recognize him at first.

"Well," Cadel said. "What was that all about? I don't even know what one would fight about in such a grand socialist society. Did he try to steal your toilet paper rations?"

"Who the hell are you?" Red Face asked.

"Oh nobody ... just a casual observer."

"Yeah, well, observing means no talking, don't it?"

Ahhhhh, a wordsmith.

"I guess I could be an observer and a commentator. The two do not have to be mutually exclusive last time I checked."

Red Face got to his feet, looked at Cadel, and right when Cadel thought there might be another throwdown in this place of peace, love, and harmony, Red Face shrugged his shoulders and turned back to the kid.

"If you ever try that shit again, it'll be different, I promise. Your ass will be gone, on the street again, got it?"

He held his hand down to the kid, who took it and got to his feet.

Red Face turned and looked at Cadel again.

"I know you. I know who you are. We all do. We're being patient with you because Alexander wanted to help you out, I guess, but make no mistake: We all have our eyes on you, and you'll be held accountable. You will. I promise. Just ask him."

He pointed to the kid, turned away, and wandered off.

Cadel looked at his cabinmate, who returned the favor with a blank stare.

"Let me guess: He's the enforcer of this place. His gruff on the outside, but on the inside, he has a heart of gold. He just has a hard time expressing his feelings."

The kid sighed, smiled, and put his hands in his pockets.

"I don't really know who he is or, I guess, what kind of person he is."

"Well, pray tell, what exactly did you do to garner the ire of such a fine, upstanding gentleman?"

"Let's just say some old habits die hard, especially after what went down today. "

Cadel understood and nodded his head. The kid probably had a stash hidden as a safety blanket around here, but never intended to use it. After today's craziness, he probably did not hesitate to go feel its escape, no matter the consequences.

"Do people normally beat up people who backslide around here?"

"No, but when you do said backslide with someone's so-called girlfriend, it does not end well."

"No, no it doesn't. You actually got off relatively easily."

"Yeah right, well, he did do a number on me I suppose. He also took what little I had left."

"Weed?"

The kid rolled his eyes. "That's hardly even considered a drug anymore, but, no, not weed."

Cadel guessed it did not matter what the kid's drug of choice was. He was up here under the guise of recovery, and he was able to keep a stash -- not a good look.

"Are there a lot of drugs up here? I mean I know this is a recovery type place, but are drugs a problem?"

"No, man, not at all -- at least not as far as I know. People here take that shit pretty seriously .... as you could tell from the crowd who did nothing as I got my ass beat. They thought I deserved it."

"Well, did you?"

"I guess so. I mean it's not like I want to do it. I mean, I do, but it's different. I don't know. I don't like myself when I'm using. I don't like who I am. When I'm not using, I feel a sense of pride, you know, like, hey, I did it. I'm clean. I can finally feel good about myself. And, then, that sense of pride kinda takes over, and I feel like I can do anything. Then, I hear this little voice in my head that says, hey, I kicked the shit. I have it all figured out. I could even smoke a joint here and there, and I'd be OK. Well, you know what happens next. It becomes all I can think about."

"Hey, I'm just fuckin' around man. I know. I know. I also know that the only thing that works is the program -- not coming out to some deserted farm and hoping to avoid it all. I mean, do you people even have anything remotely resembling the program out here?"

"No, not really. I wouldn't know, though. I've never tried it. I'm not really sure how I got here to be honest. I met this guy, who said he could help me get off the street, get a job, get clean, and I thought I'd give it a shot. What did I have to lose? Since I've been up here, though, I haven't exactly fit in."

"What do you mean? No offense, but this place is a little like The Isle of Misfit Toys. No one really fits in, and that's kinda the point, right?"

That stopped the kid for a moment.

"Yeah," he said after a moment of contemplating that thought. "Maybe. Honestly, I really don't want to get clean. I sure as fuck don't want to live on a fucking farm for the rest of my life. I sure as fuck don't want to live my life with no music, no pussy, no drugs, no alcohol, no cigarettes, no weed … no freedom. I'd rather be a druggie loser, living on the street, than living like a fucking Quaker, having people tell me what to do all the time."

Damn, Cadel thought, the kid had a soul after all. The pod people had not eaten his brain away … yet. "Well, yeah, I guess you don't fit in, then."

The kid started to walk away, and Cadel watched him leave.

"Wait. Wait," Cadel said.

The kid turned back around and held his hands out. "What? What now? What the hell do you want from me? Do you want to give me some fatherly advice? Do you want to tell me some quote that'll somehow solve all my problems, that'll put everything in perspective for the first time in my life, that'll tell me something I don't already know? What?"

Cadel thought for a moment. He had an idea, but he did not want to show all his cards just yet. If everyone was indeed gunning for him here, as Red Face just implied, he needed an ally. He needed someone to give him some insight. He admitted to himself the one thing he hated to admit to himself: He needed help.

"No, I'm not one to give you any advice. Obviously, I don't exactly fit in here either. As you heard from your friend just now, I'm not exactly the most popular person."

The kid looked away for a moment.

"So, you want something from me? What? Intel? An inside man? What? Yeah, everyone knows you're not here to contribute. What are you? A cop or something? Or a part of the mafia? That's one of my favorite theories: You're part of the mafia, and that's why that crazy guy came in here shooting people, to kill you."

The kid laughed.

"You, some washed-out Gen-Xer, is somehow a criminal mastermind. Yeah, right."

"Damn, am I that easy-to-read?"

The kid turned again to leave.

"OK, OK, OK!" Cadel limped after him. "Stop, please. You're right: I'm not a criminal mastermind. I'm not a member of the mafia. I'm not a cop. I'm not a drug addict. I'm nothing. I'm nobody. I am a Gen Xer, yes, and, like all other Gen Xers, I'm just trying to survive. I'm not trying to manipulate anyone. I'm not trying to get something for nothing. I just need some help. I don't know why I'm here, and I don't know what's going on. Could you just help me understand what this place is about, so I can get out of here?"

When all else fails, play the victim card, Cadel thought to himself. People could not help but be the one with the upper hand.

"Please?" Cadel asked again as the kid slowed down.

"Look," he said as he turned to face Cadel, "you're different, and, yes, I'm different too, but you represent something to everyone here -- something that makes everyone else uncomfortable -- something that represents what they've all been trying to escape from their entire lives.

You're not a threat necessarily, but you're a decent-looking guy, and you're funny. You're kinda smart, and, most of all, you seem normal. You seem like you're part of the American Dream. You seem like the world was made just for you, that you can float by, with little-to-no effort, and the world will flower before you."

"I've only been here a day," Cadel answered, exasperated for some reason. His calm demeanor was starting to show cracks in the armor, and he did not like it.

"Not you specifically, but you in general. But you specifically a little too. You represent what we all hate: normalcy. You represent what we've seen our whole lives, as we have struggled and failed and fallen down, you've floated by on a cloud, strumming a gold harp, deeming all the rest of us unworthy."

"Wait. I struggle too. You don't know the shit I've been through."

"No, but it doesn't matter because everyone thinks they've been through more shit than everybody else."

"So you just want to destroy someone because you think he's doing better than you, even if he's not? That sounds rather pathetic to me."

"Here's the deal: I am pathetic. I'm not a good person. All of us here are pathetic people, who come from pathetic lives. Yes, I don't care anymore, and, no, I don't want to get better, but most of the rest of the people here do. They don't need some asshole like you coming around and trying to relate to them or, worse, trying to convince them that your life has been just as hard or that you are just as bad or that you understand their feelings. It just doesn't work that way. People like you want to be with people like me because it makes you feel better about yourself."

"No, you've got me wrong. I don't want that at all. I'm not like that at all."

"You still don't get it. It doesn't matter if you think you're that way or not."

"Look at me. I'm 45 years old. I'm disgusting. I'm out of shape. I've never had a serious relationship with anyone. I've never been able to hold down a job. The only difference between me and you and everyone here is that I don't have the addict gene. Frankly, I don't even know if it's that. I think I'm just too lazy to be an addict. I'd rather watch TV on my couch than go outside and search for a score."

"You're too lazy to be an addict? Is that really what you're going with?"

"No, no, that's not what I'm saying at all. I'm too lazy to do anything other than barely get by. It's not even being lazy. It's that I just don't really care enough about anything. It's why I don't play golf, or hunt, or gamble, or follow a sports team, or quilt, or anything that requires any sort of effort -- I just don't care. I don't know what's wrong with me."

The look on the kid's face told Cadel all he needed to know. The kid would not be an ally of his, the way things were going. In fact, he would probably end up hating Cadel more than the rest of the folks in this place, if that was possible.

And then it really hit him: He had failed. He would not have much of a story after all -- at least, not on this place. He would never be able to find out exactly what was going on here.

Sure, he could still write a pretty good story on Mookie and his influence and his ties to his many lackey politicians. He would not be able to connect all the dots, though. Of course, as most half-assed journalists do, he could bring his readers right to the edge and let them draw their own conclusions. He wanted something much deeper, though, and he had not been able to get it.

"Oh, well, fuck it," he said still looking at the kid. "You know what? You're right. I don't know what you're going through. I don't understand your pathetic existence. I never will. You dumbasses live in the richest country in the history of the world. You have access to running water, decent shelter, education, a justice system, police … everything that just about 99 percent of humans who have lived on this planet have not had, and yet you find something to bitch about. You don't have an authoritarian despot, murdering your family or stealing your children to be slaves. You live at a time in our world's history when you can worship whatever you want in whatever way you want without being put in jail. Yet all you can do is whine about not having as much as what you think your neighbor has."

Cadel took a deep breath, but kept going.

"Guess what? Everyone has demons. Everyone has addictions. Everyone has troubles. Everyone has pain. Everyone feels like they don't belong. Everyone feels like they aren't heard. Everyone feels like they aren't pretty enough or handsome enough. Everyone feels like they have been left off the guest list. Everyone. Do you understand what I'm saying? You're no different than anyone else.

"I'm sorry all of you are addicts. I really am. But it has nothing to do with me. There's no cosmic yang/yang in the universe, where just because I'm not an addict that somehow means you've got to be one. It just doesn't work that way. There's no synchronicity. There's no butterfly flapping its wings that is causing tsunamis on the other end of the world. That is complete bullshit. So get the fuck over yourself.

"I'm sorry, but I'm so fucking sick of watching people walk around like they are masters of the universe, acting like what they do and say mean anything or affect anyone. You are nothing. You mean nothing. It's all so pathetic."

Cadel caught himself. He was out of breath. He had lost himself.

The kid's expression had not changed the entire time Cadel had been going off on him. He was probably used to older males screaming at him. Hell, he'd just had one try to beat his ass. Cadel knew that screaming and criticizing people never, ever accomplished anything, and yet he had lost his shit. In the process, he had lost the kid. So much for his plan. So much for his ally.

But damn it felt good.

"You done?" the kid asked in a deeply monotone, almost robotic, voice.

"Yeah, I guess so."

"Well good. I would like to help you if I thought you could help me, but you can't. No one is going to let you leave. In case you haven't figured it out yet, you are a prisoner here. Yeah, Alexander decided to let you out of the Barn, but you were never going to leave. You were going to be a prisoner here until whoever was supposed to come for you came."

The kid stopped and took a breath himself. He looked around as if to make sure no one else was listening and continued, leaning into Cadel's personal space and pointing at his chest, "The question is why would you stick around when you already had your perfect chance to escape?"

"Well, in case you couldn't tell, I'm injured," Cadel tapped his bum leg in an exaggerated fashion and shrugged. The kid was right, though, but Cadel had made the decision to stay, even if it meant he was a prisoner -- even if it meant he was probably going to fail. He had to figure out what was going on. He could not help himself. He would just have to suffer the fate of being a pariah until things shook out a little more. Yeah, he was a prisoner for now, but his gut told him this place would not be around much longer. He just had to remain patient and let things play out.

He had to make one last run at the kid, though. He really needed his help, if he had any hope of exposing this place and Mookie. He quickly thought of a plan.

"Listen, you obviously don't want to be here anymore than I do. I'm not suggesting you betray anyone or get yourself in trouble, but I was brought here for a reason after a couple of goons beat the shit out of me. I just want to figure out why. You say I've got shit figured out, and that's why people around here resent me. I may not be an addict, but I was living on the fringes before this. I was working in a coffee shop for God's sake. It wasn't like I was a Wall Street douchebag or anything."

"Wait, were you working at a Starbucks or something?"

The bait was cast. Now, he just had to wait and see if the kid would take it.

"No, no, no. Nothing like that. It was a kind of place for people down on their luck to make some money and get their bearings straight."

"You were working for Mookie before this?"

Ahhhh, yes, the kid was nibbling.

"Yeah, that's right. Wait a minute. How do you know Mookie?"

Almost there, Cadel thought. The kid was quiet. Cadel watched the gears turning in his head.

"OK," the kid said. "Look, I don't really know who this Mookie is, but I've heard a lot about him. Everyone seems to understand that he is behind this place somehow, or at least has a very important role, but no one talks about him really. I just know you don't want to fuck with him. You definitely don't ask questions about him."

The kid looked down and kicked the dirt at his feet. "It doesn't make sense for him to beat the shit out of one of his employees and then send him here as a prisoner. I will give you that. I don't think it's ever happened before. At least, I haven't heard about it happening before."

He took the bait, but now Cadel had to bring him back to his side.

"Well, I did smart off to him a few times. As you've probably seen, my mouth tends to get me in trouble. I don't know. Maybe he'd just had enough. "

That should just about do it: put just enough doubt in the kid's head where he would not see him as an existential threat.

"Have you had other prisoners here, then?"

The kid looked trapped. He did not know which way to turn. His loyalties were being put in play. Just a few minutes before he had been punched in the face by someone here, he had admitted he was different than the others, he had confided he did not want to stay here, and yet something was holding him back from telling the truth about what was going on. Cadel doubted the kid knew everything, but he knew something -- something about which he was conflicted telling Cadel.

"OK, look," the kid said, rubbing his face with his bony hands. "This place actually does a lot of good for a lot of people."

Oh, goodie gumdrops, Cadel thought to himself. He's justifying what he's about to say.

"Yep," Cadel said. "Look, I've been hard on this place, but I know it does do some good. I've only been here a short time, but even I can tell that."

OK, it was time to go in for the kill.

"Mookie, on the other hand, I'm not sure he does much good at all. He runs his Coffee Shop under the guise of its being a refuge for addicts and the homeless and an opportunity for people to get back on their feet. But it's not that way at all. There's something else going on there -- something much more sinister. I got a little too curious and asked some questions, and the next thing I know I'm beaten up and in the trunk of a car. You tell me. This place might be great, but if Mookie has his fingers in it, he's using it for something else. And eventually he will destroy it."

The kid looked at his feet. Then slowly, as if he had made a decision about which he was still not so certain, looked back at Cadel. He looked into his eyes. Cadel noticed a little speck of black in his otherwise perfectly blue ovals.

"OK, what do you want to know? I might not know as much as the others, but I have heard things."

Cadel smiled, took the kid by the arm, and they both limped in tandem towards the farmhouse.

8.

Mookie slowed the car down as he got closer to the Farm's entrance. As he eased the car through the open gate, Mookie knew things were different. He rolled down the driver-side window and slowed the car to a halt. Everything was eerily quiet. He did not see any of the orderly groups of people walking around with a purpose. He did not see any workers in the fields. He did not hear any of the usual chatter and other background noises.

Something was definitely off. He put the car in park, but left the engine idling. He had to think for a moment.

He put his hand up to the key in the ignition, but put it back down again. The car kept idling. He knew it would be better for him to get out of the car and stroll around the place to see what was going on, or what had exactly happened, but his gut told him to stay put for now.

The girl next to him still did not say a word. She just kept staring straight ahead. She had the slack-jawed look of someone, who was lost deep in his or her mind, and Mookie assumed she was too. Nonetheless, he did not want to leave her in the car by herself if and when he decided to get out.

The car kept on idling, and the girl kept staring ahead. He still did not say anything, and the Farm remained quiet.

Maybe this is how it should be: everything calm and quiet. Maybe he was the one who was injecting chaos and pain where there was none. Maybe he was not the pragmatic soul, skirting along on the fringes of chaos, taking what was extra, mining what was already corrupt. Maybe life was calm, rational, and orderly, and it was he who was the drop of bleach in the Petri dish. Maybe somewhere along the way he became what he thought he was exploiting.

Maybe.

Maybe, but he did not think so. No, calmness and quiet were unnatural. It meant something else was coming. Something on the horizon was about to come and tear life up by its roots and toss it around until there was nothing left but death and destruction.

The quiet before the storm. The eye of the hurricane. The way animals stopped making noises seconds before an earthquake. No, silence was deadly, and calmness was an illusion.

Yet here he was, heading right back into it all. He should leave; he should not be here. It did not feel right.

Mookie look closely at the Farm. It looked like it normally did, even though he had not been here in a while. Rustic. Gravel roads. Wood cabins. Natural beauty. He had to admit it was nice here, especially compared to what he saw on an everyday basis. He could understand the appeal of the place, especially to those who had lived a good portion of their lives on the street.

There was still no movement, though, and he got that odd feeling he was being watched.

He listened to the birds' chirping over the quiet hum of the engine of his car, as well as the other sounds of nature that never made any sense to him. Where did these noises come from and what were they? Crickets? Frogs? Squirrels? He was more used to city sounds: horns honking, sirens blaring, people yelling, garbage trucks reversing. Although they could be annoying at times, he had to admit those were the background noises with which he felt most familiar. They composed the soundtrack of his life.

It was also busy in the city. Things were always moving. There was so much life and activity. Mookie felt alive there, and he felt on top of his game. Here, he felt lost, out of his element. He could appreciate the beauty, and he could see how someone could love the outdoors. It just was not him.

But he wondered if the people here really liked it too, or if they would all prefer to go back to their old lives. Alexander did not seem to think so. He seemed convinced the people here were all taking advantage of their second chances at life. He had shown them a cleaner, more simple way to live, and in turn, they turned their lives around by giving up drugs, alcohol, etc., in the process. They had been given the chance to become completely new people, and they had taken it. All they ever needed was a chance.

Maybe.

Mookie was not completely buying that either. Alexander had oversold it slightly, and Mookie knew it, but he continued to give Alexander the money and supplies he needed. Mookie did not really care as long as the place would provide a good photo op and news story, and, more importantly, the place would continue to provide a good cover for his other business ventures.

Speaking of that…

If the maniac was here, then Mookie would definitely know it. The man with unlimited wealth and power made sure that everyone else knew how much more wealthy and powerful he was. He certainly would not stay in this place longer than he had to.

Mookie looked a little closer at his surroundings. Yes, other than the quiet, there was something else a little off, but he could not quite put his finger on it.

He saw some movement behind one of the buildings. It looked like someone trying not to be seen. Well, that is not a good sign, he thought to himself. He reached inside his jacket and put his hands on his gun. He felt the contours of the handle and clicked the safety off. His gut had told him not to come here, and now it was telling him to leave.

No, not yet, he told himself. I'm not going until I have a handle on what's going on here.

He turned the engine off and put the keys in his jacket pocket, while keeping his other hand on the gun. He looked over at the girl, who was still staring straight ahead.

He reached across her and opened the glove compartment. She did not flinch. He pulled out an old Swiss Army knife he had since he was a kid. He opened the blade right in front of her face. Again, no flinch. He reached down to her feet and cut the binds from her ankles.

He straightened himself upright in the driver's seat and looked at her again. She just kept looking straight ahead.

He thought about leaving the binds on her wrists, but then considered how impressed his client might be to take a willing participant rather than a prisoner. It would be a nice touch and worth the risk of her trying to flee. The way she was acting he doubted if she would try to escape anyway.

He shrugged and cut the binds from her wrists with a jolt that seemed to surprise even her.

"OK, let's get out of the car," he told her, even though he was not sure she heard a word. "I have a gun pointed right at you, but I really don't feel like killing another person today."

She looked up at him, and, for a second, he thought he saw some life in there. But then it was gone, replaced by that familiar dullness.

He hated that he had to kill those two dumbasses -- he really did. He never considered himself a killer, as strange as it seemed, considering he had done his share over the years, even if, for the most part, it had all been at arms' length. He definitely did not enjoy it.

To take another person's life, no matter how much they deserved to die, was not as easy as the other pragmatic sins with which he had become all too comfortable over the years. All those deaths still weighed on him. Sure, he had forgotten the names and the faces of some of them, but the gravity of its being his decision to take something no one could create seemed so unnatural to him. He had never gotten used to the feeling he felt when he learned a death was final.

Still, he always did what he felt needed to be done, but after all these years, the choices he made and the way he decided to live did not seem real to him. Although he had taken advantage of the world and lived life to its fullest, had more money and more power than 99 percent of the world, he still had the nagging feeling that he did not do it right, that he never truly lived up to his potential, that he never became who he was supposed to become. He thought back to that young, skinny black kid in a cheap suit, who showed up at college with a full scholarship, full of hopes and dreams -- as well as the dreams of his parents, grandparents, uncles, aunts, cousins, and friends.

Sure, he graduated from college, but he had let them all down. He did not become whom they wanted. He did not become a preacher, or a politician, or a banker, or a lawyer -- he had rejected all of those expectations. He had reached for something greater, something outside the path laid before him.

He got out of the car and waited for the girl to get out as well. He leaned down and looked inside. She was still staring straight ahead.

He walked around to the passenger side and opened the door.

"Come on now," he said. "Let's go ahead and get out of there. We have things to do, places to see."

She did not move. Mookie did not have time to deal with her mental issues right now. She needed to get out of the car and on her own volition. He did not want to drag her out. He was too old for that shit.

He reached in, but before he could put his hands on her, she looked at him with a furiousness that took him aback. He pulled his hands away and stood up straight.

"Well, get the fuck out, then," he said.

She looked back in front of her, and the fury dissipated from her face. She kept looking straight ahead, but right when Mookie was about to reach back in for her, she put her feet to the side of the car and slowly eased her way out.

By the time she got on her feet Mookie could have walked all the way around the first few buildings and back, but he was patient. He could not leave her in the car for obvious reasons, but he also needed her as a bargaining chip if the maniac was here. If he had already left, Mookie needed her to stay here at the Farm, so the maniac could come back for her.

At least, that was his very loosely structured plan.

He was still ready and willing to chunk it all, and if he did that, the girl would not be a part of the plan.

In short, he needed her ass out of the car.

She stepped toward him looking at the dirt road. He grabbed her arm and started walking toward the first structure on the grounds. It was a storage area with farm equipment in one part of an open area with the other part walled off and a door to the inside. He walked to the door and looked at it. It was always locked, and Mookie knew why. This is where he would make his deliveries. This is where that dumbass would have put the girl if he had done what he was supposed to do.

I mean, what was the dumbass thinking? Mookie asked himself the question for the first time. He had been so focused on what he had to do to try and salvage the situation he realized he had not taken a step back and tried to understand what really had happened. Frankly, it was out of his character ever to ask why something was the way it was. He just did what needed to be done, yes, but today was a strange day. He let himself asked the question.

Why?

Mookie resisted the urge to say what he would normally say: It does not matter why. Instead, he let the question marinate in his brain.

The dumbass's stepfather?

He did it for him?

He did it to ease the pain of a dying man?

He did it, so his stepfather would have some sort of human connection in his last days?

Good Lord, if that was the case, how pathetic. Mookie knew the old man personally and from stories he heard from others. The old man had his own so-called business back in his day, although unorganized and redneck in nature.

He was a bastard. He never treated his stepson with any sort of compassion or genuine affection, at least from what Mookie saw. The old man was a bully who took every opportunity to exploit the vulnerability of others, including his stepson's.

And even in his middle age, the dumbass was still trying to please the old bastard, to gain his approval.

No, no, no. It did not make sense. With the old man's connections, he could have gotten any girl out there at any time. Hell, with the dumbass's own connections, he could have gotten any sort of girl the old man wanted.

No, this was sinister in nature. His gut reaction had told him something was off, and it had been. Mookie had been lured there. He had been lured there by all three of them. He knew that was the case. He just could not figure out why. What had they been planning? Why did they want him out of the picture? What did the old man have to do with it all?

Mookie stared at the locked door to the room. What was his brain trying to tell him exactly? Why was he thinking all this now?

Alexander?

The thought hit him hard.

He had never considered that Alexander might be behind it all. Not that Alexander deserved more loyalty than anyone else, even if he did, but Mookie never considered him as someone, who was motivated by power or greed.

Mookie put his hand on the door handle.

No, Alexander had always been someone Mookie never really worried about in that regard. He had his own little kingdom carved out here. Mookie never thought Alexander would want anything other than what he had here. In all the time Mookie knew him, Alexander never asked for anything that was not directly related to the well being of the Farm.

Mookie turned the doorknob. It was not locked. Mookie assumed it would be, and he hoped it would be. He did not want to know any answers. He did not want to know whether Alexander was living up to his side of the bargain.

Mookie pulled his hand away.

No, maybe Mookie had not lived up to his potential, maybe Alexander was behind the betrayal of one of Mookie's most loyal employees, maybe the maniac would try and take him out.

Maybe, maybe, maybe.

Mookie put his hand back on the doorknob and turned it. He again let go of the doorknob and let it click back into place.

"Fuck it," he said out loud.

He looked at the girl. She seemed to understand what was going on. He smiled. She was probably playing him too. So she somehow knew Alexander or something?

Or something.

Nope, that was it. He was done. Hello, Mexico.

"Well, have a good fucking life."

He turned from the girl, from the door, from the Farm, from it all, and headed back to the car. Paradise was just one turn of the ignition away.

Nah, maybe he never lived up to his potential, and maybe he let a lot of people down, but it did not matter now. It was finished, and so was he.

7.

Alexander finally reached the Farm's front gate. He was injured and out of his mind, but he made it. Now, he just needed to get to the Big House. He could get someone to come and give him some painkillers, and he could just try and heal his injuries. It would take a while, but it could happen. He would have to try and heal the Farm as well. He had to make sure everyone was OK. He had to contact the families of those killed and those critically injured. He had records on everyone, but some of them were more scant than others. Most had some sort of number to contact, though. It would take a while, but, yeah, he could do it.

He knew he would have to deal with Mookie first, though. He assumed Mookie was already inside the Farm somewhere. He had seen him drive by earlier, so he knew Mookie would be inside looking for him now, wanting answers for what had happened. Alexander did not know what he would say to him. He was still unsure himself about what happened.

He thought he could reason with Mookie. He would be mad, yes, but once he calmed down, he would hopefully see that Alexander did not have much to do with what happened. Alexander would still be blamed somewhat, and that was OK. It came with the territory.

Alexander walked through the gate and turned toward the Big House. He wanted to get there first before he saw Mookie, even though he knew that was probably not going to happen. He was tired, he was in pain, and he did not want to think about what needed to be done. He did not want to be the responsible one right now.

He knew what he really wanted. He wanted her. He wanted her to lay down with him and feel her body mold into his. He wanted her all to himself. More than anything, though, he wanted not to feel ashamed about having these thoughts. He had taken the high road for so long. He had rejected her advances time and time again, and he was tired of it. He was not better than anyone else, and he was tired of trying to be something better than he was. He wanted to sink into her and feel her warmth and smell her and lose himself. He could almost taste her wet, pale skin pressed against him as her red hair fell all around him.

He wanted to be with her and not think about the Farm anymore. He did not want to think about what he had to do to prepare for what was coming. Maybe he had taken them as far as he could, and now it was all over. Maybe it was time to hang it up.

Yet, he knew, Mookie would not let him quit. Mookie would make him stay aboard and continue doing the shady things on the side -- the things Alexander turned a blind eye to time and time again.

He did not want to think about that now. He just wanted to rest. He knew he was close to the brink of passing out.

He really did not want to see Mookie.

Yet here he was, walking right toward him.

The look on Mookie's face told Alexander all he needed to know. Alexander had seen that look more times than he would have liked. He was in trouble.

The painkillers would have to wait.

The girl would have to wait.

He felt the adrenaline kick in and flow through his brain. His senses heightened, and the pain took a backseat.

"What the fuck? What the fuck, Alexander? What the fuck happened here?"

Even though Alexander had only seen it a few times, when Mookie was like this, he was like a bull, charging and fighting, running people over. It made no sense to fight him or reason with him. Alexander just had to engage him slightly, step out of his way, and hope he tired out before doing any real damage.

"Nice to see you too, old friend. You know who did this, and it wasn't me. He shot up this whole place, took me prisoner, and dumped me on the side of the road without so much as stopping his car. So, yeah, I can see why you'd be mad at me right now."

That caused Mookie to stop in his tracks.

"What do you mean shot up the place?"

But before Alexander could gather his thoughts, Mookie was back in his face. Mookie was as desperate as Alexander had ever seen. He was taller than Alexander, and, even though he was slightly overweight and sagging in the places he should not be, was intimidating in a much different way. He harnessed an energy that crackled from within. From his eyes and jawline to the way his upper back slumped forward. It reminded Alexander of a boxer coming out of his corner when the bell rings, ready to land the first punch.

There would be no reasoning with Mookie, Alexander realized. He would just have to let Mookie be Mookie. Once the ranting was over he would remember who Alexander was and what they had accomplished together.

At least he hoped so.

Mookie grabbed Alexander by the shirt and pulled him close to his face.

"He shot up the place? What do you mean? Did he kill anyone?"

"Uhhh … yeah."

"Where are the bodies?"

"I don't know."

Mookie let go of Alexander's shirt and retreated back into his mind. Alexander knew he was processing what had happened and what to do next.

"Did he say anything to you? Did he say anything at all?"

"No, not really."

"What do you mean 'not really'?" Mookie again grabbed Alexander's shirt. "What the fuck did he say? Did he say anything about me? Did he say anything about where he was going? Did he say he'd be back? Think! Think, you fucking dumbass. It's important."

Alexander had seen Mookie lose his temper before, but it always seemed to be a controlled anger. He was completely unhinged at this moment. Small specs of spittle landed on Alexander's face as Mookie continued to rant. He had completely lost it.

And he was scared.

Alexander had never seen Mookie scared -- at least, not like this. Alexander realized he himself had not been scared or felt fear in a very long time -- real fear, that is. Mookie had protected him, as much as Alexander hated to admit it. Mookie had been the umbrella keeping him dry, the wall that kept the bastards at bay.

If Mookie was scared, Alexander realized, then he should be terrified.

The truth hit him hard, how close he had been to dying. Even when he had been in the car with his tongue down the barrel of a gun, he realized he had never truly thought about dying. It had all been so surreal, and he guessed part of that was just shock. He thought it was something else, though, too: He never thought Mookie would let him be killed. That somehow a completely insane person had in his head he could do whatever he wanted, by whatever kind of rationale his brain allowed, except harm Alexander.

Maybe he was not invincible after all.

"No, he didn't say anything at all like that. All I remember is trying to talk rationally with him, or wanting to, and he just … well, he took me captive … and then all hell broke loose. He shot and killed so many people in such a short time, and he never even came close to getting injured himself. It was crazy … I still quite can't make sense of it. I don't know why he didn't kill me when he killed so many others with hardly a thought. I thought maybe it was because you…"

Alexander dropped to his knees and began retching all over the ground. He did not have much in his stomach, but that did not stop him from dry heaving, with every muscle in his body clenching up at once.

He looked up from the ground once he was done, and even though the sun was beginning to set, a ray of light hit Mookie's face perfectly. The look of disgust on his face poured all over Alexander, and he felt the shame he knew all too well.

But Alexander could deal with that. He was used to people being disappointed in him. What he could not take was seeing it in Mookie in his current state: frantic, nervous, desperate, and scared.

"You done?" Mookie asked.

Alexander wiped the gritty mixture of vomit and dirt off his face, pushed the long, thinning gray hair back from his forehead, and started to get back on his feet, but stopped and fell back to his knees.

"I guess so," he said. "It's just been a really long day."

"Well, you got many miles before you sleep, motherfucker. He didn't kill you because he wanted to send a message to me."

That was the first thing that made sense to Alexander in this crazy day. It was a relief to hear truth. The maniac would have killed Alexander without blinking an eye, but he wanted Mookie to know he had been here and was not a happy camper.

"OK," Alexander said and started to pick himself up off the ground. "Yeah, I can see that."

As he got to his feet, Alexander continued looking at Mookie, whose face continued to metamorphose from fear to anger to quizzical to frustration. Alexander guessed he was trying to make sense of the situation too. If the maniac was sending a message to Mookie, what would Mookie's response be?

"What now, then?" Alexander asked, hoping that the plan would not include him or at least allow him the chance for some sort of rest.

Mookie stood in front of Alexander, deep in contemplation. His face stopped contorting and settled into the usual poker face he maintained daily.

"You know," Mookie began and paused, giving what he was about to say a little more thought. "Right before I saw you I was about to get into that car and leave this place, this state, even this country. I was going to leave all this behind."

Mookie kicked at the dirt and seemed to relish keeping Alexander in a state of suspense.

"Then, I saw you walking over here. I didn't know where you'd been, and I didn't care. I just knew that, whatever happened, you were ill equipped to handle all this by yourself. No, I don't know what happened, but from what I can tell, some pretty bad shit went down, and you weren't able to stop it.

"Worse, you didn't have the capacity to stop it before it even got started. You see, that is the difference between someone like you and someone like me. You live in La-La Land, dreaming of the way it could be or, in your simplistic mind, the way it should be. You don't realize or even try to comprehend the way things actually are."

Alexander had heard Mookie pontificate before about "the way the world works" and how pragmatic one has to be to succeed, but he had never seen Mookie take it to this extreme: that he was the only person in the world who could anticipate and prevent a maniac from doing crazy things, that he was the only person who could reason with someone who happened to be insane.

He understood it was human nature to look in the past and blame people for a tragedy -- to see the patterns so clearly and wonder out loud how stupid someone must be not to have seen them. And Alexander knew Mookie had reached the age where, faced with a failing memory and failing capacities, and wanting so desperately to hold onto relevance, would blame everyone else for his fuck ups, never taking responsibility and never, ever apologizing.

The search for relevance never ends, even when your life is coming to an end. Alexander also knew Mookie would never give up his "business," no matter how much he tried to fool himself into thinking he was "ready to give it all up." No matter how screwed up it was, his "business" gave his lonely, miserable life purpose. He was in control of something, and people did what he said. He was the master of his own little universe, and, in his mind, he was the only one who could run it the way it should be run. If he walked away, he would just be another over-the-hill black man, complaining his food was too salty.

Alexander had to let it play out. He knew Mookie would never leave, would never relinquish control of his true love: his life. No matter how much he might try to convince himself otherwise Mookie would rather die than live a life in which he was no longer relevant. No matter how scared Mookie was at the moment it was not enough for him to walk away. Alexander also had a suspicion that as much as Mookie liked to pretend he was a detached individual, he deep down loved the thrill of it all. He enjoyed feeling the rush of being alive -- being right on the edge of living or dying, being free or being in jail.

Alexander had to let Mookie do his thing, then, and Alexander in return would be a good First Mate. He first had to gain Mookie's confidence back, and then, maybe, Mookie would leave him alone again.

"OK, you're right," Alexander said while nodding his head. "I do sometimes get caught up in my 'La-La Land,' here, but other than that it's been pretty successful, right? I mean look what we've built together. There was nothing here but farmland and a rundown house when you bought this place. Now, look at it. I know I didn't handle this situation the right way, I realize that, but I mean, come on, he was a lunatic after all."

Mookie shook his head.

"I just don't think you get it. What we do, who we are -- all these moral dilemmas and ethical quandaries -- none of it means shit. You've been so wrapped up in justifying or rationalizing the true meaning of why we built this place that you lost sight of who you are. This place is nothing but a cover. I want you to hear me. Nothing else. You forget that. You forget the kind of people we are dealing with.

"Yeah, the asshole is a fucking maniac, but if you'd been on guard, if you'd remembered who you are, I guarantee you would've done things differently. You're not Jesus Christ, you don't walk on water, and you certainly don't have the capabilities to talk sense into a maniac criminal, who likes nothing more than to do sexual, violent acts on young girls and then ... well..." Mookie let his sentence drift off into the vapor.

Alexander was dumbfounded. He never heard Mookie speak in such blunt, specific terms about him or the Farm.

"OK, then, well, you're right," Alexander said, again trying to appease him, while thinking about what to say next. He was beginning to think that maybe Mookie was going to do something out of character, something Alexander was not anticipating, and he had to be, using Mookie's words, "on guard."

"I see that. I suppose I did lose sight of our purpose here," Alexander said as his mind was racing. He saw the furtive glances of Mookie's eyes, and it was scary. He was usually so calm. He was obviously battling some extreme thoughts in his head and was barely paying attention to Alexander anymore.

"Well, then, tell me what to do, Mookie," Alexander said, trying to get his attention back. "What do you think the next step is here? He's gone, and he's not coming back. Can't we just go back to normal, to the way things used to be?"

Alexander needed Mookie engaged in this conversation. If Mookie was close to panic, Alexander hated to think what he was planning, if he was capable of planning anything at all. Alexander needed Mookie to slow down and think clearly. He needed him to look at the big picture and not just obsess over the situation.

Of course, Alexander did not know what the situation was, exactly, so he had to be careful.

But Mookie's mind still seemed to be in another place, another time. Alexander's presence was barely registering with him now.

"Mookie. Mookie. Hey, did you hear what I said? Now, that he's gone, let's get things back to normal. What can we do to get things back to normal?"

Mookie snapped out of it and looked at Alexander.

"There ain't no normal."

6.

Junie watched the two men arguing just out of her hearing. She knew this was her opportunity to get away from Mookie and to safety, but she could not help herself. She still held out hope she could bust this whole thing wide open, even though she still did not know quite what this thing was.

The man to whom Mookie was speaking looked vaguely familiar, even though he did not seem to be the type of person with whom Mookie would normally cohort. He did not have the look of someone who had lived on the streets for a long time, and he did not look like one of Mookie's powerful and/or rich contacts, who would mosey into The Coffee Shop from time to time.

No, he was completely ordinary, but cute in an aging hipster kind of way. He had a longish, unruly gray head of hair and was thinner than the normal late-50s-year-old man. If in another life, he was wearing Birkenstocks, a tie-dyed shirt, and grooving to the Dead, she would not have been at all surprised.

She tried to hear what they were saying, but she could only understand a few words here and there. It was more the tone of the words and body language that interested her. Mookie was much more engaged, even to the point of aggression, than he normally was, pointing at the man, waving his arms, and leaning into the conversation, as if he wanted to make sure his point was made and understood completely.

Junie had heard enough about the Recovery Farm during her time as an "employee" of The Coffee Shop to know this must be the place. Her research of the Farm was enough for her to know that, while it was a good idea in theory, the place did not offer quite the salvation reported by the mindless media, which relied on press releases and unsubstantiated quotes to craft feel-good stories to get more internet clicks.

The stories always concentrated on Mookie's selflessness, his charity. People who had long been homeless and addicts got a chance to work in his Coffee Shop and, then, maybe at his Recovery Farm to learn new skills, even though she gathered that these new skills did not do much to teach them how to live in their previous environments. Yes, agricultural skills were great and necessary and even pure, but she doubted that they would find much real employment once they left the Farm.

She had read all the stories and had seen the same patterns, the same quotes, and, notably, the same omissions. No reporter had ever taken the time to follow up with anyone who had actually "graduated" from The Coffee Shop or the Recovery Farm into normal society. It was a huge black hole in Mookie's feel-good narrative.

Then she recognized the guy to whom Mookie was speaking. Even in his disheveled appearance, Junie knew he must be the one who ran the Recovery Farm. She recognized him from a few of the newspaper articles. That was another warm and fuzzy story in Mookie's narrative. The guy was an addict and homeless, but he went through Mookie's system and was now a productive member of society, giving back by helping those who were previously like him.

So maybe there was one person who graduated from Mookie's School for the Hopeless and Despot. The only problem was that he was now part of a crime organization that exploited and abused more people than it helped.

The two continued to talk, and Junie continued to try and hear what they were saying. She wanted to walk a little closer, but if she did, she would lose the cover of the little building. She knew she was still in danger and knew she should probably do everything in her power to get away from these two. She had to know what was going on. She had to find out what they were saying, even if it meant risked being seen. She looked at the structure. She was safely in its shadow. She knew if she made any sudden movements or made any loud noises, she would break the flow of the conversation between the two. She did not want that. She wanted them freely conversing with each other, and she wanted to hear all the details. She did not want their intimate conversation to be sanitized in any way.

She looked around the structure again. It was basically a big lean-to with what looked like a storage facility on either side. One side was open. She could see sawhorses, tools, and other random farm machinery. The other side, though, was walled off with a door. The only way to get closer to the conversation without drawing attention to herself was to walk out the back, to the other side, and hope she was out of their line of vision.

She began walking back through the open area of the structure and looked at the door to the closed-off room. She thought she could get closer if she could get into the room and find a window or door or air vent or something that would allow her to listen. She did not remember seeing a window or a door on that side of the building, but she had to check.

"Why not?" she thought to herself.

She put her hand on the doorknob and turned it clockwise. There was no resistance. She turned the knob further and felt the door release from the inside.

Unlocked.

OK, that's a break, she thought to herself. She would just scan the room quickly. She pushed the door open and immediately felt light-headed. The smells overwhelmed her senses, not because they were putrid or strong, but because they pulled her back to a place she was not prepared to go. She grabbed the doorframe to steady herself. She smelled the feminine B.O., as well as the faint tinge of cheap perfume: the same smells that enveloped her so many years ago from the sliding back door of the moving van.

She thought she might be sick for a moment, but righted herself. She strained her eyes to look inside the room. There was no window. There was no vent. There was no other door. There was no light switch. The heavy and stuffy air that encapsulated her as she stepped into the room told her there was no ventilation of any kind.

"Hello?" she whispered.

She heard no stirring and felt no life presence lurking.

She stepped further inside and let the light from the door spill in the room, so she could see inside -- even though she already knew deep down what this room was.

She let her eyes adjust to the darkness even more. Yep, there were the deflated, old mattresses. Yep, there was the pile of trash with ripped pieces of cloth and grease-stained paper plates. Yep, there was the metal chair.

She saw the ghosts of the girls standing before her with the same vacant look in their eyes from long ago. Girls who were dirty, sweaty, greasy, and clothed in hand-down clothes from Goodwill that did not fit just right, but would be discarded anyway as soon as they got to their destination.

She saw the gross, disgusting middle-aged men. The ones she saw time after time, who probably would overdose on Viagra if their little red nubs would not blister away first. She caught too many of them with their cheap suit pants down to their ankles, pleading they would lose their wives and families if arrested, that she now assumed a cheap gray suit with a red tie down to the thigh was merely a cover for every sexual deviant roaming the earth. She saw them in front of her, and she wanted to kill each and every disgusting one of them.

Then she saw those in power, those who loomed over the girls and the deviants. Those who exploited everyone and everything to get what they wanted. They probably did not even partake in the sexual favors the young girls were offering, but they would rape them in other ways. The deviants at least knew they were wrong and deep down felt shame for what they were doing. These bastards not only knew they were evil: They reveled in it. Junie wanted to kill them too, but more than that, she wanted to root them all out. They were faceless and shapeless, floating listlessly among all of us, and, unlike the deviants, there were no defining characteristics to set them apart.

They were yellow, brown, black, and white, yet were anything but children of God. Mookie played footsie with them for sure, but he was not one of them. He was different. She could not quite put her finger on why, but he was. He did not seem to want money or even power in the traditional sense. He did not have a nice car. He wore practically the same thing every day: raggedy jeans, a white button-down, and some sort of black beret. He lived by himself in a nondescript apartment, which took Junie a long time in recognizance even to find. He did not have a cell phone, but Junie suspected that was so he could stay off the grid. His calm demeanor was only interrupted by small bouts of annoyance.

God, how she hated him.

She felt the anger pulse through her body. She hated so many people. She wanted them all dead. She could not even think of one person she liked. She had been fighting so long to be respected, and, if she was being honest with herself, liked by her peers in the police department. It took a while, but she now understood that was never going to happen. Was it because she was a woman? Maybe. There were other women in the department, who seemed to be accepted, but, oddly, she felt the most hated by them. She did not know what it was about her that made her so hated, and it used to drive her crazy. She remembered the early days in the department when she would wake up at 3:23 a.m. every morning and stew, trying to understand why she was such a pariah.

She thought it might be her directness with those around her. She could not stand B.S. and was always trying to avoid office politics as best she could. Sometimes that meant coming into work, not speaking to anyone, plopping down at her desk, putting on headphones, and working as hard as she could on a case. She saw the other women in the office, mostly in administrative positions, walking around with their powdery faces and bright-red-lipstick-stained coffee mugs, wearing their cheap "power suits," and arching their backs for every human with a penis. She could never be that way, and it made her sad. She did not like being alone. She did not like being ostracized. She wanted to connect with people ... hell, just one person. But she would not allow herself to sell her soul just to avoid loneliness.

The smells of the room awoke her again. She thought of the van with the girls. She did not hate them, but they did break her heart. She was not naïve enough to think the girls liked her back. She remembered the scared and frightened looks, but she also remembered the looks of defiance and pride. Those looks they had, in the face of all they had been through, made her love them all the more. Whenever she became bummed out because of the leering detectives or the lipsticked Aunt Janes, she remembered those looks of defiance. They fed her soul.

She inhaled the smells of the room deeply. She knew they were not the same girls, of course, but she felt a connection to them. She breathed in their defiance, their resolve. She felt like she could reach out and touch their sweaty, grimy flesh.

She went deeper into the room and let the gravity of it all swallow her whole. She had a dim recollection of what her life outside of this room had been, and she knew she was allowing the conversation between the two men slip through her fingers. She did not care. She sat down on one of the flat mattresses and felt the floor hit her tailbone.

She wondered where they were, the girls who had been here. Were they somewhere on the Farm? Were they transported somewhere else? She had a feeling it was the latter.

She tried to piece it all together in her head. Mookie would get the girls from somewhere, transport them here, keep them here, and someone else would pick them up and take them to God knows where. He was probably paid a lot of money to be this type of holding station. She always assumed he recruited girls at The Coffee Shop to put them in the stream of commerce. It threw her off because it did not seem to be a very efficient business model. But she knew girls who disappeared from The Coffee Shop. She let herself consider that maybe, just maybe, those girls actually got on with their lives or maybe they moved here or maybe they just left. Maybe they did not get sucked up into a sex trafficking black hole.

She was now beginning to realize that all of it -- The Coffee Shop, the Farm, the feel-good stories -- all of it was just a cover for the big money maker: being nothing more than a conduit to an international highway of young girls streaming into this country for gross, old men to have one last chance to sip from the Fountain of Youth. It was all so disgusting. She thought for a long time that Mookie was the mastermind behind the whole ring, but he was not. He was a small cog in the whole grand machine. Even if she busted him, it would not stop anything. Someone somewhere else would just provide another place to store the goods.

There was just too much demand, and, sadly, there was just too much supply. There was too much money, and there were too many people willing to look the other way for a tiny bit of cash.

She had never felt so hopeless, at least, that is, in her adult life. She laid herself flat down on the mattress and let herself go. She felt herself giving up, surrendering. She was tired of fighting, and she was tired of caring. Nothing she did would ever make a difference. She might as well buy a pair of pants with an elastic waistband and do what everyone else did: the bare minimum.

She imagined herself on the mattress as a lone traveler on a raft floating down a river. Where she used to fight the currents, now she was willing to go wherever the river took her, even if it was over a waterfall to plummet to her death. She did not care. She just wanted to be another amoeba. She wanted to tell the masses of people with whom she came in contact exactly what they wanted to hear, not so they would like her, but so they would leave her alone. She wanted to go to church and believe everything that came out of the preacher's mouth. She wanted to nod her head, lift her hands in the air, and say, "Amen," without one skeptical thought popping into her head. She wanted to put 10 percent of her earnings, pre-tax of course, in the offering plate without a concern about where the money was actually going.

Most of all she did not want to care about these girls anymore. It hurt too much, and there truly was no reward in it. She wondered if this is what growing up was all about: learning how not to care.

"Hey, what the hell are you doing in here?"

Junie sat straight up. She could not believe she let herself go like that. What was she doing?

She strained her eyes to see the figure in the doorway. She shook her head and felt a smile crawl across her face.

5.

Cadel and his new buddy walked across the opening to the farmhouse. Once he got his tattooed friend to start talking he could not get him to shut up, even though he was not "saying" much. That was fine, though. Just keep talking. He might eventually say something relevant. In the meantime, Cadel was hoping they could get to the farmhouse without drawing any attention, so he continued to feign interest in the mundane conversation. If anyone saw them, it would look like they were discussing something very important, not the dinner schedule for the past week. He did not want to get mixed up in any more drama, and Cadel knew the best way to do that was to act as if he already belonged to a drama of his own.

He just wanted to get to the farmhouse. Cadel guessed that because the old hippie was out of the picture, at least for the moment, it was the perfect time to do some snooping in the man's abode.

They walked to the front door without any attention, he thought so at least, and went inside. Cadel looked around the room. It was sparse as far as furnishings went. He guessed this was some sort of "walk-through" area rather than any sort of destination.

In his mind, he was past the fact-gathering stage of his story. He knew, though, there were always holes to fill, logic gaps to close. And he knew he had to be ever so vigilant to do so, or he would be just another USA Today hack with no respect for the rules of journalism or, hell, for just reporting the truth.

He scanned the room for anything -- bills, letters, receipts, random affidavits confessing guilt unequivocally. Nothing. He decided to expand his search and look in the adjoining rooms.

Meanwhile, his tattooed counterpart kept talking in a nasally voice of which Cadel had only now become acutely aware. Cadel gave up trying to pay attention to the conversation. His mind was now focused on getting information as quickly and efficiently as possible.

He walked into what must have been a kitchen/dining area at some point in the house's previous life. Now, though, other than the kitchen sink, gas stove, and green-pastel colored refrigerator, the room looked more like a storage area. There were milk crates with random pots and pans, brown cardboard boxes with black writing on top, and stacks of books with worn covers.

He thought for a brief second that maybe he had stumbled across some receipts or documents that would tip him off, but, no, they were just random clutter piles of junk mail that should have been thrown away long ago. The envelopes were even addressed to "current residence," so he could not even find out the hippie's last name.

He looked around the room one more time. Nope, this had not been used as a kitchen in quite a while. In his mind, he pictured it as a place of food, family, and fellowship in its previous incarnation. It was now just a place for stuff that did not fit anywhere else.

"Hey, where did you go?" Cadel heard his friend inquire from one of the other rooms.

"I'm in here," he yelled back toward the voice. He really just wanted to be alone and look through the house without having to babysit anyone, but he knew he would need his new ally if he was discovered.

"OK, hold on," his friend said and appeared in the kitchen. Cadel looked up at him, "So have you been in this house before?"

"No. I don't know anyone who has now that you mention it. Usually, I'm not on this side of the Farm anyway. It doesn't look like many people live here either."

The kid was stating the obvious, but he was right. The place had the feel of not being a place at all: empty, forgotten, and disregarded.

He peeked into a few more rooms downstairs and saw the same thing: Rooms that used to be one thing were now storage rooms for mostly useless items. If this house was not the nerve center of the Farm, Cadel wondered what was.

The whole bottom floor was well lit with natural light coming in through big glass windows. He looked outside and saw people still scurrying about in the aftermath of the bloodbath. He looked for places he might recognize, but unfamiliar buildings and structures blocked his vantage point. He also looked for familiar faces, but saw none. They were all busy little worker bees, looking concerned and with a purpose. They all had their little jobs to do, and, by God, they were going to do them. They would accomplish task after task after task until their time on Earth was complete. It always made him sad to see so many people who do not have the word, "why," as a part of their vernacular.

"Yeah, like you got it all figured out," he said to himself. He looked for his friend, of whom he had lost sight momentarily. He looked around, went back into the kitchen area, and did not see him.

"Hey," Cadel called out. "Where you be?"

Nothing.

The farmhouse had a wraparound porch, and Cadel stepped through the front door to, well, walk around. He thought his friend might have stepped outside for a smoke. He had a theory that smokers, more than actually putting tobacco to their lips, liked going outside to get away from everyone. He knew several, who, after quitting, still went outside to get away from the big crowds in big buildings to be by themselves for a few minutes.

Cadel did not want to be seen by the worker bees outside, but he also knew they probably had other things on their collective mindset than some stranger standing on a porch. Still, he knew he had to be careful.

He walked onto the porch and looked around. His friend was nowhere to be seen.

"Strange," he whispered.

He walked back inside. "Hey, man," he said out loud, but, suddenly getting the heebie-jeebies, thought he needed to be quiet and maybe even leave the house altogether. After all, this was the part in the movie where he would stumble upon his friend with either a gun to his head or a knife in his back.

The redhead stepped into the former kitchen area ever so quietly and, well, gracefully, that Cadel did not even startle. It was the most natural thing in the world for her to be there.

They looked at each other for a few seconds without saying a word. She did not change her facial expression, as she looked Cadel over.

"You're not supposed to be here," she said in a calm, but confident voice.

She did not seem mad or angry in the least, but Cadel could feel that by his violating some unspoken taboo, he had provoked a certain revulsion deep within her. She despised him, that much was clear, even though the neutral expression on her face did not change.

"Really? Well, ya know, I was helping out in the infirmary, and I saw where they were running out of supplies, so I thought ..."

"Stop it," she said and raised her hand ever so slightly, as if she knew that was all she had to do to make her point.

"So, where is…"

"I told him to go back to his cabin. He knew he wasn't supposed to be here, so he didn't put up much of a fight. He was relieved he didn't have to keep doing what he knew was wrong."

Cadel looked at her closely. She possessed the type of natural beauty that made men do exactly what she wanted. Her beauty was, also, not the type to threaten other women, so the inevitable resentment of her, Cadel guessed, was not the type to boil over into jealousy. They would just secretly seethe at her and their luck of the draw while also doing whatever she wanted.

And here he was. Busted. In trouble. Yet all he could do was think about how pretty she was and how, yes, he also was probably going to do whatever she wanted.

She continued to look at him as if waiting for him to explain himself, truthfully this time.

He smiled and thought to himself that he might as well go for it. He did not have much else to lose at this point.

"OK, I admit it. I'm in here looking for something, anything, that will tell me what the hell this place really is. You tell me one thing. The hippie tells me something else. Then, I see a shootout. Then, people are beating each other up. And, oh yeah, before all that I was kidnapped and tied up in a barn."

Her facial expression never changed. In fact, she looked around her and began fidgeting with random objects within her grasp -- as if his conversation was so boring, she had to do something just to keep herself awake.

He waited for her to say something, and he waited some more. Finally, she looked at him and with a calm determination pointed to the door.

"Get out," she said. "This is not for you. This house. This place. You don't belong. Leave."

His whole life, whenever someone told him to do something, he would do the exact opposite. He at least knew that about himself. Yet here he was about to obey the command of someone who had no authority over him, had no physical advantage over him, and had no other bargaining power over him. He also knew he had no chance for the proverbial romp in the hay. Was he really that simple of a person? Was he really just going to do what she said because she was kinda cute?

"OK," he said. "How the hell do I get out of here?"

"The door," she said.

He sighed. He deserved that. He had lobbed the softball, and she had jacked it over the fence. He looked behind him at the door and then back at her.

"OK, and then…"

"You can just walk out the front gate. Just walk between those two buildings there, and you cannot miss it."

He turned to look at where she was pointing. Yeah, that would make sense he supposed. The shooting had been over that way. He guessed that was the only entrance/exit to the place. He looked at her again.

"At the risk of destroying my only chance to get out of here, though, I would like to point out that I was kidnapped and brought here. I stayed out in that barn tied up like an animal. I'm assuming I was freed from my bondage because someone believed I would not leave. Don't you think that someone, somewhere, will be mad to have gone through all that trouble just for me to leave?"

"Nobody cares about you anymore," she said with such frankness and honesty it took him aback. He usually had to peel back multiple layers of bullshit to get to what someone actually meant or wanted. He had no doubt she was telling the truth and nothing but the truth so help her the great bush god or jolly green giant or mother nature or whatever the hell they worshipped out here.

"Well, then, I guess I best be on my way, my lady," he said while giving an exaggerated curtsy. "Through those two buildings you say? Right where a maniac drove in here and shot up the place? OK, I think I can remember how to get there. Just follow the trail of blood-stained hippie tears."

The look on her face changed. Contempt spread over her cheek-bones, mouth, and jaw line. "Friends of mine are dead or seriously injured and you're cracking jokes. You need to leave. You disgust me. Leave. Now."

Her calm demeanor now gone, Cadel wished he had the energy to take her on. He wanted to confront her with all he knew. He wanted to show her that her beautiful oasis of kumbaya and campfire songs was nothing more than a front for dangerous men, who did bad things.

He was too tired, though -- not just physically and mentally, but spiritually as well. His fight for truth was all but over. Nobody wanted the truth. He was a dinosaur, a dying breed, fighting for survival against the inevitable flaming asteroid blazing toward him.

"OK," he said and turned to leave.

He walked out the front door and onto the porch. He admitted to himself that he wished she would chase after him and ask him to stay, but he was self-aware enough to know that was only the strange side of himself that always wanted approval -- the side of himself that was in a constant state of tug-of-war with the other part of himself: the desire to be honest. He could not be both, so he lived with the constant state of feeling torn apart at worst and just feeling discontent at best. He tried to land on the side of being honest, but he would be lying to himself if he did not at least acknowledge how good it felt to make people smile or laugh or nod their heads or give him the proverbial thumbs-up.

He was a whore for approval, and the girl had given him none.

Fine, then, he thought to himself. It was time to cut his losses. With the redhead against him, his tattooed friend back in the barracks, and no one on his side, he knew his time at this place really was coming to a close. He had enough to write a story. He could fill in the blanks with assumptions and innuendos like the rest of his colleagues. It was a compromise, sure, but he was suddenly tired of fighting an unwinnable war.

He also was in danger whether he wanted to admit it to himself or not. The longer he stayed at the Farm the more likely he was going to be called out and the more likely he would get his ass handed to him once again.

He tried to look casual and invisible as he shuffled across the open area between the farmhouse and the other structures. He did not want to bring any attention to himself. He had made the decision to leave, and he did not want to give off any weird vibes now that he was desperate to get the hell out of here. He made himself take deep breaths and not make eye contact with any of the worker bees.

His leg was keeping him from being too nonchalant, though.

The pain came in waves, but he tried to ignore it. He was not doing a good job, though. He felt like he should rest too. His energy was leaking out of his body at an alarming rate. He guessed there was some sort of correlation between his time here coming to a close and his sudden tired and painful existence. He had decided to quit, and now his body was quitting on him?

Oh sure, he thought. Rub it in.

He could always rest, though. He doubted he would get much flack if he just stopped and sat down for a minute or three.

Yeah, right.

He was getting closer to the clearing where the massacre occurred. He guessed that once he left here, he would be walking for quite a while until he got to any sort of civilization. He definitely needed to find a place to rest before leaving. It might as well be here, instead of out in the woods somewhere. He still felt the dangerous vibes from the body snatchers, but rest suddenly seemed to be the higher priority. It really would not take that long. Really, it wouldn't, he tried to convince the inner voice telling him to get the hell out of here … now.

OK, OK, OK, he rationalized, I'll try to find a place out of sight of everyone else, and if it is not perfect, absolutely perfect, and I don't feel completely safe, I will leave.

He reached the last, small building before the clearing, where he last saw the car with the maniac. He knew this would be his last chance to sit down and take a breather. As luck would have it, he saw a door as he walked onto the porch breezeway, which appeared to be open. Maybe a storage room? He would at least be able to sit down on the wooden floor out of sight of everyone and close his eyes before his long journey to nowhere.

Perfect, he thought.

He stumbled closer and looked inside.

4.

Mookie felt the earth melt beneath him. This was the end. Everything he had worked to establish was slipping away, and there was nothing he could do to stop it. There was no logical, pragmatic way to get out of this mess. He was done. Even if he got in the car and drove away as far as possible, he would never escape the nagging feeling he could not yet quite swallow: He had failed.

It was not that he failed that let him know he was finished. It was that he cared that he failed. He now knew he was just like every other dumbass on the planet. His ego and pride had been ruling him, obscuring his judgment, all along.

He was done.

The fact that he was now screaming and yelling at someone was the most telling. His emotions had gotten the best of him without his knowing it. He felt the anger consume him as he recognized he was acting in a way that served nothing. He was not going to change anyone's mind, including his, by being angry, by yelling and screaming. It would just make people either scared or defensive. They would not listen to why he was angry. They would only see a screaming black man with veins popping out of his neck.

Worst of all, by letting himself become angry, he knew he would miss something. He would miss some small detail or observance that would harm or even destroy him later.

He could not help himself, though. And the man in front of him had not done anything wrong; he was just not that bright. There was not much he could have done to prevent what had happened. People get killed every day all over the world for reasons that do not make sense. It was just the way of the world. Of course, people always want to look back and try to determine why a tragedy occurred in order to prevent it from ever happening again. But, of course, it would happen again -- over and over and over again. All one could do is try to survive.

Mookie had always prided himself on being a survivor … until now. He was beginning to realize, though, albeit slowly, how he had become a non-survivor.

And that was why he was so angry.

His pride had caused this -- not to come here today, not to chase down a worthless junkie, not to suspect and kill two of his most loyal employees, not to get his butt off the cheap plastic chair at The Coffee Shop. No, his pride had let his operation get too big, too complicated, too much for one person to run without exposing himself to the leeches, jellyfish, ostriches, sheep, and whatever other lame-ass metaphor he could conjure in his head that equated to the weak-minded, weak-willed majority of people in this world, with whom he would at some point have to do business, have employed, or just be around.

He should have kept it lean and efficient. He did not need this Farm, and he did not need The Coffee Shop. He could have worked in the shadows like so many of his colleagues, never exposing himself to the light. He probably would have made just as much money, and while he would not have had the power he enjoyed today, he would have had enough sway with the right people that it would not have mattered.

But it was too late now; he had made a mistake -- a fatal one. His pride had sunk him. He had to be smarter than everyone else, stronger than everyone else, to prove he could get whatever he wanted whenever he wanted by exploiting weaknesses, prejudices, and perversions that no one else perceived.

His need to be right in the face of his crumbling empire had finally done him in.

He looked at the man in front of him. The man was weak, but he had been loyal and hard-working. He had just now been abducted and thrown out of a car, yet he had walked all the way back here to make sure everything was OK.

So why did Mookie hate him so? Could it simply be because the man represented the weak-minded addicts Mookie saw on a daily basis?

No, it was something else entirely. It was the man's sincerity that drove Mookie up a wall.

Was he really that naïve to think he could save the world, let alone save one person, let alone save himself? Mookie had explained time and time again that this place was nothing more than a cover for his operations and for Alexander not to get too caught up in the place. Mookie had given him so much leeway, though, because frankly he just did not want to deal with it all. He understood that Alexander had a God complex, but Mookie always expected him to slip up, whether it be drugs, money, or girls. And when Alexander started requesting to keep a random girl here and there, Mookie assumed his weak nature was taking over, but, no, that never seemed to be the case.

It was baffling to Mookie, and he guessed that was why it made him, oh, so mad.

And here Alexander was, not saying a word as Mookie's spittle splattered on his face.

Why wasn't he upset? Why wasn't he arguing? Was he in shock?

Oh, Mookie thought to himself, he thinks he is playing me.

And, Mookie realized, he was.

Mookie stopped screaming.

He looked around the Farm quickly. What was he missing? What detail had he put on the backburner as he threw his little hissy fit?

Had Alexander been in on the whole deal? Had he made an arrangement with the maniac? Was all of this just a ploy to smoke him out?

Mookie could not think straight. The fog of anger, confusion, and paranoia had settled in on his brain.

"What?" Alexander asked him.

Mookie thought hard. He tried to force away the cloud in his mind. He wanted clarity, and he was not getting it.

He looked closely at Alexander. The longhaired freak knew something and was keeping it from Mookie, but what was it?

Nothing was making sense anymore. Mookie could not connect the dots. He could not figure out what was happening.

The fog in his brain became thicker, and the more he tried to clear it out, the cloudier and darker it became. He could not make sense of anything, and he felt the panic racing up his spine. How long had it been since he panicked about anything, he thought for a brief second.

Alexander looked at him strangely, quizzically, and even had a look of concern on his face. Now, that was odd. He also seemed to be talking, maybe asking Mookie something, but no sounds were coming out of his mouth. Why was Alexander fucking with him?

Oh.

Mookie did not even feel the ground as he hit. He was still trying to see through the fog, even though he now knew what was happening.

Then, everything was clear, and the panic was gone.

And, he realized, as he could finally see everything so clearly, how wrong he had been all along.

3.

Alexander stood over the slumped-over body and attempted to make sense of what just happened.

What should he do?

Call an ambulance?

Get help?

CPR?

He did not know. He had never been in such a situation before. He had seen people die before, usually from an OD, but there had always been others nearby who took control of the situation. He would just step aside and let those who seemed to know what they were doing do their thing.

It was just so surreal to see the mound of flesh in front of him. There was no life. He could tell it just from the way Mookie's body was positioned, the way his facial expression was frozen, and the grayness of his skin. There was no doubt he was dead. The question was whether he should put on a show, so everyone here would believe he actually cared the man was dead.

He realized he did not care, which was strange in and of itself. He had always gotten along with Mookie, who had given Alexander plenty of freedom and, of course, had funded this Farm. Alexander knew deep down, though, that he was just a tool for Mookie, and the moment he was no longer useful to Mookie, he would be discarded and discarded quickly.

And he had been fine with that.

He knew his relationship with Mookie had only been contractual, and Alexander was very comfortable in contractual relationships. He liked the certainty that came with them. If he did something for someone, he liked knowing he would get something equal in return. Simple. Easy. Predictable.

He did not like being in non-contractual relationships at all and had fought his whole life to stay out of them.

If he told someone he would do something without assurances that he would get something equal in return, he knew he would never get around to doing it. It was the same with love. True love was supposed to be unconditional, right? A person was supposed to love another without expecting to be loved in return. Well, that was just bullshit, Alexander knew.

At least, he had never been able to love someone that way.

He had never been able to trust the people in his life, who had, at some point, told him they loved him.

He knew if he relied on someone just because they said they would do something, or they would always be there for him, or they would not go fuck the first coworker who winked an eye, or they would take care of him if he got sick, he was setting himself up to be mightily disappointed.

He found the opposite was just as true. He was never able to follow through on anything, unless he knew he would get something in return. As a result, he let those who cared about him the most down time and time again -- friends, lovers, all of them. At the top of the heap, of course, were his parents, who looked at him like an alien creature after he would forget to follow through on something.

And it would happen over and over and over again.

He had fooled himself, thinking he had matured -- that he could now do something purely because it was the right thing to do. He knew, at his core, everything he did, he expected to receive the equal in return.

And that was exactly the type of relationship he and Mookie had.

Or did have.

Annnnnnd he bent down just to make sure.

The eyes were wide open in a creepy, lifeless way that neither movies nor TV shows ever got quite right. His chin jutted out as if stuck in some weird post-life gear.

His contract with Mookie had thus ended.

Alexander smiled in spite of himself. He looked around and realized for the first time that this place was essentially now his. There would be no more "pit-stops" for young girls or random people tied up, bloody and beaten.

It could finally be his. He could finally be the person he always wanted to be. Yeah, he knew he would always long for those quid pro quo relationships, but he also knew he had to break out of that pattern. He had been trying to for so long. He knew innately he had to break out of all of it -- all the failed patterns, systems, loops -- everything he had repeatedly failed at over and over and over. All the books he read at the library and all those recovery facility pamphlets had, in essence, all preached the same thing: He had to transcend. He had to rise above it all. He had to leave the pettiness and jealousies and grievances far behind.

Maybe he finally was going to start a new chapter in his life.

The already rotting corpse in front of him had given him a gift, and he could not begin to give something of equal value in return.

Maybe this unrequited gift was the catalyst that would catapult him far above everything.

He wondered if he was up to the task. He wondered if he had the courage to push himself outside his comfort zone -- to do what was right for the first time in his life. He wondered. He wondered if he had it inside him.

He wondered if karma, or God, or the great quid pro quo deity in the sky would allow him to do it.

He didn't think so. The ripple effects of all the bad he had done in this life would continue no matter what behaviors he decided to modify. He didn't care, though. He was tired of living a contractual existence. He wanted something more. He wanted something deeper. He wanted something meaningful.

Or did he?

He hated to admit it to himself, but all that "meaning" sounded kind of, well, boring. Was it worth all the exhaustive time and energy he would have to spend to get to a place where he really did not want to go?

Worse, he now understood consciously what he had felt innately his whole life: It took courage to live outside his way of thinking, and he had none.

He really was a pussy.

He did not want to let go of his need to get something in return. He would never be able to reach that next plane of human existence. He would always be a simpleton, fighting the choppy waters on the surface of life, instead of letting it all go and sinking to the bottom, where true meaning existed. He just did not have it in him to give up the artifices of meaning he had created for himself.

He ran his hand through his long, greasy hair and laughed. After all the work, after all the time, after all the putting up with Mookie, after giving up drugs, after getting off the street, after all that, he was still no better off inside.

He did not want to change.

And just as quickly as that self-awareness came to him, it floated away, and in its place was a newfound euphoria: He did not have to change. He could continue to be himself.

It felt so good that he almost forgot why he had been so anxious just a few moments before.

Yes, he was a good person, and he did not have to prove it to anyone.

He looked back down at the body. He let himself believe this was how it was supposed to be. He was in charge now, and he would make a difference. He would change this place, and it would reflect the way society should be. He would show everyone how it should be done.

He somehow knew, out of all the people in the world, he was the only person who could do it the way it needed to be done.

Well, the first step is to get rid of the body and car, he told himself. Knowing Mookie, he doubted the man told anyone what he was doing or where he was going.

Alexander would let the police come to him, if they came at all. Who would file a missing person's report, after all? Mookie's cronies? Not bloody likely. They would be glad to get rid of him.

The workers? Sure, they would be disappointed, but they would easily move on to something else. They certainly would never call the cops. Alexander remembered vividly that kind of mentality, and his lingering distrust of the police still ran deep. They would never call the police for any sort of help.

The greatest risk would be Mookie's clients: the rich and the powerful. Alexander knew, though, that no client of Mookie's would ever want the police to look too much into his whereabouts. Any investigation would run the risk of exposing who Mookie really was, which would also cast aspersions on those who did business with him.

So, maybe, just maybe, Alexander could live on in perpetuity this way. He felt hope and optimism overcome him. He knew he should not get too excited, but he could not help himself. It felt too good, so he allowed himself this brief luxury.

And things would change. He would allow himself the occasional dalliance, and the first would be that redhead. He was sick of denying himself things, and now that Mookie was out of the picture, and Alexander's responsibilities would necessarily increase, he would not feel too bad about partaking in the spoils of such leadership and power.

He was even willing to accept that maybe it was just the natural order of things.

He was finally in charge.

He let it sink in.

He had made it. He had won the race.

Whoa, calm down there, he told himself. He still had a lot to do to make this thing work, to make it truly self-sufficient.

OK, and, yes, first he had to decide what to do with the body on the ground in front of him. He also had to give himself as much plausible deniability as possible and that meant making sure no one else knew Mookie had died.

Next, he had to get rid of Mookie's car. That would be more tricky, and he might need someone's help. Who could he trust to help? No one he could think of off the top of his head.

Well, wait a minute, as he thought again of his previous analysis. There was no hurry to get rid of the car. No one would be reporting Mookie as missing for quite a while. He could just hide the car for now and, at some point, get rid of it. Wow, he thought to himself, the pieces of the puzzle actually seemed to be coming together. He could not believe it. Things never seemed to go so easy for him. Usually, he would think he had solved some problem, and, just as quickly, everything would fall to pieces all around him.

Well, how about that?

Yeah, but he still had to get rid of the body.

He reached down and put his hands under the armpits of the body formally known as Mookie and began dragging it towards the nearby storage facility. The building was one of the first built here, so he always had a soft spot in his heart for it. Building it had taken him a lot of time and a lot of trial and error to get it right. He had help from others, of course, but they, at the time, had as little experience as he had in building things. Former contractors and construction workers would come onboard later, and eventually it would take no time at all to put up a small building like this one.

This first building, though, did take time.

The foundation itself was rebuilt twice. He had to cut the boards for the floorboard twice because he had cut the original sizes wrong by almost a foot.

He had been determined, though, to do it right. He still remembered the pride he felt when it was finally finished, even though it took three times as long as it should have and cost twice as much.

But he had done it.

It was a pretty standard building, but he loved the layout: a breezeway right through the middle with rooms on either side. He had decided for it to have a tin roof to match the Big House, even though it had been such a pain to put up there. During construction, he kept expecting a long piece of tin to slide off the roof and slice his head right off. But, luckily, there were no injuries at all. He had been so extra careful and patient and methodical he never allowed the opportunity for anyone, including himself, to get hurt.

It was a source of pride for him, this building. And now it would be the perfect place to hide the corpse of his former business partner, who had given him the money to build it.

He dragged the body closer and closer. He looked around to see if anyone was watching and did not see a soul. He had an excuse if anyone did -- he was just taking Mookie somewhere safe to treat him and get him medical care. Yeah, it was lame, but it was all he could think of at the time.

As he pulled the body closer, he felt someone was watching him. He had not done any drugs for a long time, but he still felt that ole-time paranoia from time to time only serious drug users knew all too well.

This was different, though.

He dropped the body with a thud and turned around to face the structure.

Something was off, but he could not tell what exactly.

He thought he heard something from inside the storage area, where the "deliveries" were usually made. He did not want to leave the body out in the open like this, but he definitely wanted to know who or what was in the structure first ... and he did not want to turn his back to whoever or whatever was in there.

He stood still and listened. From out of the shadows of the breezeway, two figures rushed out at him before he could understand what was happening.

They leaped down the stairs and were on him before he could even raise a hand in self-defense.

The blows against his face initially stung, but then, oddly, he did not feel anything, as his body went numb. He was suddenly in another reality altogether. While he saw the faces of those on top of him, and vaguely recognized one, his mind drifted away from the fists raining down on his body to his parents.

It was odd, yes, but also strangely comforting.

His mom really did love him, and his dad did the best he could. He, for so long, simultaneously blamed them for screwing up his life, with their Midwestern religious dogma and accompanying guilt and shame, while also longing for their approval. Now, he just wished he could see them again, be in their presence, even if it was in a crowded room or sports stadium from afar. They did not even have to know he was there, if he could just see them and watch their mannerisms. He might even be able to walk past them unnoticed, smelling his dad's old musty smell that used to repulse him and the essence of moisturizer and cheap hairspray that unmistakably belonged to his mother.

He would give just about anything to see them and smell them, to experience them, once again. They had been the only stable presence in his life he had ever known. He longed for that stability, that peace, that safety -- never having to worry about what was coming next or having the rug pulled out from underneath him.

He had a vision of himself as an adult, naked and soaking in a tub of good, warm amniotic fluid. It was the most comforting thing he had ever felt in his life. It made the blows on his face seem insignificant, as one after the other landed over and over and over again, and the soft, cool mud cradled the back of his head.

2.

Junie could not believe her eyes. Her old friend was standing right in front of her.

And the dumbass did not even recognize her.

Even the good ones, she sighed to herself.

"Hey, are you OK in there?" he asked as his eyes adjusted to the darkness. She let him take his time to realize who she was. After all, the last time he had seen her, she was a recovering smartass junkie, not a beaten, bloodied pile of flesh, lying on the floor in a random shed on a farm in the middle of nowhere.

The recognition came slower than she thought it would, though, and right when she was about to remind him who she was, the realization spread over his face.

"Hey, is that … what … are you…?"

She nodded her head, and she slowly got to her feet. She felt the tears behind her eyeballs heat up, and, the next thing she knew, her vision blurred as the water ran down her face.

How girly of you, she thought briefly, but did not care.

He walked toward her with a slight limp and before she could say a word he grabbed her in his arms and held her tight.

She always wanted to be strong and always made sure her male counterparts knew how tough she was in just about every situation. Here, though, she let herself go. She sunk into his arms and let the tears flow.

It was an ugly cry.

In doing so, though, she realized why she was allowing herself to weep: This was not about a male rescuing a female, or a female surrendering to a male's dominance, or the weaker sex showing its true colors. This was, she understood, two human beings' connecting.

They were two people, who happened to find each other, out of all the pieces of shit in the world, who actually liked each other and trusted each other and could talk to each other -- even though they did not truly know each other. He did not even know she was police, she remembered with a slight pang of guilt.

She buried her face deeper in the crook of his arm and let herself continue to weep openly. He did not say a word. He just held her tight and let her get it out of her system.

She eventually stopped, and after she let the burning of her embarrassment go, looked up at his face. He had a look of concern, or was it worry, over his face, but she could tell it was not really about her. It was a look of anxiousness, maybe, as if he was allowing her the time to get her shit together, but knew if she did not pull it together quickly, he would have to do it for her.

"Kopowski, what the hell are you doing here? Who in the world is making that delicious, Artisan coffee in our absences?"

She laughed through the tears. "I don't know, Patasky, but I bet, whoever it is, cannot quite get that essence of pig swill you perfected."

"Look, I will explain everything when I can, but right now I ... well ... we just have to get out of here."

Then, without thinking about what she was saying, but, again, not really caring, blurted out, "I thought I could do this. I thought I could help. I cannot, though. I cannot. It's over. I just want to get out of here."

When she realized what she said, she looked up to see whether the inconsistency in her story had registered with the man in front of her.

Something had changed in his demeanor, yes, but it was not what she expected. He had a look of bemusement, as if the cosmic joke of it all was overriding the dire position in which they had found themselves.

"Hey," he said, and stopped himself, then tried again. "Hey, look, I don't know what's going on right now with you, but I don't care. I'm just glad to see you. You can explain to me later what all happened, but, right now, I'm with you: Let's get out of this place."

Even though they both had decided it was time to leave, they did not. They continued to stand together, in each others' arms, instead.

Junie allowed herself to feel safe for just a few more seconds. She had a brief insight that maybe that's all people wanted, whether it be through family or religion or whatever, just a way to feel safe, even if it was for a few moments -- to feel that maybe, just maybe, someone, somewhere, a god perhaps, actually had their backs.

She felt the tears heat up again in her eye sockets. Why was this thought making her cry, she wondered, as she tried to get the strength to pull away, to stand on her own.

And, more specifically, why did she feel that this person, who she was actively deceiving, was the first person in her life who actually did have her back?

It made her sad, and so she decided, at the very least, she would try and return the favor. "OK," she said and finally pulled away from him, feeling good that, as absurd as it sounded, she could actually stand on her own.

"Mookie's here. He's outside. He brought me here. He killed two of his goons without batting an eye. He's dangerous…"

She stopped because he did not seem surprised at all. He just nodded his head in affirmation. He had always made fun of Mookie as an incompetent, lazy loser, but now he had no problem accepting him as a dangerous, coldblooded killer. It did not make sense.

"What?" she asked. "What do you know?"

He looked away and then back to her eyes and held her stare for a few seconds.

"Listen," he said. "We don't have much time, but I promise I'll explain everything once we get out of here. Just please believe me. I know. I know he's dangerous -- very dangerous. And you say he's here? Where?"

"Right outside."

"Shit."

He turned from her and went to the door. He made a motion with his hand for her to be quiet or still or something. He then peered outside and eased himself through the doorway. She watched as his outline disappeared into the bright light. She waited for it to reappear.

And she waited.

Finally, she heard a whisper.

"Hey, come out here ... quietly."

She walked to the door, let her eyes adjust the brightness, and walked onto the porch.

What she saw next was not what she expected: The long-haired man from earlier was awkwardly dragging Mookie across the open area, heading, apparently, towards them. She could tell it was Mookie from his big, black belly, hanging out from underneath his shirt.

She looked closer at Mookie's body and felt horror creep up her spine. He was dead. She could tell even from where she was. She thought she would feel relieved, she was probably safe now, but, no, she was angry. All the time and effort she had spent over the last year to bring Mookie down, to save those smelly, sweaty girls in the back of the van, all of it was for nothing.

This asshole had taken it all away from her.

As illogical as her anger was, and she did recognize it as such, she let it all hit her. She was pissed off, and she had a new target for her anger. She might not ever save those girls now, but she could make sure this no-name middleman piece of shit paid the price.

She looked at her compadre. He displayed no emotion at first, but after he looked at her and returned her glare, she realized he was experiencing some of those same emotions.

He did not look happy at all.

"If we have any chance of getting out of here, we have to take that fucking hippie out. There's no one around. It's now or never."

He was whispering, but his voice was getting louder. Junie had never seen his calm, smartass demeanor stripped away before. Maybe he was like the rest of us -- just one big ball of rage barely covered from the outside world.

"OK," she said, partaking in the nectar of unbridled anger herself. "Let's take him out."

He turned and ran down the steps from the breezeway, even though his athletic-body-gone-soft with a pronounced limp was one of the least intimidating things she had ever seen. She was sure that a pale, freckled hundred-pound girly girl with dried blood all over her was only slightly scarier, but for the wrong reasons. It was too late to back down now, though. Adrenaline pumped through her body, and she no longer felt any pain. She had only one thought on her brain now.

"I'm gonna beat the shit out of that motherfucker," she heard herself say out loud.

She did not even feel the steps under her feet as she flew down from the porch. On the ground, she ran after her friend and overtook him right before they got to the creep.

If this was a movie, the picture would freeze with her stuck in midair. The camera would zoom in on her face, pausing briefly to marvel at her rage, exemplified by her eyes' bugging and neck veins' popping.

This was not a movie, though.

Instead, her timing was off, and she awkwardly tripped over her own feet and fell into the man. She landed a weak punch on his face before she lost her equilibrium, but, luckily for her, Mookie's body broke her fall, while the long-haired freak show crashed hard to the ground.

He probably did not feel the pain of his falling, though, because her only friend in the world was already on top of the man, punching his face over and over and over again.

She had seen people get the shit beat out of them before, she had even seen a few country-boy ass whippings in her life, but this was different than all of them.

It was a slow and methodical pummeling, and the man on the receiving end was accepting it, as if he knew he deserved it, as if he was voluntarily taking part in some sort of unholy communion. He was not even raising his hands in self-defense.

And the hits kept coming and coming and coming until the face taking the beating quit looking like a face at all.

She picked herself up off the ground and gently put her hand on the back of her friend's head. She began stroking his hair to calm him down, to let him know it was OK to stop.

He was in another world, striking the tomato face in front of him. He did not even act like he knew he was so close to killing the man and, in some ways, had already passed the threshold of irrevocable injury. The man would never fully recover from this. Neither man would ever fully recover from this.

He slowly woke from his slumber and stopped.

He got up and looked at his hands. They were bloodied and obviously causing him severe pain.

"That's the first time I've ever hit another person in my life."

"You definitely made up for lost time."

They stood in stunned silence a few more seconds, looking at each other.

The first gunshot startled her, but she did not quite understand she was the target, or at least one of the targets, until she heard the yelling behind her.

"Oh shit, let's go," her partner in crime said as he grabbed her arm.

Mookie's car was not that far from them, maybe a hundred feet or so, and it would at least provide cover if not an escape for them.

As they headed toward it, she felt the air from the whizzing of the bullets around her and saw the mud and dirt pop-up around her.

They weren't going to make it.

She dove for cover and found it in a small ditch close to the road. Her friend, though, continued running to the car, and he almost made it. She saw his left leg tighten, as if he was having a leg spasm, and watched the dark red spread over his pants leg. He fell to the ground and rolled to the bumper of the car. She watched him crawl to the driver side door as pings and pops rang out from the car and cracks appeared in the windows.

And just like that the shots stopped.

She did not allow herself time to wonder why or look to see. She made a run for the car as fast as she could. She felt the pain in her own leg and her shoulder almost immediately, but somehow kept going.

She made it to the car and opened the back door and crawled in, but not before she felt another sharp pain in her hip.

She closed the car door and climbed into the backseat. New cracks in the car windows started appearing.

"Come on, let's go," she heard herself whisper and then angrily yelled, "Go! Go! Go! Let's get the fuck out of here!"

She let herself sink all the way down on the floorboard. She could not see anything other than the tree line through the cracked rear window. She could not see the front seat and did not know if her partner in crime was alive or dead. She thought about climbing over the front seat herself, when she heard the jingling of keys and the click of the car's ignition. She assumed he was on the passenger-side floorboard and was fumbling around trying to start the car from his blind vantage point.

The engine turned over, and she felt the car start moving forward. The pings and pops on the side of the car increased, and she heard voices outside growing louder and more frantic.

"Come on, let's do this," she heard him yell. He was in the driver seat now and hunched over, with his hand over his face, as if the flesh and blood and bones of his hand could stop any random screaming bullet from piercing his scalp or plunging right into one of his eyeballs.

"Come on! Come on!" he kept yelling. She guessed he was talking to the car.

As the car moved and gained momentum, she felt it turn around back towards the gate and pick up speed. The pings and pops lessened and finally stopped altogether. She heard the familiar sound of gravel hitting the undercarriage and sides of the car, and she felt the tension in her body slowly fade away.

It was only then that she realized she had been lying in a pool of blood. And with that realization she felt the pain the adrenaline had been trying to hide from her.

"Hey, are you OK back there?" she heard her friend say. "We made it out. We made it. I think some buckshot got me in the back of the leg, but it should be fine. We need to get to the hospital. We need to call the police."

He kept talking, but she stopped listening. His adrenaline was obviously still flowing. She knew he had been hit by more than just buckshot, but she agreed that he would probably be OK.

She, on the other hand….

"I'm a cop," she heard herself say.

He stopped talking.

"Say what, Kapowsky?"

"I'm a cop. I've been working undercover to bust Mookie. He runs a sex-trafficking ring, probably drugs, other stuff too, and The Coffee Shop was just a cover ... the Farm too."

She stopped talking. The blood was pooling now in the space beneath her. She would not make it to the hospital. It was over -- all of it.

She thought she heard her friend say something that registered surprise in some distant part of her brain, but she did not have the energy to figure out what it was. She was tired and figured that it would be OK if she just shut her eyes for a few seconds.

First, though, she smiled. She was finally honest with her friend … her only friend. He was the only person with whom she had allowed herself to be herself, even though she had pretended to be someone else.

She chuckled and heard the gurgling of liquid deep inside her chest, as she let her eyes close.

1.

Fuck me.

Cadel took a long inhale from the cigarette and then let it just hang from his lower lip. He looked across Pier 27. It was a foggy day, but he still thought it was beautiful. It had been nine months since he had last been here. He smiled at the thought of that person he had been: stupid, yes, or naïve maybe, thinking he could change the world by typing words on a computer screen.

As predicted, his story did go viral, but more for the salacious details than the truth of the matter. By the time he had gotten around to writing it, other papers and news outlets had reported on Mookie and his criminal enterprise. The Coffee Shop was no more and neither was the Farm, at least in its previous form. Whereas The Coffee Shop closed immediately, the Farm was around for another month or so until it all went up in flames in a Janet-Reno-style blaze of glory -- all captured on cameras in the sky and social media.

He kept up with it all in his hospital room, watching his story -- the one he had worked on for so long -- break all around him, but without him.

Of course, it all came out about Mookie: the political corruption, the drugs, and the sex trafficking. Politicians, who had taken newspaper-ready photo ops with him over the years to satisfy the required appearance of social consciousness, quickly discarded him and scurried under the rocks like vermin. It did not help, though. As careful as Mookie was, the politicians were not, and it did not take long for investigations and reporting to expose some of the offenders. After all those kind folks were exposed, and they spilled the beans, other offenders and worse crimes were discovered.

Every day it seemed as if another layer of the onion was peeled back, and, as it often happens, the whole thing became a media feeding frenzy. And all Cadel could do was watch it unfold in his dank hospital room with a tube up his dong.

The police did come speak to him, as did the FBI. Apparently, the FBI had Mookie and the Farm on its radar for quite a while -- at least that's what the agents who came to visit him said. They naturally had to act perturbed that he had disrupted their investigation, and, yet, they did not seem too concerned that he had been kidnapped, beaten, and shot as a price for his sins.

Eventually, though, they left him alone. They had bigger fish to fry. The ATF was honing in on their jurisdiction, and they had to take control. The real trouble came after the FBI stopped coming to see him. Whereas, the FBI had been somewhat annoyed at his "interference," the local police -- San Francisco's finest -- were outright hostile, which was odd, considering one of their own had been killed.

Cadel felt the pit of his stomach turn at the thought. It still hurt, and it still pissed him off.

He learned more about her in the aftermath. She had been an undercover cop working at The Coffee Shop for several months before he strolled through its front door. Cadel did not know all the details, but the notes and research she mailed to her desk at the SFPD had been what laid the foundation for most of the prosecutions that came later. If it was not for her, the investigations probably would have stopped at the surface level, not moving much beyond Mookie and his immediate contacts. As for her personal life, Cadel learned little from a few half-ass internet searches and news stories. He had guessed correctly that she was from a poor, uneducated family unit, but he was somewhat surprised, and, yes, even proud, to discovery how well she had done, and how well respected she was, in the SFPD. Most of the anecdotes were from younger female officers, who saw her as an inspiration, how she came in and did her job every day, but never attempted to pander or look for the political glad handling or affirmations, that most of the others intuitively felt like they had to do. She had done it all on her own terms.

So it was understandable when the SFPD detectives, all male, all older, had walked into his hospital room with the air of injured animals: mad, hurt, and ready to bite. He assumed they were just angry that one of their comrades had been killed, and they were going to lash out at everyone involved, including him.

That assumption quickly faded once the questions began. And the questions were not questions at all. They were accusations. They were accusations that he was lying, that he was stupid, that he had an agenda, that he did not know what he was talking about, that he was in over his head, that he was the mastermind of an intricate conspiracy, that he was a bit player, that he was an evil genius, that he was a typical ignorant journalist, that he was everything and nothing at the same time.

Soon after these "interviews," the top brass of the police department started to fall, followed by others in leadership roles, lieutenants, captains, and detectives. He only then realized the cause for their hostility: They had wanted to expose him as the fall guy. They did not care about her. Unfortunately for them, he was too boring, too poor, and too much of a failure on which to hang anything. Also, unfortunately for them, there were actually good detectives in the police department, who knew where the real corruption was.

News reporters came by his room too, but he held back most of what he knew from them, other than what he knew had already been reported, so he could salvage a little bit for his own story. They got most of it right, but missed some key details, so he knew there would still be an interest in what he had to say if he could ever get started on it. He figured he had a three-month window to write it and get it out there. So he kept his mouth shut, for the most part, and, as a result, they, along with everyone else, stopped visiting him in the little hospital room. He was left alone with the TV, doctors, and nurses, who seemed determined to wake him every time he drifted off to sleep with an order for blood, tests, or medicines -- anything to keep him from a full night of sleep.

He flirted with the nurses, though, and faked an interest in what the doctors said, and thus things proceeded as smoothly as they could. Eventually, he was released with a long list of medications and an even longer bill, which he knew he would never get around to paying anyway.

He went back to his apartment, the same one that Mookie's thugs had ransacked, which seemed like such a long time ago, and carefully put together all his notes, evidence, and background research. Only then did he start to write.

It was intoxicating once he got going. The words flowed, and the caffeine kept him going. He cranked up the music in his headphones and, once again, lost himself.

He did not partake in alcohol, though, as he used to do.

In fact, he quit taking the pain medicine too. It was not too much of a conscious decision. He had always assumed he might be an addict or an alcoholic with the way he would lose himself with a big bottle of whiskey in those lonely nights a year ago in his apartment. Now, he knew he was not. He had just been self-medicating, thinking he was exposing others' truth while actually avoiding his own.

Pathetic.

It felt good, though, in some strange way now to feel something, even if it was pain. If nothing else, it gave him the clarity to finish the story.

In two weeks, he had a rough draft, and after another three weeks, he had the whole thing written: just a smidgen over 50,000 words. It could have been a novella in a different time.

He shopped it around to a few of his contacts and went with the highest bidder: a small, but reputable, news blog out of LA. Within days his story got picked up by the AP and other news organizations. He even appeared on CNN and some smaller TV news programs.

He made enough cash to pay most of the bills he had accumulated over the last year or two (not including the medical bills), and put the rest in savings ... that is, in his pocket. He was set to move to the East Coast and dig into a couple leads he had received on random corruption stories sent to him by those who had seen his byline, when he read the Farm was being converted into a true place for recovering addicts. It would be run by the State thanks to a huge donation from a donor who chose to remain anonymous.

An anonymous donor, you say?

That caused his Spidey Sense to tingle, so he started doing a little digging with no plan whatsoever.

It was not long, after a few calls were made, and a few trips to downtown LA were had, that he started getting a little momentum going.

That was when the call came and why he was here today.

He received a job offer from the largest paper in California -- and not just any job either: the "corruption/city government" columnist, which also meant a spot on the editorial board. The salary was decent, and the health benefits were even better. Even though he had never longed for it, the possibility that he could work at a normal job with normal hours and live a stable existence, appealed to him in a way he never saw coming.

This was a good thing, right?

This was a normal progression, correct?

This was just a coincidence, hmmmm?

His gut told him, "No," to all the above, but he was getting tired of listening.

He allowed a smile, despite himself, and took one last drag off the cigarette. He flicked the butt to the ground and got ready to leave. As he put all his weight on his cane, so he could pivot around and walk away, he stopped himself. For a moment, it was all too real. All the life, all the possibilities … all of it gone. He tried to think what that meant, but instead found his mind drifting, as he watched the horizon swallow the ocean and a cruise ship outlined in the suddenly sunny sky.

Acknowledgements

First, I want to thank my son, Austin, for being the first person to read this novel -- front to back -- and give me the constructive criticism and encouragement, especially, I desperately needed at the time. I cannot tell you how much I appreciate it, buddy. I am so proud of you.

Many thanks to Michael Hewes for being the person who has given me the most encouragement and advice throughout this process. Other than Austin, he was the only other person who I trusted enough to read the first draft of the book. It was his encouragement at many low moments that kept me going. If not for him, this novel would not have been published.

Thanks also to Charlie Webb, who told me I needed to research what sort of ships were docking in San Francisco, which led me to discover the history of cruise ships at Pier 27.

Thanks to my sister Jenny Wilson for taking my picture for the back cover. She is immensely talented, and I'm so proud of her (I'm also SO grateful for our friendship and relationship -- even if I did "ruin her life").

So much gratitude, more than I could ever express, goes to my family (Kim, Cate, Austin, Mom, Jenny, Bekah, Nate, Nana, Pop, Cary, Allen, Aaron, Rebekah, Cohen, Marion, Jacob, Christopher, and Sterling). I'm so thankful for your love and support over the years.

Thanks to the two biggest influences in my life: Tay Gillespie and Steve Clements (and the rest of the Strong River family -- you know who you are. I love all of you).

Thank you to all the teachers who put up with me over the years, but specifically to Dr. Richard Patteson and Dr. John Tisdale, the only two who actually believed in me … for some odd reason.

Thanks to Butler Snow and all my colleagues who continuously teach me, challenge me, but more than anything support me every day. I am very grateful for everything I have learned from each of you.

As weird as this sounds, thanks to Spike Lee (as if he will ever read this) and his discussions in the early 2000s about the "Magical Negro." I'm a white guy, so I'll never know the depths of the prejudice and racism African-Americans experience every day. When I decided to write from the perspective of an African-American character, the temptation, to be safe, was to make the character as "sin free" as possible. However, Lee's talks and interviews stuck with me and challenged me to make the character as whole and complex -- and, yes, flawed -- as any other in the book. It was for that reason I named the character, "Mookie," who, of course, is the lead character in Lee's Do the Right Thing, another of his works that had a tremendous effect on me.

And, lastly, thanks to Chris Berge and Berge Design for the beautiful cover. It was exactly what I was hoping for but had no idea what it could look like. You captured the book perfectly.

See Gavin -- I wrote a book!

Made in the USA
Coppell, TX
05 August 2020

32406869R00166